Praise for the *Diagnosis Murder* novels

"*Diagnosis Murder: The Past Tense* is the latest—and arguably the best—original mystery based on the popular Dick Van Dyke TV series, which Goldberg wrote and produced. What makes it more than just another spinoff is the way Goldberg takes the reader—and his hero, Dr. Mark Sloan—through forty years of Los Angeles history, a journey that captures the unique flavor of the city so many of us used to call home."

—*Chicago Tribune*

"*The Past Tense* contains all the elements of a fine mystery novel: good characters, interesting plot, surprising twists and, above all, crisp and enjoyable writing. With books this good, who needs TV?"

—*Chicago Sun-Times*

"This novel begins with tension and ends with surprise. Throughout, it is filled with gentle humor and a sure hand. . . . This is not just a novel for fans of the television series; it is a nifty, creative take on the tradition of great amateur sleuths with a cast of quirky characters."

—Edgar® Award–winning author Stuart M. Kaminsky

"A whodunit thrill ride that captures all the charm, mystery, and fun of the TV series . . . and then some. . . . Goldberg wrote the very best *Diagnosis Murder* episodes, so it's no surprise that this book delivers everything you'd expect from the show. . . . A clever, high-octane mystery that moves like a bullet train. Dr. Mark Sloan, the deceptively eccentric deductive genius, is destined to join the pantheon of great literary sleuths. . . . You'll finish this book breathless. Don't blink or you'll miss a clue. A brilliant debut for a brilliant detective. Long live Dr. Mark Sloan!"

—*New York Times* bestselling author Janet Evanovich

"Can books be better than television? You bet they can—when Lee Goldberg's writing them. Get aboard right now for a thrill ride."

—*New York Times* bestselling author Lee Child

continued . . .

W9-BXW-212

To Sheri~ Readers this is

DIAGNOSIS MURDER

THE DEAD LETTER

Lee Goldberg

BASED ON THE TELEVISION SERIES CREATED BY

Joyce Burditt

Ⓢ
A SIGNET BOOK

SIGNET
Published by New American Library, a division of
Penguin Group (USA) Inc., 375 Hudson Street,
New York, New York 10014, USA
Penguin Group (Canada), 90 Eglinton Avenue East, Suite 700, Toronto,
Ontario M4P 2Y3, Canada (a division of Pearson Penguin Canada Inc.)
Penguin Books Ltd., 80 Strand, London WC2R 0RL, England
Penguin Ireland, 25 St. Stephen's Green, Dublin 2,
Ireland (a division of Penguin Books Ltd.)
Penguin Group (Australia), 250 Camberwell Road, Camberwell, Victoria 3124,
Australia (a division of Pearson Australia Group Pty. Ltd.)
Penguin Books India Pvt. Ltd., 11 Community Centre, Panchsheel Park,
New Delhi - 110 017, India
Penguin Group (NZ), cnr Airborne and Rosedale Roads, Albany,
Auckland 1310, New Zealand (a division of Pearson New Zealand Ltd.)
Penguin Books (South Africa) (Pty.) Ltd., 24 Sturdee Avenue,
Rosebank, Johannesburg 2196, South Africa

Penguin Books Ltd., Registered Offices:
80 Strand, London WC2R 0RL, England

First published by Signet, an imprint of New American Library,
a division of Penguin Group (USA) Inc.

First Printing, March 2006
10 9 8 7 6 5 4 3 2 1

Copyright © 2006 Viacom Productions Inc.
All rights reserved

The Edgar® name is a registered service mark of the Mystery Writers of America, Inc.

Ⓟ REGISTERED TRADEMARK—MARCA REGISTRADA

Printed in the United States of America

To Paula Block and Phyllis Ungerleider,
for making it happen.

ACKNOWLEDGMENTS

The inspiration for this story came from Lisa Klink, so this book is all her fault. I am indebted to Dr. D. P. Lyle, who gives kindly of his medical knowledge, which I then use for nefarious purposes. I'm also grateful to William Rabkin, Tod Goldberg, Paul Bishop, Tom Mayes, Larry Hill, Al Navis, Robert M. Greber, Bill Fitzhugh, Tom Becker, Lewis Perdue, Robin Burcell, James Lincoln Warren, and Richard Yokley for their help and technical assistance. Finally, to my wife, Valerie, and my daughter, Madison, for not complaining about having to look at my back all the time.

I would love to hear from you.
Please visit me at www.diagnosis-murder.com
and say hello.

PROLOGUE

The cliché goes that a picture is worth a thousand words. That might be true, but the pictures splayed out on the desk in front of Bert Yankton were worth about five hundred dollars each, based on what he paid the private detective who took them.

Even that figure didn't calculate their true worth once he factored in the cost of a divorce, the dismantling of his business partnership, and his own considerable pain and suffering, the magnitude of which, he feared, would be extreme. So, when it came right down to it, Yankton decided that figuring out exactly what a picture is worth was a complicated endeavor.

He glanced at another set of pictures, displayed in silver frames on the bookshelves that lined his home study, and pondered their worth. Like the other photographs in front of him, they also were of his twenty-nine-year-old wife, Vivian.

The first photo was taken five years ago, before they were married. It was her headshot, the glossy photo she paper-clipped to her acting résumé when she went out for auditions. He had met her at a party at the Hollywood Hills home of one of his clients, actor Flint Westwood, who'd become an overnight sensation on *Sexual Surrogates*, a cable drama about a bunch of smug, self-absorbed sex therapists and their patients in Miami.

For reasons Yankton didn't understand then, but certainly understood now, Vivian lavished her attentions on him, even though she'd crashed the party to meet the casting directors, producers, and actors in the room. Yankton was Flint's financial manager, so there wasn't really anything he could do for her career besides teach her how to invest her money, of which she had little. He was also ten years older than she was. Despite all of that, Vivian had clung to him that night and almost every night since.

What was that picture worth? It was hard for Yankton to calculate. It was taken before he knew her, before they made a life together. He supposed its value was the potential for happiness he saw in her perfect features, her radiant smile, her vibrant eyes.

The second photo was taken after they were married and not long after she had surgically upgraded her breasts from a B cup to a C, narrowed her nose, capped her teeth, and plumped up her lips with collagen injections. He hadn't thought she needed any surgery. On a beauty scale of one to ten, she rated herself a seven, and to make it in Hollywood, she believed, she had to be a ten. In his eyes, he told her, she already was. Your eyes don't cast movies, she said. So he did what any good husband would do. He made her happy. He found her the best plastic surgeon in Hollywood.

What was that picture worth? If he combined the cost of the Mercedes convertible he bought her as an engagement present, the Harry Winston diamond ring, the wedding ceremony at the Hotel Bel-Air, the honeymoon at the Four Seasons in Hawaii, and the plastic surgery, he was looking at a half a million, easy.

But being a ten didn't get her the roles she wanted. She was relegated to playing waitresses and models and nurses who had, at best, one line. Vivian felt that with her looks, and her husband's close relationship with some of the most powerful people in Hollywood, she should be doing better. But

Yankton couldn't bring himself to nag his clients to hire his wife, although he made sure he had plenty of her headshots and résumés on hand when they came in.

Of course Vivian interpreted his unwillingness to pressure his clients on her behalf as evidence that he was ashamed of her, was embarrassed by the way she looked, and had no faith at all in her talent. None of that was true except for the bit about her talent. He knew she didn't have any, at least not for acting, though he would never admit that to anyone, except perhaps Jimmy Cale, his business partner and oldest friend.

The third photo was taken only a few months ago, one of many seductive poses from a spread commissioned by Trelayne, a famous fashion photographer from Paris. Vivian modeled clingy and revealing designer clothes and bathing suits that made the most of her body, which she'd spent months "sculpting" with a personal trainer who actually called himself Michael Angelo and "freshening up" with the plastic surgeon.

What was that picture worth? If it was all totaled up—her personal trainer five days a week, and her cosmetic "freshening," and the designer wardrobe, and the photographer, who had to be flown in from France and put up in a suite at the Hotel Bel-Air for two weeks—he'd guess close to two hundred thousand.

It was after writing those last few checks that he began to realize why she had picked him out of that crowd at Flint Westwood's party. And it was also when he began to wonder if a woman who saw herself as an eleven on a scale of one to ten could really be satisfied being stuck with paunchy Bert Yankton, a man who was, in his own conservative estimation, a four at best.

So, to ease his growing insecurity, and to prove himself a fool, he hired a private eye to follow his wife for a few weeks. His fear, of course, was that she'd found herself a younger man who was her equal in terms of physical perfection. An actor, perhaps, with washboard abs. A hot producer with a rich development deal. A high-level studio executive who could green-light movies. Or a powerful agent who could make her a star. Maybe her lover was even one of his own clients, someone whose long-term financial security Yankton had cleverly assured and loyally protected.

But in his worst nightmares—and he'd had many of them—Yankton never imagined just how deep the betrayal could be.

His wife, Vivian, was sleeping with his partner, Jimmy Cale. The graphic nature of the pictures the private eye took left no doubt at all.

In many ways, it was Cale's betrayal that hurt Bert Yankton the most. The two of them had met twenty years earlier as students at the UCLA Graduate School of Business. Yankton had the intelligence and the financial acumen, but Cale had the charisma, the charm, and the creativity. They both knew that separately they wouldn't amount to much, but if they teamed up, they might have a chance at something beyond their individual promise.

Cale knew he would never fit into a corporate structure. He chafed at authority, at anything that restrained his creativity and his freedom. But Yankton could have gone right from UCLA into the accounting department of some huge company. In fact, he would have been assimilated into the Borg collective of corporate America, his identity lost, his true earning potential left untapped.

It was Cale who came up with the brilliant idea that the two of them should make a living investing other people's money. Not as mere stockbrokers or accountants but as financial managers or, as Cale liked to call it, Wealth Generators. Cale didn't want to deal with anyone smarter than they were, so they decided to court The Talent, Hollywood-speak for actors, writers, producers, and directors, basically people who lived off their imaginations rather than intelligence.

Cale looked like Talent, though his creativity was limited to money and how to exploit it. He would bring in the clients, do all the courting, seducing, and hand-holding, while Yankton concentrated on the business itself, coming up with the investment strategies for their clients.

And that's about the way it worked, though each was deeply involved in the other's area of expertise as well as his own. Yankton would bring in the more conservative, thoughtful clients who weren't susceptible to Cale's charms, while Cale would come up with outrageous, edgy, out-of-the-box business strategies that Yankton might otherwise not have considered.

They started their business by going to equity-waiver plays in ninety-nine-seat theaters on Melrose and screenings of student films. They targeted aspiring actors, writers, and directors and offered their financial management services for free until the clients got on their feet. Gambling that a few of them would become stars, Yankton and Cale helped them deal with their credit card debt, manage their student loans, and apply for unemployment until their big breaks came.

The gamble paid off.

First, one of their actors got a regular gig on a sitcom that became the surprise hit of the season. Then a writer sold a spec feature for "the high six figures." Then a director got a music video, and that led to a lucrative contract with a major advertising agency. And all those clients remembered who'd been there for them when they had nothing, and who was going to turn their newfound something into something more.

Success bred more success, luring clients who were already established in The Industry. Soon, Yankton and Cale had stunning offices on Wilshire Boulevard in Beverly Hills, lavish homes, and expensive cars.

Surprisingly, it was Cale who married first, had a child almost immediately, and settled into a life of privileged domesticity in Brentwood, right down to the golden retriever and the Jeep Cherokee. But the marriage collapsed within a few years, as his wife, Betsy, was unable to forgive his constant and unrepentant womanizing.

Yankton had been there for his friend, letting Cale stay with him during those first few painful weeks. He even brokered the equitable division of their assets.

Betsy was the kind of woman Yankton should have married: sensible, practical, family-oriented, and totally authentic, physically and emotionally. The idea of getting breast implants or collagen injections would have appalled her. Yankton liked her immediately and remained friends with her long after the divorce, continuing to manage the family's money and their daughter's college fund. He was the only person both Jimmy Cale and his ex-wife trusted.

Vivian was definitely more Cale's type, or at least the kind of woman everyone expected him to be with.

And now he was.

How could Cale do this to him? It wasn't something that happened by accident. Cale had to know the magnitude of his betrayal and the destruction it would cause. Was that the thrill for him? Was that what made the affair irresistible?

Yankton could understand Vivian's motives. First, there was the physical aspect. Cale looked like a movie star and dressed the part, too. Cale had money, at least as much as Yankton, and would gladly manipulate his Hollywood clients on Vivian's behalf without their even being aware that they were being played. And sleeping with him was the perfect way to act out her fury that Yankton hadn't done more to help her career.

But why would Cale do it? Why didn't he rebuff her advances instead of giving in to them? Or was it Cale who pursued her? How could he put his own gratification above their partnership? Their friendship?

Yankton just couldn't make sense of it. Having an affair

with Vivian was a premeditated act of cruelty. Of hatred. There was no other explanation.

What had he ever done to Cale to deserve this?

It made Yankton want to cry.

But the self-pity passed quickly, evaporating in the heat of a stronger, more consuming compulsion.

The need to kill.

When Vivian came home that evening, clutching two shopping bags from Neiman Marcus, her husband was nearly finished remodeling the living room with a sledgehammer.

All the paintings had been driven into holes in the walls where they'd once hung. The canvases and splintered frames looked as if they were being chewed up by the house.

Anything made of ceramic or glass had been smashed into shards and covered the floor like glittering confetti.

The couches and chairs had been pummeled into piles of broken wood and twisted chrome draped in torn leather.

Yankton was in the process of destroying the dining room table when he noticed Vivian standing in the doorway, her mouth hanging open, either in shock or from the unnatural weight of the collagen in her lower lip.

"I never liked what you did with this place," Yankton said. "I only wanted to make you happy."

He used to think she was a stunning beauty. But tonight she looked grotesque to him, a mockery of a woman, with her catfish lips, bowling-ball breasts, and permanently arched eyebrows.

"Not that you give a damn," he said, giving the table a final whack with the sledgehammer that brought it crashing to the floor.

Yankton nodded, pleased with himself. His skin was damp with sweat, his clothes sticky and itchy. His tailored suit was dusted with plaster and sawdust. There were blisters on his hands from wielding the sledgehammer, which was far heavier than his usual weapon of choice, a fine fountain pen.

"What the hell has gotten into you, Bert?" she said, trying to sound angry instead of afraid. "Do you have any idea what this is going to cost?"

"Matter of fact, I do," he said calmly.

He motioned with the sledgehammer towards the coffee table, the only piece of furniture left standing in the wreckage. In the center of the table was the stack of pictures the detective had taken and, beside it, a thick document.

Vivian's breath caught in her throat as she saw the picture on the top of the stack. It was the most graphic one of the set, which is why Yankton put it on top. He didn't want any arguments. He didn't want any denials. Her grip tightened on the handles of her Neiman Marcus shopping bags as if they were life preservers. She couldn't look away from the picture. She couldn't look at him.

"You can keep the pictures for your portfolio. They're sexier than the crap the French guy shot and a lot cheaper. The document beside them is our prenup," Yankton said. "I've highlighted the key points with a yellow marker so you can't miss them. I'm going to La Quinta for the weekend. Be gone when I get back on Monday."

Still hefting the sledgehammer, he headed for the door. She flinched as he walked past, as if expecting him to take a swing at her. But he didn't. He took a few swings at her Mercedes in the driveway, though, leaving it bleeding antifreeze and wailing for help as he got into his BMW and drove off.

When she was certain he was gone, she slowly set down her shopping bags, reached into her Louis Vuitton purse, and took out her cell phone. Her hands trembled. The phone rang twice, and then he answered.

"Jimmy," she said, but then she couldn't say anything more. All she could do was sob.

* * *

On Monday morning, Bert Yankton showed up promptly at seven A.M. at his Wilshire Boulevard offices looking fit and rested. He smiled at the receptionist, picked up his mail, and sauntered into his bright corner office.

He emerged a few moments later to get a cup of coffee and a donut from the snack room, then went back to his desk to check the stock market, catch up on his e-mail, read the newspaper, and go over his calendar for the day. This was all part of his morning routine.

Ordinarily Yankton would spend the next two hours preparing for his first meeting of the day, which would be with either a client or members of his staff.

But this morning he had a meeting that wasn't on the books.

The man who strode uninvited into Yankton's office looked like he would be much more comfortable wearing a tank top, shorts, and sandals than an off-the-rack suit and scuffed Florsheims. He had the even tan and sun-bleached hair of a surfer, but there was nothing laid-back about his attitude. The man radiated authority and probably would have even without the badge and the gun clipped to his belt.

"Bert Yankton?" the man asked.

"Yes." Yankton rose from his chair. "How can I help you, Officer?"

"It's detective. I'm Steve Sloan. LAPD Homicide."

"Who died?" Yankton asked.

"People who die aren't my problem, Bert. Just the ones who are murdered."

"All right," Yankton said. "Who has been killed and what does that have to do with me?"

"Where have you been since you left the office Friday night?"

"I went home for a few hours, and then I drove down to La Quinta," Yankton said. "I have a place there."

"Is there anybody who can confirm your whereabouts?"

"I was by myself. But I stopped for gas in Montclair on my way down, got some groceries at Jensen's market on Saturday night, and filled up the tank again on the way back this morning, at a Chevron in Redlands. I used my credit card for all those transactions, if that matters."

"It will."

"Are you going to tell me what this is about?"

"Where's your partner?"

Yankton's face tightened, and he glanced at his watch. "Jimmy doesn't come in until ten."

"When did you last see Jimmy Cale?"

"Not since Friday," Yankton said. "We met with a client for lunch at Le Guerre in Studio City. Jimmy had other meetings in the Valley and I had an appointment back here at the office."

"Who did you meet with?"

"I'm not answering any more questions until you tell me what's going on."

"You met with a private investigator who calls himself Nick Stryker," Steve said.

"What should he be calling himself?"

"Zanley Rosencrantz. That's his real name, but it doesn't sound half as cool as 'Nick Stryker,' does it? Think about it for a second, Bert. Would you have hired a guy with a name like that to follow your wife?"

Tiny beads of perspiration were beginning to make Yankton's brow shine. "If you already knew who I met with and why, what was the point of asking me?"

"To catch you in a lie, of course," Steve said. "It's a big part of what I do."

"Has Stryker been murdered?"

Steve shook his head. "No such luck."

Yankton shifted his weight in frustration, clearly trying to keep his voice steady and his demeanor professionally aloof. "Then who has?"

"That's a tricky question," Steve said. "We aren't entirely sure yet."

"We?"

"Me, your wife, and the La Quinta police," Steve said. "I'll tell you more about it on the way down to the parking garage."

"What's in the garage?"

"Your car," Steve said. "Which reminds me, you better bring your keys."

The two men didn't speak to one another again until they were alone in the elevator. Yankton hit the button for the parking garage and turned to Steve.

"You mentioned my wife and the La Quinta police," Yankton said.

"I don't know what your weekend has been like, but let me tell you about mine," Steve said. "After you trashed your house with a sledgehammer, your wife, Vivian, called her lover, your partner, Jimmy Cale, who set her up in an apartment in Marina del Rey. He was supposed to join her there Saturday night. When he didn't show, she got worried and went over to his place. His car was parked in the driveway, but his front door was wide open. She went inside and found everything smashed, blood on the floor, and no sign of Cale. That's where I come in."

Yankton cleared his throat. "Is Jimmy dead?"

"You tell me," Steve said. "But if you're going to confess, wait until I read you your rights."

"I didn't kill Jimmy," Yankton said.

"Did you trash his house?"

"No," Yankton said.

"It must have been another angry husband with a sledgehammer," Steve said. "Right, Bert?"

Yankton didn't answer. He reached into his jacket for his cell phone to call his lawyer, but thought better of it after remembering two things: There was no reception in the parking garage, and his lawyer didn't know the first thing about criminal law.

The elevator reached the garage and stopped with a disconcerting jolt. The doors slid open like the curtains on a stage at the opening of a play. Yankton gasped involuntarily at the drama that was already unfolding.

His parking space was cordoned off with yellow police tape. The trunk and all four doors of his BMW were wide open. Several uniformed officers were standing guard as a team of half-a-dozen crime lab technicians in blue jumpsuits went over his car.

"I guess I won't need your keys after all," Steve said as they stepped out of the elevator.

"You better have a search warrant," Yankton said. He'd watched enough TV cop shows to know that much.

Steve reached into his pocket, pulled out a piece of paper, and handed it to Yankton. "Here it is. Hold on to it for your scrapbook. It will go nicely with the one they issued down in La Quinta, where the police are searching your place as we speak."

"What are you looking for?" Yankton's voice was barely more than a whisper.

"Evidence of murder," Steve said.

"This is crazy. Jimmy could be anywhere. He could be in Vegas right now, have you thought of that? He goes up there for quick trips all the time. Flies up, gambles all night, and straggles in here at ten o'clock looking like hell." Yankton glanced at his watch. "He could be here any minute."

One of the crime lab techs motioned Steve over to the trunk. Her name was Leslie Stivers, and the tech squad jumpsuit didn't do her any favors. But Steve was one of the few in the department who didn't need to use his imagination to know what she looked like without it.

Steve went over to her, gesturing to Yankton to follow.

"What have you got?" Steve asked her.

She aimed a special light into the trunk. Several spots glowed bluish-white.

"What's that?" Yankton asked.

"It's blood, Bert," Steve said. "We sprayed the trunk with luminol, which detects hemoglobin and makes it glow when hit with the right light."

"I spilled some spaghetti sauce in there once," Yankton said. "Maybe that's what it is."

"It's not," Steve said.

"Someone attempted to clean it off, but whoever did it missed a few spots in the back," Leslie said. "He also missed this."

She reached into a dark corner with a pair of tweezers and picked up something, holding it up for them to see.

"Is that a thumb?" Steve asked.

Leslie shook her head. "Tip of a big toe. Hacked off the left foot, I think."

Steve glanced over at Yankton, whose face was ashen.

"Mondays are hell, aren't they, Bert?" Steve said.

CHAPTER ONE

On another Monday, nearly five years after the most miserable morning in Bert Yankton's life, Monette Hobbes stood in line at the Tarzana post office, waiting to send all the stuff she'd sold on eBay.

Monette's hobby was shopping and, thanks to eBay, she'd found a way to subsidize it. She visited the outlet malls in Camarillo, Ontario, and Cabazon when they were having sales. She would use her AAA Club card to get free discount coupon books at the mall offices, and then she'd hit the stores, scooping up tons of brand-name items at rock-bottom prices.

She always kept a few things from her shopping sprees for herself and her twenty-year-old daughter, LeSabre, who could wear anything with that body of hers. Monette listed most of the clothes and shoes she bought for auction on eBay as soon as she got home. Whatever she couldn't sell, she simply returned to the stores on her next visit for a full refund or store credit. That was rarely necessary, since she usually sold most of what she listed, and the profits from her little entrepreneurial enterprise financed her own discretionary shopping fund above and beyond the household allowance her second husband, Lowell, gave her each month.

She was very pleased with her ingenuity and the success of her business. Monette wasn't going to make the cover of

Forbes magazine anytime soon, but it made her feel good about herself anyway. Besides, it was fun, something to do now that her daughter wasn't living at home anymore and, for the first time in nearly two decades, Monette was a homemaker with no home to make.

The only downside was the twice-weekly chore of going to the Tarzana post office to send her goods and pick up mail from the box she rented for her eBay business. But she even found a way to turn the chore into something that made her feel special.

Monette always spent her time in line looking at the display case full of Edgar Rice Burroughs' memorabilia that ran through the center of the lobby. Burroughs wrote the *Tarzan* novels, and he used all that money he made to buy a huge ranch, which he subdivided in the twenties into a housing tract named after his most famous character.

She never tired of studying the sales brochures for the original Tarzana subdivision, the yellowed *Tarzan* novels, comic books, lobby cards, and toys, the faded photos of Burroughs, various actors playing Tarzan, and the Tarzana area when it was still farmland.

Looking at everything in the display case made it seem like living in Tarzana was something romantic and steeped in Hollywood glamour, which by extension, meant that so was she. It meant that her fifties-era Tarzana tract home wasn't simply a disposable example of mass-produced housing—it was something of cultural significance, built on hallowed ground. It meant her post office was more than a post office—it was a museum, a place that tourists might travel hundreds of miles to visit but that she could go to anytime she wanted. It meant that Monette Alicia Hobbes was privileged.

Lately, Monette had needed those self-esteem boosters wherever she could find them. She was feeling unappreciated at home. Abandoned. Forgotten. And fat. Her husband, Lowell, was never around, and now her daughter, LeSabre, wasn't either. Perhaps that was why she checked her positive feedback score on eBay every day and why, a year ago, she'd hired a private detective to follow Lowell and see what he was up to.

She had been afraid that Lowell was having an affair. It cost her fifteen hundred dollars of her hard-earned eBay profits to find out that her fears were unfounded, that her second husband wasn't going to abandon her for some waitress the way her first husband, Desmond, did (the one who impregnated her in the backseat of his father's Buick LeSabre, the nicest car she'd ever been in).

It was a silly fear, really. Lowell ran a Pep Boys auto supply store. His hands were always greasy and covered with calluses. Every day he wore the same drab uniform, a baseball cap and a stained gray shirt with his name written on a dirty white patch. He was thin, with a flat chest and a lazy belly.

It was silly of her to think Lowell was stepping out on her. What kind of woman was going to fall for him anyway?

He was lucky to have her. It made her sick to think about all the things she could have bought with the fifteen hundred dollars she'd spent to discover the obvious.

She finally reached the front counter and chatted with Rene, the huge Polynesian postal worker, about his six kids while he weighed her packages and applied the correct postage. Then she strolled back across the lobby to unlock her mailbox and get whatever checks and money orders had come in from customers too afraid of identity theft to use PayPal.

But the only thing in her box that day was a fat manila envelope with no return address that had been bent in half and jammed inside by some uncaring postal employee.

Monette carried the envelope back to her Windstar minivan, sat in the front seat, and opened it up. There was no note inside, just a dozen eight-by-ten glossy photographs with a crease down the middle.

She pulled them out and propped them between her lap and the steering wheel so she could look at them.

There were pictures of Lowell and her sweet, beautiful little LeSabre walking hand in hand down the street. Monette smiled—the two of them looked so good, and it warmed her heart to see the affection between the two most important people in her life. She couldn't believe how fast her daughter was growing up. LeSabre looked so adult, so confident, so sexy. Monette's heart swelled with pride, but then she wondered why neither of them was looking at the camera, and who took the picture and why she wasn't in it, too. She quickly swapped that picture for the next one.

It was a photo of Lowell and LeSabre embracing outside a motel room door. It wasn't the kind of embrace a father gives a daughter. It was the kind of embrace Monette kept hoping Lowell would give her again one day. She felt her chest tightening up, and she flipped through the remaining photos so rapidly it was almost like frames of a film passing through a projector, the movie playing out in her hands. An X-rated movie. The remaining photos showed Lowell and LeSabre in bed.

Monette flung the photos onto the passenger seat and grabbed the steering wheel for support.

The bastard was cheating on her. With her daughter.

It didn't matter that LeSabre wasn't his flesh and blood.

It didn't matter that LeSabre was an adult now.

LeSabre was his *stepdaughter*. The child he'd raised since she was twelve years old.

Monette knew it wasn't her daughter's fault at all. LeSabre was a victim of a vile, perverted sicko who took advantage of her trust, her obedience, and her love.

Lowell had ruined her sweet LeSabre's future. His despicable acts were something the girl would never forget. It would be with her every moment of her life.

It was unforgivable. It was unbearable.

Monette gripped the steering wheel until her knuckles were white.

She couldn't breathe. She couldn't think. She couldn't see.

Monette felt as if she was being buried alive, deep in the cold, dark earth. She was being smothered. There was nothing she could do to save herself.

And then, as quickly as all the panic had descended upon her, it disappeared, leaving perfect clarity and calm.

Monette didn't feel angry. She didn't feel hurt. She didn't feel anything. She didn't need to feel anymore. She was a creature of single-minded purpose who existed now to do just one thing.

The man on the gurney was in his early forties and looked pretty relaxed, considering his situation. He was bleeding from a deep gash on his forehead, a cut on his lip, and a scrape on his prominent chin. Both of his arms were obviously broken, tucked close to his chest and supported by crude cardboard splints made by the paramedics who wheeled him into the Community General emergency room. He wore a bloodstained aloha shirt, baggy shorts, and leather flip-flops. Judging by the tan lines on his face, he'd only recently started cutting his hair very short in a futile attempt to hide the sprinkling of gray and halt the eternal march of time.

Dr. Mark Sloan, Community General's chief of internal medicine, had seen a hundred patients with injuries just like this during his four decades in medicine. He could guess what had happened.

"Motorcycle accident?" Mark asked.

The man shook his head. "I tripped over the handicapped ramp at McDonald's."

"You're joking," Mark said and glanced incredulously at

the paramedic, Nestor Cody, a seasoned fire department veteran who'd been wheeling patients into the ER for years.

"It's true, Doc," Nestor said. "Mr. Copeland was walking out of the restaurant with his Happy Meal and tripped. He hit his head on the curb, but didn't lose consciousness. His elbows must have broken his fall—no pun intended."

Mark turned back to the patient on the gurney. "I don't understand, Mr. Copeland. How could you possibly trip over a ramp? They're flat, with smooth edges. That's what makes them *ramps*."

"Not this one," Copeland said. "It goes down the middle of the sidewalk, parallel to the curb, gradually declining towards the front of the building. You have to walk across it to get to the parking lot and I didn't see it."

"It wasn't painted or anything?"

"It is now," Copeland said. "With a pint of my blood."

"That's very vivid," Mark said.

The man shrugged and immediately winced at the pain. "I'm a writer."

Mark glanced at Nestor. "Where's his child?"

"What child?" Nestor asked.

"The one he was buying the Happy Meal for," Mark said.

"It was for me," Copeland said.

"You seem a little old to be ordering from the kiddie menu," Mark said.

"I collect the toys. I have a complete collection of McDonald's toys going back to 1967," Copeland said, and then a look of panic washed over his face. "Where's my Earthquake Kitty?"

Nestor reached into his pocket and pulled out the toy, still in its plastic wrap. It was a chubby blue-plastic cat with a jet pack on her back. "Right here."

Copeland sagged with relief. "Thank God. That's the hardest member of the Kitty Crew to find."

Mark turned to the paramedics. "That's one Happy Meal that didn't do its job."

"A Happy Meal of Doom," Copeland said.

"Speaking of which, a Big Mac sounds pretty good right now." Nestor looked at his partner. "What do you say we go back and grab lunch?"

Mark shook his head and motioned to Teresa Chingas, one of the youngest nurses in the ER. She was also the only person on staff at Community General Hospital who found Mark Sloan intimidating. No matter what he did to try to put the woman at ease, it never worked.

She hurried over to them. "Yes, Doctor?"

"Teresa, please take Mr. Copeland in for X-rays and call Dr. Wiss down for an orthopedic consult," Mark said, making some notes on a chart and handing it to her.

"Certainly, Dr. Sloan," she said. She took charge of the gurney from the paramedics and rolled it right over Mark's foot.

He yelped in surprise. Teresa looked back at him, horror-stricken. "Oh my God, are you okay?"

"I'm fine." Mark winced, hopping on one foot to one of the waiting room chairs. "Hardly felt a thing."

"I am so sorry." She rushed over to him. "Can I get you some ice?"

"You want me to take a look at that for you, Doc?" Nestor asked with a grin.

"No, thanks," Mark said, sitting down and pulling off his tennis shoe.

Nestor chuckled and headed back outside with his partner.

"Hey," Copeland called from his gurney, "what about me?"

Teresa looked back at him, as if noticing him for the first time.

"He has a point, Teresa. You better get going." Mark

tipped his head in the general direction of the radiology department. "I'll be fine."

Teresa, her face red with shame, went back to the gurney and wheeled the patient away, careful to steer clear of Mark's chair.

Mark was about to take off his sock and examine his aching toes when Susan Hilliard called out to him from the nurses' station, where she stood at the emergency console, communicating with paramedics in the field.

"Dr. Sloan," she said, "I need your help."

Susan was as young as Teresa, but more confident, more skilled, and not the least bit intimidated by Mark or, he suspected, anyone else. Then again, even Teresa would be hardpressed to be intimidated by a white-haired man in his sixties, hopping over to the nurses' station on one foot.

"A guy was crossing an intersection when he was hit by a minivan. Paramedics are on the scene," she said. "The victim is male, approximately forty years old, unconscious, with negative vitals. He's in full arrest."

The voice of one of the paramedics came over the speaker. "We're administering CPR, oh-two via ambu at one hundred percent, and an IV, five percent dextrose in lactated ringers wide open."

Mark glanced at a monitor that showed the victim's EKG. The pattern of the man's heartbeat looked like a straight line drawn by a trembling hand.

The patient was in v-fib. His heart was failing.

Mark took the mike from Susan and gave the paramedics a quick series of orders. "Give him a hundred milligrams of lidocaine. Shock him. Four hundred-watt seconds."

"Ten-four," the paramedics replied.

Mark studied the EKG monitor to see if the drugs and cardioversion caused any change in the patient's condition. They didn't. He looked at Susan. "How far away are they?"

"Five minutes," Susan said.

Mark spoke into the mike again. "Continue CPR and bring him in." He turned to Susan. "Page Jesse, set up a major trauma room. Call X-ray and the lab. Get a crash cart ready and pulmonary down here so we can get some ABGs done stat."

Susan hurried away to make the preparations.

Mark continued giving instructions to the paramedics en route. As soon as he knew they were pulling into the parking lot, he left the nurses' station, hopped back to his seat, and put on his tennis shoe. He didn't think he'd broken any toes—not that there was much he could do about it besides taping the injured toe to the one next to it for support.

He finished tying his shoelaces just as the paramedics came rushing in with the man on a gurney, nearly running over Mark's foot again.

Mark gave the man a quick visual examination. His legs were crushed, his clothes were covered in blood, and he was in full cardiac arrest. One paramedic was giving him CPR while the other pushed the gurney. The situation was bleak.

"He's still in v-fib," said the paramedic who was giving CPR.

"This way," Mark said, leading the gurney to the trauma room, where Dr. Jesse Travis was already waiting, pulling a pair of rubber gloves on with a loud snap. The X-ray and lab techs were there, too, ready to do their work.

Jesse's boundless enthusiasm and boyish eagerness often made patients wonder if he was old enough, and experienced enough, to be their doctor. But here in the trauma room he was a different person. He projected a natural confidence and authority that eluded him in every other aspect of his life, including his long-term relationship with Susan Hilliard. He immediately started giving orders to the team of nurses who streamed in behind Mark, the patient, and the paramedics.

"We need five units of O-negative, lidocaine, an amp of bicarb, and an amp of calcium gluconate," Jesse said, taking over the CPR from the paramedics as they transferred the patient from the gurney to the trauma table.

Susan had anticipated Jesse's order and was already rushing up to Mark with the ampoules, which were standard doses of medication in glass tubes, prepackaged with needles at the tip to save time in emergencies.

Mark removed the needle covers, inserted the ampoules into the IV line and injected the drugs while he ordered X-rays and the standard labs, though he knew this patient's fate would be decided long before tests could be done.

He kept his eyes on the EKG monitors. Flatline. "Asystole," Mark said, turning to Susan. "One milligram of atropine."

Jesse took the defibrillator paddles and prepared to shock the patient. Susan administered the atropine and stepped back.

"Clear!" Jesse said and applied the paddles. The man's body jerked as the electricity coursed through him. Life, however, did not.

The round of drugs was repeated and more shocks were given, but the patient's heart simply refused to beat. Mark and Jesse shared a look without saying a word to one another. Jesse dropped the paddles back on the crash cart and peeled off his gloves, declaring defeat.

"Time of death, one twenty-two p.m.," Jesse tossed his gloves in the biohazard can. "The poor guy was as good as dead when he came in."

Mark couldn't argue with that. He studied the patient for the first time and noticed a white name patch on the man's bloody work shirt. The patch read: LOWELL.

He looked up and saw his son, Steve, in the corridor, watching them through the glass of the trauma room doors.

Jesse followed Mark's gaze. "The only thing worse than a homicide detective outside your door is a mortician. It's like having the Grim Reaper peering in your window. It doesn't exactly make a patient feel good about his prospects for recovery."

"I don't think this gentleman had much of a chance to worry," Mark said.

The two doctors went out and met Steve in the hall. He was holding a large manila envelope in his hands.

"He looked dead to me before the paramedics even left the scene," Steve said. "But I'm no doctor."

"Have you ever thought about carrying a scythe?" Jesse asked.

"A *what*?" Steve said.

"Did you catch the guy who ran him over?" Mark asked, ignoring Jesse's comment.

Steve nodded. "It was a woman. Mr. Hobbes here was walking across the street when she plowed into him, lost control of her car, and slammed into a light pole. Not a scratch on her, thanks to her seat belt and the air bag. Some Good Samaritans yanked her from the car and were restraining her when I arrived."

"Why?" Jesse asked. "Did she try to drive away?"

"No," Steve said. "She tried to back up and run over her husband again."

Mark and Jesse both looked at the body in the trauma room, then back at Steve.

"That's her *husband*?" Mark asked.

Steve nodded. "Isn't my job glamorous?"

"This is why I am in no hurry to get married," Jesse said.

Steve gave him a look. "Because you're afraid Susan is going to mow you down with a car?"

"Women are irrational," Jesse said. "It's a medical fact."

Mark raised an eyebrow. "Is that so?"

"You've got to keep up on the latest advances in medical research, Mark. These are the results of an exhaustive study conducted over years and years."

"And where was this study done?" Mark asked.

"My apartment," Jesse said.

"I'm not advocating vehicular homicide," Steve said, "but I think Monette Hobbes had a good, rational reason for being upset with her husband."

Steve opened the envelope wide enough so they could take a discreet peek at the photos inside.

"We found these pictures all over her front seat," he said.

Mark and Jesse glanced at the pictures. They didn't leave much to the imagination.

"Whoever took this was inside the motel room. How does someone get a picture like this without the couple knowing about it?" Mark asked.

"The same way you get pictures inside someone's heart," Steve said. "You can snake a tiny camera under a doorjamb or through an air vent. Or there's always the low-tech approach. If you know the hotel the couple likes to go to, you can hide the cameras ahead of time and slip the guy at the front desk a few bucks to book the couple into the room you've rigged up."

"I take it that isn't the woman you arrested," Jesse said, pointing to a photo showing a woman walking to a room at the Movieland Motor Inn with the late Lowell Hobbes.

"I don't know who she is," Steve said, "but I noticed she's a lot younger and a lot prettier than his wife."

"I'm sure Mrs. Hobbes noticed it, too," Mark said.

"I guess motive isn't going to be a big mystery in this case," Jesse said.

Mark looked past Steve to the admittance desk, then motioned to his son to follow his gaze. "Whoever the woman in the photo is, she's right behind you."

Steve turned to see. It was definitely the woman in the pictures, though she seemed older and more mature than she did in the grainy eight-by-tens. She looked like a fashion model who was dressing down so she wouldn't be recognized in public. She wore an oversized sweatshirt and loose-fitting pants that resembled pajama bottoms, casual clothing that did nothing to diminish her beauty.

"Why doesn't everybody come to me like this?" Steve said. "It would really cut down on the time I spend in traffic."

As he started to approach the woman, he noticed that both doctors were accompanying him.

"What do you two think you're doing?" Steve asked.

"I was the attending physician," Jesse said. "I need to ascertain her relationship to the patient and determine whether she has the legal right to be informed of his condition."

Steve looked at his dad. "And you?"

"I'm supervising the attending physician to see that hospital protocol is strictly observed in this sensitive situation."

Steve shook his head. "I don't know why I even bother to ask."

"Neither do I," Jesse said.

The three men reached the desk. Up close, Mark could see that the woman was agitated, tapping her foot and biting her lower lip. Before Steve could open his mouth, Mark spoke up.

"Excuse me. I'm Dr. Mark Sloan, chief of internal medicine. May I help you with something?"

"Yes, my name is LeSabre Brower. I was told that my father was brought here. He was in a terrible accident. Somebody ran him over."

"He's your *father*?" Steve said.

"Stepfather. What difference does it make?" she said, becoming more irritable and anxious by the second. "Who are you?"

"Lieutenant Steve Sloan, LAPD. I'm investigating the incident."

"Have you reached my mom? I've tried calling her at home and on her cell, and I can't get her."

"We've been in touch," Steve said. "I can assure you that she's aware of the situation."

LeSabre turned to Mark. "Where is he? How badly is he hurt?" Before she could say anything, she read the expression on his face. "Oh my God. Is he going to be all right? I want to see him. Now."

"Maybe we should go somewhere quiet where we can talk, Miss Brower," Mark said, putting his arm around her as she started to cry.

CHAPTER TWO

It took LeSabre about twenty minutes to cry herself out after Mark told her that her stepfather was dead. She sat slumped, exhausted, in the center of the couch in the doctors' lounge, her eyes bloodshot, her cheeks flushed, embracing herself and rocking gently back and forth.

She was comforting herself.

Mark had seen this behavior many times before. Giving people tragic news was something he did every day. Within seconds of performing the awful task, while the words still moved through the room like a breeze, he shifted out of himself. It wasn't so much an out-of-body experience as it was a change in perspective. He stopped being a participant in the drama and became a member of the audience, watching how people handled what he had told them.

What he observed was that the others in the room shifted perspectives, too. But not in the same way he did. They didn't step out of themselves. A different self took over instead.

After years of watching this phenomenon, he decided that perhaps everybody has a mild split personality, one part responsible for living, the other for survival. The living self was the more emotional part, while the survival self was pure logic and necessity.

It was LeSabre's living self that was mourning, it was

her survival self giving her comfort, embracing her, and rocking her.

He had no empirical evidence for his hypothesis, but he believed it nonetheless. It was true even for himself. His living self delivered the bad news; his survival self slipped him into cold, observational mode the instant the task was complete.

Mark glanced at his son, who sat beside him facing LeSabre in one of the chairs they'd taken from a lunch table. The three of them were alone; Jesse had been called back to the ER in the middle of her crying jag.

Steve dealt with a lot more ugliness in his job than Mark did. Mark assumed that Steve's survival self was the dominant personality, at least while he was on the clock. It was why Steve appeared to be remote and unfeeling to people he encountered while doing his job.

It wasn't that he was unfeeling. It was that he couldn't risk feeling too much.

"Did you catch the person who did this?" LeSabre asked in a weak, distant voice.

"It was your mother," Steve said.

LeSabre looked up, her eyes pleading.

"No," she said.

Steve opened the manila envelope, took out the stack of pictures, and handed them to LeSabre. "I think this is what provoked her."

LeSabre glanced at the top photograph and her hands began to shake. She let the pictures slip from her fingers onto the floor.

"I don't understand," she said.

Steve glanced at his father, as if to say, What is there to understand? He took a deep breath and let it out slowly.

"You were having an affair with your stepfather," Steve said in a tone that was more than a little patronizing. "Your mother found out and was enraged. So she ran him down with her car."

LeSabre looked up at Steve. "But it was over."

"It doesn't look over to me." Steve motioned to the photos spread out on the floor. But she didn't look at them. She just shook her head.

"I fell in love with him the same time my mom did," LeSabre said. "He was so charming, so funny. When she said she was going to marry him, I couldn't have been happier."

"When did your affair start?" Mark asked cautiously.

"Nothing happened, not while I was growing up, if that's what you're thinking. Lowell isn't some sort of pedophile. Our relationship didn't change until after I left home and got my own place," LeSabre said, anger bringing some strength back to her voice. "He came over one afternoon to help me move some furniture. Afterwards, he stopped and looked at me in this peculiar way, as if seeing me for the first time. There were tears in his eyes. I asked him what was wrong, and he said, 'Nothing, it's just that you aren't a little girl anymore.' For the first time, he saw me as a woman. And when he said that, I knew I was a woman, and that I wanted him to love me as a woman, too. So I kissed him."

Mark thought that a stronger man, a better man, would have gently rejected her and seen to it that she got some professional help for her inappropriate feelings. But Lowell Hobbes wasn't that man. He was weak. Worse than that, he was sick. He went from being a father, someone who should have been protecting and nurturing LeSabre, to being a predator, someone who manipulated and harmed the girl for his own needs.

Once again, LeSabre read the expressions on Mark's and Steve's faces and didn't like what she saw. Anger flashed in her sorrowful eyes.

"You're looking at me like it was incest or child abuse," she said. "You're wrong. He wasn't my birth father and he didn't adopt me. We were two consenting adults who fell in love. He didn't break any laws."

Perhaps not anything in the penal code, Mark thought, but he violated plenty of social, moral, and ethical codes of behavior. It wouldn't help to argue that point with her now, though.

"Who ended the relationship?" Mark asked.

"Lowell did," LeSabre said sadly. "He said he couldn't go on living two lives, it wasn't fair to me or to Mom. He broke my heart."

That wasn't all he broke, Mark thought. The damage done to this young woman would take years of therapy to work through.

"His sacrifice made me love him even more," she said. "He set aside his own happiness for someone else's."

"When did you stop seeing each other?" Steve asked.

"A year ago," LeSabre said.

Mark and Steve shared a confused look. Steve picked up a picture of Lowell and his stepdaughter in front of a motel and held it up to LeSabre. "You're saying this was taken a year ago?"

She nodded and started to shake with dry sobs. "I love my mother. I didn't want to hurt her, either. But I did. Now Lowell is dead and my mother's life is ruined. Oh God, what have I done?"

Mark arranged for someone from the Community General psychiatric department to examine LeSabre and determine if she was potentially suicidal. If she wasn't, Mark wanted to be sure she was offered counseling and, if necessary, appropriate medication to help her deal with her emotional turmoil.

He left LeSabre in the care of the psychiatrist and joined Steve in the corridor.

"This just doesn't add up," Mark said. "If the affair was

going on a year ago, why didn't Monette Hobbes run over her husband then? Why wait until now?"

"The anger could have been building up all this time," Steve said, "and today she finally lost it. I've seen it happen before."

"That's one possibility," Mark agreed. "The other is that Mrs. Hobbes didn't find out until today."

"Why would whoever took these pictures wait a year to give them to her?"

"Good question," Mark said. "One you should ask her."

"She's not talking," Steve said. "At least not to me. I tried to question her at the scene, and all she gave me was the finger."

"That's because you're the big, mean cop who wants to punish her for going after the monster who hurt her daughter. I might have better luck with her."

"Why would she talk to you?" Steve said. "You're some doctor she's never met."

"I'm her daughter's doctor," Mark said.

"You are?"

"I am now," Mark said. "That puts Monette Hobbes and me on the same side. We both want to help LeSabre."

If any other doctor had offered to question a homicide suspect, it would have been a laughable request. But Mark Sloan's skills as a doctor were greatly exceeded by his uncanny ability to solve murders. In his years as an unofficial consultant to the LAPD, Mark had sat across the interrogation table from some of the most clever and most sadistic killers in Los Angeles history. From the Clown Killer to the Silent Partner. From the Venice Strangler to the Sunnyview Bomber.

This was a low-profile case. Nobody was looking over Steve's shoulder on this one. There wasn't any doubt who the killer was. There were a dozen witnesses and a wealth of physical evidence. Monette Hobbes was going to prison, no doubt about it, so nobody was going to give Steve a hard time if he let his father talk to her.

Steve shrugged. "I suppose it's worth a try."

Monette Hobbes sat in the interrogation room, across the table from Mark, staring into her Styrofoam cup of coffee as if her eBay listings were visible at the bottom. She hadn't asked for a lawyer and raised no objection to seeing Mark, though she hadn't said a word since he introduced himself and told her that her daughter was under a psychiatrist's care.

So they sat in silence for the next twenty minutes, Monette staring into her coffee and Mark drawing on a yellow legal pad. He didn't want to pressure her. He wanted her to feel comfortable and safe with him. And if that meant sitting quietly and doodling, so be it.

"To hell with Woody Allen," she said finally.

"Pardon me?" Mark said, looking up from his scribblings.

"It's his fault for setting such a poor example," she said. "Woody took nudie pictures of Mia Farrow's daughter and ran off with her, didn't he?"

"I'm afraid I don't pay much attention to the personal lives of celebrities, Mrs. Hobbes."

"Well, that's what he did. Lowell drags me to see all of Woody Allen's movies, even though there hasn't been a good one in twenty years. Now I know why," Monette said. "If I could run Woody Allen down, too, I would, but the pervert never leaves New York."

"It sounds like your anger has been building up for some time," Mark said, glancing at the mirror to his left. He knew Steve was watching them on the other side of the glass.

"Since about noon," she said.

"What happened at noon?"

She looked Mark in the eye for the first time. "I opened my mailbox and saw the pictures of Lowell raping my daughter."

"Do you know who sent you the photos?" Mark asked. "Was there a letter?"

She shook her head. "Does it matter?"

Mark shrugged. "Someone wanted to destroy your family."

"Lowell did that," Monette said.

"Aren't you curious who took the pictures and sent them to you?"

"It doesn't change what Lowell did to my daughter," Monette said. "And what he would have kept doing if I didn't stop him."

"But it was over," Mark said.

"What was?"

"The affair between Lowell and LeSabre," Mark said. "She told me it ended a year ago."

"That's not possible," Monette said.

"Why not?"

"Because that's when I was having Lowell followed by a private detective," she said. "Lowell was working all the time and finding any excuse at all to leave the house. I was afraid he was having an affair. But the detective watched him for weeks and said Lowell wasn't cheating on me."

"Maybe the detective wasn't very good," Mark said.

"He's the best," Monette said. "I got his name from the *National Enquirer*."

"What's his name?" Mark asked.

"Nick Stryker," she said with dramatic emphasis, as if she expected to hear his theme song begin playing the moment she was finished speaking.

Mark knew who Nick Stryker was—and not because the detective's name showed up a lot in the gossip magazines, usually in connection with embarrassing photos of celebrities doing things that they shouldn't be doing.

Stryker was in his thirties, tall and long-limbed. He had

the build and the casual gait of a golf pro and dressed like one, too.

He'd met Stryker while investigating the murder of movie producer Cleve Kershaw, who was executed in bed with a young woman who wasn't his wife.

After Kershaw's murder, Stryker tried to sell Cleve's wife incriminating photos documenting her own extramarital affair, a blackmail scheme that Mark and Steve foiled. Stryker later became a key player in a little drama Mark devised to unmask the killer.

Those events unfolded about the same time Stryker would have also been following Lowell Hobbes.

Although Mark had serious doubts about Nick Stryker's ethics, he was confident of the detective's ability to discover, and document, infidelities and indiscretions of all kinds.

If Lowell Hobbes was sleeping with his stepdaughter a year ago and Stryker was following him, Mark was certain that Stryker would have found out all about it.

And that's the opinion Mark shared with Steve as he emerged from the interrogation room and walked with him to the squad room.

"Which means LeSabre Hobbes is lying," Mark concluded. "The affair didn't end a year ago."

"Yes, it did," Steve said.

"You say that as if you have more than LeSabre's word for it," Mark said.

"I do," Steve said.

"You've been doing some detecting," Mark said.

"Just enough so I can still call myself a detective," Steve said as they reached his cluttered desk, where the pictures of Lowell and LeSabre outside the Movieland Motor Inn were laid out. "I tracked down the motel and contacted the manager, which wasn't easy."

"You couldn't remember the number for directory assistance?"

"The Movieland Motor Inn changed hands," Steve said. "It's a Comfort Inn now."

"How long has it been a Comfort Inn?"

"About a year," Steve said.

"So LeSabre isn't lying," Mark said.

"It looks that way," Steve agreed.

"So we don't know who took those pictures or why they waited a year to send them," Mark said.

"No, we don't," Steve said. "But we know who killed Lowell Hobbes and why, so my job is done."

Mark motioned to the photos. "But that's still a mystery."

"One that doesn't have to be solved," Steve said, gathering up the photos, dropping them into a file, and snapping it shut with finality. "My favorite kind."

CHAPTER THREE

Mark called Nick Stryker's office from his Mini Cooper convertible as he steered a well-practiced zigzag course of streets between Santa Monica Boulevard and Wilshire, working his way north from the West LA police station to Community General Hospital. But he wasn't able to reach Stryker. He got the detective's voice mail and left a message asking Stryker to call him back.

It was frustrating. He'd hoped he could get answers to most of the questions that bothered him from Stryker on the drive back to the hospital and be done with it. But now he knew the mystery would nag at him, an intellectual itch that would get worse with each passing hour until he could think of nothing else. It would become an obsession.

This was his great personality flaw, his curse and his addiction. At the same time, he knew it was also the foundation of his skills as both a physician and a detective. It made him tenacious in his quest to find answers.

His self-awareness did him no good. If anything, it made his inevitable, and incessant, mental gnawing over the unknown even more frustrating for him. He felt he should be able to master his compulsions with reason and logic. This was one of those instances.

Intellectually, he knew Steve was right. There was no pressing need, or any need whatsoever, to find out who took the volatile photos and why whoever it was waited a year to send them to Mrs. Hobbes. The police knew all they needed to know. Lowell Hobbes was having an affair with his stepdaughter, a fact confirmed by the photos and LeSabre's own admission. Monette ran over Lowell, a fact that no one was disputing either—not Monette and certainly not the dozens of witnesses who saw her do it.

But acknowledging those facts didn't ease his suffering. Mark wouldn't stop thinking about the mystery until he had the answers, no matter how irrelevant the information might be to the police. He needed to solve it for his own peace of mind.

Besides, as far as Mark was concerned, whoever sent those photos was morally responsible for the violence and tragedy that the pictures provoked. Whoever did it had to know that, at the very least, the revelations contained in the photos would tear the Hobbes family apart.

Mark could think of two possible motivations, one misguided and the other purely malicious, for sending the photos to Monette Hobbes.

One explanation was that someone close to the family stumbled onto the affair between Lowell and LeSabre, was horrified by it, and felt it had to be stopped. Since LeSabre was an adult, notifying the police or child protective services wasn't an option. So the misguided do-gooder sent the photos to Monette, not realizing just how angry she would become.

The other possibility was that some hateful person wanted to destroy the Hobbes family and knew that sending Monette the compromising photos of her husband and stepdaughter would certainly do that.

Instinctively, Mark felt that malicious intent was the most likely explanation, but regardless of whether he was right or wrong, he couldn't let go of it until he found the answer.

It was a pointless, selfish pursuit. He couldn't really do

anything with the knowledge besides satisfy his own curiosity. Taking pictures of someone having an affair and alerting the aggrieved spouse wasn't a crime. Some would even say it was a community service.

Who could have known that the pictures would provoke Monette Hobbes to mow down her husband?

Nobody.

So what gave him the right to hold someone morally responsible for what Monette had done? And who cared what he thought anyway?

Nobody.

Acknowledging those truths didn't put the mystery out of Mark's mind either. He was who he was. If he couldn't accept it, he'd just have to endure it.

Since Mark couldn't answer the big questions—who sent the photos and why—he put his mind to the other riddles related to the mystery.

Why didn't Nick Stryker discover the affair when he was following Lowell Hobbes?

Perhaps it was timing. The affair started shortly after Stryker's surveillance ended. Or, less likely, Lowell Hobbes managed to elude Stryker but not someone else.

There was another answer.

Stryker knew about the affair, but for some reason didn't tell Monette about it.

But Mark couldn't see why Stryker would keep the information to himself. It was the man's business to catch cheating spouses and expose them to his clients.

Whatever the explanation was, Mark would know Stryker's side of the story soon enough. Stryker owed him a favor or two after the notoriety Mark helped him achieve on the Lacey McClure case. For a couple of weeks, Stryker was a celebrity. There was even talk of a TV series based on his life, though as far as Mark knew nothing ever came of it.

Mark pulled into his space in the Community General

parking lot and hoped that chaos awaited him inside. It was the only chance he'd have of getting some relief from all the nagging questions.

Steve Sloan was not a big believer in coincidence as a twist of fate. In his experience, a coincidence was conclusive evidence that fate *wasn't* involved. It was proof of intent, a glimpse at the pattern behind someone's premeditated actions.

Behind every coincidence, he usually found someone who benefited from it.

Or he found a corpse.

He was finishing up the paperwork on the Hobbes case when the call came in from the fire department's arson investigation unit. A strip mall in West Los Angeles had burned down around five o'clock that morning. By the time the firemen arrived, the building was fully engulfed. Once the fire was extinguished, arson investigators began carefully picking through the charred rubble to determine the cause of the blaze.

The investigators found traces of an accelerant, proving that the fire was no accident. And they discovered a body buried in the debris.

The strip mall was only a few blocks from the police station. It was one of those ubiquitous urban eyesores, with a convenience store, a greasy-fast-food joint, and a nail salon on the first floor and storefront offices on the second, all squeezed onto a corner lot with too few parking spaces, where a gas station had once stood.

He jotted down the address of the strip mall and then stared at what he'd written. Something troubled him, but he couldn't figure out what it was. By the time he was a half a block from the scene, he knew.

The strip mall was a gutted, scorched skeleton of the building it had once been. The smell of smoke was still heavy in the air, the intersection inundated with soot-blackened water, the storm drains clogged with burned debris. He didn't remember what stores had been in the mall, but he knew somebody who rented one of the offices upstairs.

Nick Stryker. The same guy whom the woman he'd just booked for murder had hired to follow her cheating husband. Now somebody had torched Stryker's office, maybe even killed him.

Coincidence?

No such thing. As Steve parked his car behind the medical examiner's windowless black Suburban, he made a mental note to check on Monette's whereabouts at the time of the fire—not that he really figured she was responsible.

The area was roped off with yellow caution tape, and members of the LAPD Scientific Investigation Unit, affectionately known as the crime scene mice, were on the job.

The work of the mice had been popularized on shows like *CSI*, where the forensic team tooled around in Humvees, wore designer clothes, and carried guns. If the mice expected any of that Hollywood glamour to rub off on them, they were mistaken. They drove old Ford vans and wore unisex jumpsuits. The only weapons they carried were tweezers and baggies. And if Steve had ever caught them questioning a witness, he would have shot them.

He flashed his badge at the LAPD officer securing the scene, stepped under the tape, and began looking for Dr. Amanda Bentley among the investigators swarming over the debris. She was a pathologist at Community General Hospital, where the morgue doubled as the adjunct county medical examiner's office. So she wore two lab coats, one as pathologist, the other as medical examiner, handling overflow for the beleaguered county morgue and the chronically understaffed ME's office. She juggled the inhuman demands of both of her jobs, as well as single motherhood, with astonishing ease and efficiency. Steve wished he knew how she managed it. Even more, he wished he could find her. She didn't seem to be anywhere.

Steve approached one of the arson investigators, flashed his badge by way of introduction, and asked him where the ME was. The investigator directed him to the alley behind the building, where he found Amanda and another arson investigator peering into a scorched trash bin.

"What's the story?" Steve asked as he stepped up beside them.

"That's what we're trying to figure out," Amanda said, motioning towards the trash bin.

He followed her gaze and saw a charred corpse, vaguely recognizable as human, curled up amidst the burned trash, his fists clenched under his chin as if preparing for a blow from a boxer. Steve knew from experience not to read anything into the position of the body. The tremendous heat from the fire had dehydrated the victim's muscles, causing them to contract and twist the body into the pugilistic position.

When Steve looked up again, Amanda introduced him to the arson investigator, Tim Lau.

With his LAFD baseball cap and wraparound sunglasses, Tim looked less like an arson investigator than a Hong Kong movie version of an American cop.

"What can you tell me about the fire?" Steve asked, shaking Tim's hand.

Tim glanced at the building behind them. "Well, Steve, it started on the second floor—"

"The third office from the left," Steve interrupted.

Tim smiled. "I'm impressed. What tipped you off? The pattern of spalling on the concrete?"

Steve shook his head. "The office belongs to Nick Stryker, a PI who likes to catch philandering husbands in the act. I'm surprised someone didn't lob a Molotov cocktail through the window years ago."

"That wouldn't have been enough accelerant to cause the amount of spalling I saw," Tim said. "It was too widespread."

"Spalling?" Steve asked.

"Pockmarked concrete. The flammable liquid seeped into minute cracks in the concrete and ignited, creating fissures, holes, and flakes."

"That's why you don't want to line a campfire with wet rocks," Amanda said. "The rocks will explode."

Steve gave her a look. She shrugged.

"I was a Girl Scout," she said. "And a troop leader."

"Of course you were," Steve said.

Amanda cocked her head towards the body in the bin. "You think this is Stryker?"

"You tell me," Steve said.

"I can't—at least not yet," she said. "The victim was nearly cremated. There's almost no skin or subcutaneous tissue left. Call me in the morning after I've had a chance to do some cutting. I might even have a cause of death for you by then."

"How did he end up in the trash bin?" Steve asked.

"You tell me," Amanda said.

Steve looked back at the corpse and considered the possibilities. If the victim was Stryker, the killer could have tossed him in the trash and set him aflame to make a statement. Then the killer torched the office to destroy Stryker's files and any evidence that might lead to him.

Considering Stryker's methods and his line of work, the scenario wasn't as contrived as it might otherwise have seemed.

Another possibility also occurred to Steve. This wasn't the first time he had come upon a body torched in a trash bin. A few years back, he'd pursued a psycho who got his kicks dousing drunks and derelicts with gasoline and setting them on fire. One of the victims was found in the trash bin he called home.

Steve didn't think the two cases were related. The psycho

was dead; he'd set himself on fire as Steve closed in to arrest him. But that case reminded Steve that trash bins made sturdy, if unsanitary, homes for derelicts. The victim in this situation might have died accidentally, if the flames from the building had ignited something in the trash bin where he was sleeping.

Or the victim could have been a witness, someone who saw the arsonist at work and was killed to keep him from talking.

He would check the cars parked in the area, see if one of them belonged to Stryker. If not, he'd put out an APB.

"Well?" Amanda asked, jarring Steve from his thoughts. "What's your theory?"

"I'll know more in the morning," Steve said.

"What makes you think you'll know then?" Amanda asked.

"Nothing," Steve said. "But that seems to be the stock answer around here." He faced Tim. "There's something you can tell me. Which fire started first, the trash bin or the building?"

"I don't know," Tim said. "When the firefighters arrived, both the building and the bin were already fully engulfed. We're collecting samples from the point of origin and from this trash bin and running them through the vapor trace analyzer. But I should have an answer for you soon."

"Let me guess," Steve said. "In the morning."

Tim smiled. "You must be a detective."

Dr. Mark Sloan got his wish. There were so many patients to treat, and so many bureaucratic hassles to deal with, that he didn't have a free moment to think about who sent Monette Hobbes the photos and why the person waited a year to do it.

When he left the hospital, his mind was still buzzing with

the events of the last few hours, rehashing encounters with patients, meetings with staff, and memos he'd written.

He was halfway home to the beach house in Malibu when the mystery began to occupy his thoughts again. This time he welcomed the puzzle. He hoped the short respite from thinking about it would give him a fresh perspective on the facts and allow him to see something he missed before. Sometimes he just needed to give the jumbled bits and pieces of information a chance to settle.

But it didn't happen this time. The facts were as muddled and confusing as before.

Mark headed north on the Pacific Coast Highway, the slow-moving rush-hour traffic a ribbon of lights illuminating the curving shoreline ahead of him.

It was a warm summer night, so he was driving with the top down on his Mini Cooper convertible. He could almost smell the sea through the exhaust fumes and hear the waves under the roar of passing cars.

To his left, beachfront homes were crammed tightly against one another, their decks leaning out over the crashing surf. Every winter, the waves would swallow a house or two, but the lots were never left vacant for long. Someone was always willing to build a new home where the sea had claimed one. If Mark's beach house was ever washed away, he would probably rebuild too, assuming he could find anyone crazy enough to offer him homeowner's insurance again.

To his right were the ever-eroding hillsides of Santa Monica and the Pacific Palisades, held back by all kinds of elaborate retaining walls meant to keep the homes, apartment buildings, and parks along the cliffs from falling. But the slopes were littered with foundations, swimming pool tiles, exposed pipes, and ripped fencing, constant reminders of the futility of the costly efforts.

Mark tried calling Stryker and got sent to his voice mail again. Irritated, he checked his own voice mail for messages, but Stryker hadn't returned his call. He did, however, get two recorded sales pitches, one offering him low rates on home refinancing and another from a stockbroker with some wonderful investment opportunities to share.

He deleted the messages, recordings of recordings, and wondered if there was anybody who actually responded to cold calls from computers. His musing was a desperate attempt to distract himself from more pressing questions, and it didn't work.

When he finally arrived at home after what seemed like days on the road, there was a large cardboard box waiting for him on his front porch, his mail stacked neatly on top of it. The box was about the size of the file-storage cartons used in offices. He wasn't expecting anything larger than a book from Amazon, so he assumed the box was a mail-order purchase that Steve had made.

Mark and Steve lived together in the house. Steve had the beach-level first floor, which had all the conveniences of an apartment, including a small kitchen and a separate entrance. Mark lived on the street-level second floor, which had a gourmet kitchen, a dining room, and a family room that shared a sweeping view of the bay and opened to a wraparound deck with steps leading down to the beach.

This arrangement allowed each of them privacy but more opportunity to spend time together than a father and a son with busy professional lives would otherwise have had.

It was especially convenient for Mark, making it easy for him to pry into whatever investigations his son was working on.

Mark moved the letters off the top of the box and was surprised to see his own name on the address label. The box was from Weldon, Jarvis & Swann, a Century City law firm that he was unfamiliar with.

He carried the box inside, set it on the kitchen table, and opened it with a steak knife. The box was filled to the brim with bulging files, audiocassettes, and camcorder tapes. A white letter-sized envelope sat on top of the files.

Mark opened the envelope and pulled out a handwritten note. The first line grabbed his full attention.

If you are reading this, I'm dead.

CHAPTER FOUR

Armed with a search warrant, Steve went from the scene of the fire to Stryker's condo in a sprawling Marina del Rey complex inhabited primarily by recently divorced men, upwardly mobile singles, flight attendants, and airline pilots.

There was a reason the area was more popularly known as Marina del Lay.

Steve flashed his badge and the warrant to the forty-five-year-old property manager, a man who apparently never got the news that *Miami Vice* had been canceled. He wore a blue T-shirt under a white linen blazer and parted his hair down the middle. He tossed Stryker's key to Steve and didn't bother to escort him to the condo.

That was fine with Steve. He didn't need Sonny Crockett's uglier brother looking over his shoulder while he searched the place.

It was a typical bachelor condo, dominated by a huge leather recliner that faced a sixty-five-inch television and an elaborate entertainment system. A leather couch, a glass-topped coffee table, and several framed prints that Steve had seen before in one of those shopping mall galleries completed the living room furnishings. A camera with a massive telephoto lens was mounted on a tripod facing the closed drapes.

He parted the drapes, opened the sliding glass doors, and

stepped out onto the narrow deck overlooking the yachts in the marina. He wondered how many starlets Stryker had photographed sunning themselves on the decks of their boats.

The sky was impossibly blue and picture-perfect, sailboats drifting through the channel and seagulls appearing to float on the breeze that wafted in off the sea. He couldn't see the ocean from the deck, but he could smell the salt in the air.

Or at least that's what he thought it was. Considering how much toxic runoff ended up flowing into the sea, perhaps what he'd grown up assuming was the scent of salt air was actually industrial solvent, insecticide, and raw sewage.

On that sobering thought he stepped back inside to continue his task.

The kitchen was surprisingly clean and orderly, leading Steve to suspect that Stryker had a regular maid service. He opened a few cupboards and drawers, saw nothing unusual, and moved down the hall to the bedrooms.

One of the bedrooms served as a home office. The walls were lined with shelves filled with past issues of all the major monthly and weekly gossip and celebrity magazines, going back years.

The desk was simple and sleek, with no drawers. It held a slim computer, flat-screen monitor, printer, scanner, shredder, wireless router, and an iPod bay.

There was an empty slot in the computer where the hard drive had once been. It was unlikely that Stryker had ripped it out of his own computer.

Someone had been here before Steve.

He continued searching the office, but without much effort. He knew he wouldn't find any external hard drives, disks, CDs, DVDs, or a laptop. Whoever took the hard drive would have taken them, too.

He spent an hour searching the master bedroom, the closets, and the bathrooms and came up with nothing but a sore back. If Stryker had met his violent end here, there were no obvious signs of it.

Before he left, Steve called the crime lab and asked them to give the condo a more thorough ransacking, and to pay special attention to uncovering any hidden compartments or safes. He then called homicide and asked a junior detective to pull Stryker's phone records for his home, his cell, and his office for the last month, as well as a list of his recent credit-card transactions, and have them on his desk by morning. On his way out, he checked Stryker's parking spot. His Escalade wasn't there.

It was after eight p.m. when Steve walked through the front door of the beach house and found his father at the kitchen table, barely visible behind stacks of files.

"It's not like you to bring your work home," Steve said.

"It was waiting for me when I got here," Mark said without lifting his gaze from what he was reading.

"What's your take on coincidences?"

"No such thing."

"Then this will interest you," Steve said. "Somebody torched Nick Stryker's office last night. I think he's been murdered."

"So do I," Mark said, still absorbed in the papers and pictures in front of him.

"You do?" Steve said. "You must have been talking to Amanda."

"I haven't seen Amanda all day," Mark said.

"Then how do you know Stryker was killed last night?"

"He wasn't," Mark said.

Steve rubbed his temples, trying to massage away his exasperation. "But you just said you thought he was."

"I think it's likely that he's been murdered," Mark said. "But it didn't happen last night."

"I've got a burned corpse that says otherwise," Steve said.

"It's not Stryker," Mark said.

"How can you possibily know that?"

"The post office doesn't move that fast," Mark said.

"You think the post office put out a hit on him?" Steve said. "They must really be cracking down on people who send letters without sufficient postage."

Mark finally looked up, a smile on his face. "I'm sorry, Steve. I'm a bit distracted."

"When have you ever found hospital paperwork more interesting than a homicide investigation?"

"This isn't hospital paperwork," Mark said. "Stryker sent me all this yesterday. It was waiting on my front porch when I got home tonight. These files are probably what the person who set the fire to Stryker's office was hoping to find or destroy."

"So what makes you think Stryker is dead?"

"He told me," Mark said, holding up the handwritten letter. Steve took it from his father and read it.

Dr. Sloan,
If you're reading this, I'm dead.

The odds are that whoever killed me can be found in these files. Somebody decided to gamble that I was bluffing when I told him that if anything ever happened to me, all the dirt I had on him would go public.

He was wrong and I'm dead. Life is cruel.

You're getting all the major-league stuff, because I'm betting that's where the hit came from. All the petty domestic crap, the evidence against the adulterers and small-time embezzlers, has gone directly to the losers being betrayed or ripped off. I doubt any of those "civilians" had the guts or the means to kill me, but just in case, there's a list of them in here somewhere, too.

Before I met you, this box of explosives was supposed to go to various members of the press. I was always uncomfortable with the idea of sending my files to one man, newspaper, or TV station. Reporters can be easily bought or intimidated, and the media are controlled by multinational corporations, who are cowards.

But you, Mark, are the one guy I ever met who couldn't be bought or intimidated by anybody. I looked for dirt on you and I was never able to find any, which means you're either the most honorable man on earth or one of the cleverest.

Either way, I win. Except for the fact that I'm dead, which is lousy.

I know you thought I was a sleazebag, and that what you'll find in this box will only confirm your opinion, but I'm certain you won't stop until you find the son-ofabitch who killed me.

You can't help yourself. That's the one secret of yours I was able to find out.

Make the bastard pay, okay? And tell him I'm work-ing on my tan in hell, waiting for him to show up.

    Nick Stryker

Steve handed the letter back to his father. "Where's the box all of these files came in?"

Mark motioned to the kitchen. Steve went over and examined the box. He noted the law firm's return address and double-checked the date of the postmark.

"Do you know the law firm?" Mark asked.

Steve nodded and came back to the table. "They're criminal defense attorneys for the crook on a budget."

"We'll have to ask them when Stryker was murdered and how they knew about it," Mark said. "But at least we know from the postmark that it was a day before his office was torched."

"That doesn't mean the corpse Amanda's got on a slab

isn't Stryker," Steve said and then explained to his father about the body that was found in the burned-out trash bin. "He could have been killed a few days ago. Whoever did it could have tossed the body in the Dumpster last night and torched it with the building."

"I suppose it's possible," Mark said. "We'll know in the morning."

Steve gave his father a look.

"What?" Mark asked.

"Nothing. It's just going to be a big morning, that's all," Steve said. "So what have you gathered from all these files?"

"I know why Monette Hobbes got those photos today and not a year ago," Mark said.

"So do I," Steve said. "Stryker knew all about Lowell's affair with his stepdaughter and was blackmailing him to keep quiet about it."

"Stryker had no professional ethics whatsoever," Mark said.

"You're just discovering this?"

"I thought at the very least he was loyal to his paying clients," Mark said. "Clearly I was wrong."

"He was loyal to whoever could pay him the most," Steve said, "whether it was the client or the person he was following."

"I'm assuming Lowell paid Stryker not to tell Monette about his affair with LeSabre," Mark said. "But when Stryker was killed, his lawyers automatically sent the photos to Monette."

"The blackmail of Lowell Hobbes is probably just one example of the 'domestic crap' Stryker was talking about in his letter."

"There are a lot of people who got a very unpleasant surprise in their mailboxes today," Mark said.

Steve gestured to the files on the table. "So what makes this stuff so special?"

Mark picked up a yellow legal pad covered with his notes. "I've only skimmed a few files, but the people he was blackmailing with all these documents, photos, and videos aren't just guilty of infidelities. They committed felonies."

"What kind of crimes are we talking about?" Steve pulled out a chair and sat down next to his father, looking over his shoulder at the indecipherable scrawl on the legal pad.

"Extortion, grand theft, bribery, and manslaughter," Mark said. "The perpetrators run the gamut from CEOs to politicians, from rock stars to police officers. Stryker compiled all the evidence necessary to put them in prison."

"And put himself in the ground," Steve said.

Mark and Steve had pizza delivered and spent the night going through Stryker's blackmail files, audiocasettes, and videotapes, creating a master list of the information, photos, and tapes and what they contained.

Although Mark found Stryker ethically challenged and morally bankrupt, he had to admire the man's skills as a detective. The files showed that Stryker was a meticulous, tenacious, and inspired investigator with a keen understanding of the dark side of human nature. His natural talent at investigation should have propelled him to the upper echelons of the field. Instead, he let greed undermine his potential.

The irony, as Mark saw it, was that Stryker could have made so much more money as an ethical professional than he did as a blackmailer.

He also might have lived longer.

Mark, fascinated by the information in the files, would have liked to work through the night, but his body betrayed him. Around three a.m., he started to nod off at the table and finally dragged himself to bed. But he forgot to close the shades and was awakened only four hours later by the morning sun streaming through the window.

He trudged into the kitchen to find Steve where he left

him at the kitchen table, a laptop computer open in front of him and the files rearranged into piles on the floor around his feet.

"Make any headway?" Mark asked.

Steve yawned and leaned back in his chair. "I've separated the files into categories." He motioned to each pile as he spoke. "Cases where I can go out and make immediate arrests. Cases where I've got to get a search warrant. Cases I need to refer to other law enforcement agencies. And cases requiring further investigation or surveillance. There's enough here to keep me busy for months. I hate to say it, but I'm almost grateful to Stryker. All these arrests could knock me up a pay grade and make me Cop of the Year."

"You can pay him back by catching his killer," Mark said. "Anybody jump out at you as more likely than the others to want him dead?"

"I'm sure they *all* want him dead, but not all of them have the resources or the stomach for it or have enough to lose to make murder seem like a reasonable option," Steve said, turning the screen of his laptop to face Mark. "Anybody he was blackmailing could have done it, but these are the people my gut tells are the likely suspects."

Mark looked at Steve's notes on the screen. The details of three cases were listed, as well as Steve's rationale for picking them as suspects.

In one case, a woman hired Stryker to follow her ex-husband, a Los Angeles city housing official named Delmar Campos, who she was convinced was cheating her out of her fair share of his income.

"Delmar left her for a stripper and moved into an opulent new home, so naturally his ex wanted blood," Steve said. "Stryker discovered that the new home was built by Douglas Lorusso, a contractor who'd won millions of dollars in city contracts from Delmar to build low-income housing. He also found out that Delmar's girlfriend drove around in a Mercedes leased to Lorusso Construction. Stryker was black-mailing both Delmar and Lorusso."

"So what makes them more likely than the others to have killed Stryker?"

"Lorusso's name has come up in several organized-crime investigations," Steve said, "but we've never been able to make anything stick. He wouldn't have a problem finding someone to remove Stryker from the population."

"Makes sense." Mark scrolled down to the next case.

Weldon Fike was a convicted rapist who was paroled and given a new identity in exchange for testimony against a prison gang responsible for arranging the murders of trial witnesses. One of Fike's rape victims hired Stryker to track him down so she could expose him to the public.

"Where is Fike now?" Mark asked.

"Here in LA," Steve said. "About to marry a woman worth about a hundred million."

"That's a hundred million motives for murder right there," Mark said.

Steve clicked to the next case. "This is the file that's going to be the trickiest to handle."

"Why's that?"

"Because it hits so close to home," Steve said and went on to summarize the case for Mark.

Stryker was hired by a church to find tens of thousands of dollars in stolen computers, paintings, and rare artifacts. The police, in the opinion of the pastor and his congregation, just weren't doing enough. Stryker's search included scanning eBay, where he found several of the stolen items listed under several different auction accounts.

"He bought some things and managed to trace the items back to a warehouse in Chatsworth, owned by Harley Brule," Steve said. "Who happens to be the detective in charge of LAPD's West Valley Major Crime Unit."

"That explains why the police weren't aggressively pursuing the case," Mark said.

"It gets worse. Stryker tapped into the warehouse's own surveillance system and discovered the place is stocked wall to wall with stolen goods, hundreds of thousands of dollars' worth of jewelry, electronics, artwork, even a couple of cars," Steve said. "He also kept track of people coming and going from the warehouse, which included other MCU cops, as well as several patrol officers from ValTec, a private security company."

"Who was Stryker blackmailing?" Mark asked.

"Everybody," Steve said. "It's his most recent score. They were supposed to make their first payment this week."

"Did they?"

Steve shook his head. "If they did, it was with a bullet."

CHAPTER FIVE

While Mark made breakfast, Steve showered and got into fresh clothes. Over pancakes and bacon, orange juice and coffee, they sketched out a game plan for the investigation.

Their first stop would be to see Stryker's attorney. Then, depending on whatever warrants the DA could get them, they would move to arrest and interrogate the three top suspects in Stryker's murder and the firebombing of his office. In the meantime, they'd go over Stryker's phone and credit-card records and see if they could trace his movements over the last few days.

Steve called his captain and the DA to brief them on the Stryker files while Mark cleared away the dishes, took a shower, and got dressed.

When Mark returned to the kitchen, Steve was just hanging up the phone. He told his father there was going to be a slight change in their itinerary. Amanda had called to say that she'd finished her autopsy report on the body found in the Dumpster and that Tim Lau, the arson investigator, was on his way down to meet her with his preliminary findings.

Mark and Steve packed the stacks of files into old cardboard boxes and priority-mail cartons scrounged from the garage, put the boxes in the trunk of Steve's department-issue Crown Victoria, and slogged through the rush-hour traffic to Community General Hospital.

They walked into the morgue to find Amanda and Tim at her desk, sipping coffee and laughing together over something. They were as at ease having coffee among the corpses as they would have been in a Starbucks. Amanda seemed unusually upbeat and animated considering the early hour and the gruesome nature of her work. Mark attributed her bright demeanor to Tim's company, and judging by the scowl on Steve's face, so did his son. Steve didn't harbor any romantic inclinations towards Amanda, but he was very protective of her, as an older brother would be towards a younger sister.

"Should we have brought pastries?" Steve said.

Tim glanced at Steve, then back to Amanda. "Is he always this sour in the morning?"

"Morning, noon, and night," Amanda said, then introduced Tim to Mark.

"It's an honor to meet you, Dr. Sloan," Tim said, his back to Steve, who rolled his eyes, earning a glare from Amanda. "Your work on the Sunnyview Bomber case is textbook material in the training of arson investigators."

"Really?" Mark asked. "I didn't know that."

Tim couldn't see Steve behind him, kissing the air to illustrate his view of the investigator's comments.

"Here's my preliminary report." Amanda threw a file at Steve's head, then politely handed Mark and Tim each a copy of the file. "The first thing I can tell you is that he's not Nick Stryker."

"Then who is he?" Steve asked, picking up his file from the floor.

"He's the guy who set fire to Stryker's office," Amanda said.

"You can tell that from an autopsy?" Steve said.

"I'm amazing," she said.

"I can vouch for that," Tim said.

"Can you?" Steve said.

Amanda walked over to one of the autopsy tables, where

a body was covered by a white sheet. The three men followed her. She pulled back the sheet to reveal the blackened corpse, seared down to the charred muscles.

"The victim suffered multiple traumatic injuries. Fractures, ruptured organs, and collapsed lungs," she said. "He was nearly incinerated. The nature of his burns indicates he was near the source of the explosion when it occurred."

"What explosion?" Steve said.

"The one that blew him out the window of Stryker's office and into the trash bin," Mark said, leaning over the body to examine it closely. "These are concussive-force injuries."

"Translation, please," Steve said.

Tim looked at Steve and gave him the kind of smile a person might give an old lady he was helping across the street.

"The concussive wave from an explosion is like a fall from a high building," Tim said. "It has the same impact on a body as smacking into the sidewalk would have."

Mark glanced at Steve. He could tell his son was restraining the urge to slap the helpful smile right off Tim's face.

"And how do we know he wasn't tossed off the roof of the mini-mall?" Steve's voice was unnaturally even, betraying the effort he was making.

"A two-story fall wouldn't have produced such extreme trauma over his entire body," Mark said.

"How do we know he wasn't tossed off another building, scraped off the pavement, dumped in the trash bin, and then set on fire?"

"The burns tell the story, Steve," Tim said. "And it's corroborated by the fire damage in the building. Let me show you."

He walked back to Amanda's desk and picked up his leather shoulder bag from the guest chair. He reached inside, pulled out a stack of photos, and spread them across her desktop.

Mark, Steve, and Amanda joined him to look at the various

wide and close-up shots of the fire scene and individual pieces of twisted metal and burned wood. To Mark's untrained eye, it was all just blackened rubble. Tim took a sleek silver pointer from his breast pocket, extended it, and used it to direct their attention to individual photos.

"Judging by the intensity of the heat on these structural elements, the second-floor office was clearly the point of origin for the fire, which was started with gasoline," Tim said. "The pattern of spalling on the walls and floors indicates where the gasoline was spread. The guy splashed it everywhere, as you can see, including the wall around the door."

Tim retracted his pointer. "Since we didn't find traces of any other explosives in the office, we've developed a theory as to what happened."

"Who's we?" Steve asked.

"Amanda and me," Tim said. "We spent several hours last night fleshing things out."

"I bet," Steve said, turning to Amanda. "She hasn't fleshed in a while."

"She's very good at it," Tim said, acknowledging for the first time the tension between them.

Mark cleared his throat. "From what I understand, Tim, a gallon of gasoline equals twenty sticks of dynamite. But spilled gasoline doesn't explode, it ignites."

"True, Dr. Sloan," Tim said, turning to Mark and missing the glare of fury Amanda shot at Steve. "But imagine if someone dropped a match into a gasoline container."

"But that's not what happened here," Mark said.

"In a sense it is," Tim said. "The office was the container."

"Our theory is that the guy wasn't an experienced arsonist," Amanda said. "This was probably his first time torching anything. So he broke in, closed the door behind himself, and started pouring gasoline around the office. But he stopped for some reason, perhaps to read something or go through a file cabinet. After a few minutes, he finished emptying the canister, struck a match, and tried to ignite the gasoline."

Tim jumped in, like a relay runner taking the baton. "But the gasoline doesn't catch. Frustrated, he rolls up some papers like a torch, lights it, and tosses it across the room. What he doesn't realize is that all this time, gasoline fumes have been building up in the confined space."

"It was like walking into a house with a gas leak and turning on the lights," Amanda said. "Boom and adios."

Tim and Amanda smiled at each other, pleased with themselves. They had every right to be.

Mark went over the facts and saw the scenario clearly in his mind. The arsonist was blown out the window and landed, ablaze, in the trash bin in the alley below.

Steve could see it, too. They did such good work together, Steve could almost forgive Tim for hitting on Amanda so hard and her for succumbing so quickly.

He shook his head in disbelief. "I've got to hand it to you two. That's one incredible theory, but it all fits. Whoever this guy was, he's won himself a place of honor in the Moron Hall of Fame."

"The word around LAFD is that he's definitely a nominee for the Idiot Arsonist of the Year Award," Tim said, recognizing Steve's comment for the peace offering that it was.

"Sounds like he'll make a clean sweep of all the major imbecile awards this year," Steve said, then faced Amanda. "It would be great if we could identify him so his family can accept the honors on his behalf."

"I'm working on it," she said. "But if it helps, a few years ago he took a bullet in the shoulder."

Mark looked thoughtfully at the burnt body on the autopsy table. "Have you collected any other unidentified bodies in the last week or so?"

"Nope," Amanda said.

"Then we have a problem," Mark said.

"What's that?" Steve said.

Mark sighed. "We're one body short."

"Nick Stryker was murdered?" attorney Pamela Swann asked. She was sitting behind her desk, breast-feeding her baby daughter. "When did it happen? How was he killed?"

"We were hoping you could tell us the answers to those questions," Steve said, trying hard not to look at Swann's open shirt.

Swann was in her early thirties, tall enough to be an awesome basketball player, and surprisingly frail for someone who had just given birth to an enormous baby girl.

Her office was cramped, the furniture rearranged to make room for a crib, a playpen, and a baby-changing table. Steve's seat was right next to the diaper genie, which, from the smell, he figured was overdue for emptying.

"Maybe it's the hormones raging through my system," she said. "But I'm totally confused, Detective. If you don't know how Nick was killed, what makes you think he was murdered?"

Swann didn't seem all that confused to Steve. In fact, she somehow managed to maintain her lawyerly air even with a baby suckling her breast. He wondered if she'd chosen this moment to feed her baby just to unnerve him. If so, it was working. His father, however, appeared completely at ease.

"Because you told us," Mark said amiably. "Well, you told me, actually. I was sent a box of files and this letter."

Mark passed a copy of Stryker's note across the desk to her. She leaned forward to take it, revealing even more of her bosom to Steve, who looked away quickly.

She read it carefully and set it aside, taking a deep breath before speaking again.

"I've been on maternity leave for the past two weeks," she said. "I didn't know about this."

"Then how did it get sent?" Steve asked.

"It was all prearranged, part of a simple system we worked out. It's been going on for so long that I forgot all about it," she said. "I delegated it to my assistant years ago."

"How does the arrangement work?" Mark said.

"Nick calls on the seventh of every month and leaves a message on our voice mail. Nothing special, just a simple hello is all," she said. "If he doesn't call, we're supposed to immediately send out all the files in his safe-deposit box according to whatever instructions we find there."

"That's it?" Steve said incredulously. "You weren't supposed to even try to call him to double-check? Maybe stop by his house to see if he was okay?"

"He's always called," she said.

"Why didn't you notify the police?" Mark said.

"That wasn't part of his instructions," she said.

"You could have done it out of concern for your client," Steve said.

"I show my concern by respecting my client's wishes, which, in this case, are in writing."

"But if he didn't call, you knew it had to mean he was in danger," Mark said. "Or worse."

"I didn't know anything. I wasn't here. This is the first I've heard about it," Swann gently lifted her baby away from her breast, adjusted her blouse, and draped a towel over her shoulder. "Now maybe you can answer a question for me. Where did you find Nick's body?"

"We haven't," Steve said.

"So he could still be alive." Swann held her baby to her shoulder and gently patted her back.

"Someone set fire to his office and he didn't make his call," Mark said. "It doesn't look too good."

"He could be in hiding," Swann said.

"Those files were his meal ticket. Stryker would have found a way to call you from whatever rock he was under," Steve said. "He's dead."

Swann started rocking gently in her seat. Steve wasn't sure if it was to comfort herself or the baby.

"Do you know what case he was working on?" Mark asked her.

She shook her head. "I haven't talked to him in months. But he sent a box of chocolates to me last week in the maternity ward."

"Did you know what was in Stryker's files?" Steve said.

Swann offered him a tight smile. "Do you really expect me to answer that?"

Steve shrugged. "Stranger things have happened."

CHAPTER SIX

There was a list of things District Attorney Neil Burnside was determined to avoid in the few short months before the people of Los Angeles went to the polls and, he hoped, elected him mayor in a landslide over his opponents—the current chief of police, a city councilwoman, and the incumbent mayor.

Most of the things on his list he could control. He wouldn't drive drunk, he wouldn't cheat on his wife, he wouldn't take any bribes, and he wouldn't murder anybody.

But there were a few items that were a question of fate. He didn't want a scandal within his office. He didn't want any celebrities to murder anyone. And he didn't want anything to do with Dr. Mark Sloan.

Publicly, Burnside was on record many times declaring his respect for Dr. Sloan and his appreciation of the man's invaluable contributions to law enforcement. His true opinion of the doctor, however, was far different.

He conceded that Dr. Sloan was a brilliant detective who had been responsible for the apprehension and conviction of many killers over the years. But every one of the doctor's successes was nonetheless an embarrassment to Burnside's office and the LAPD. If a white-haired old doctor could solve more murders than professional homicide investigators, what did that make them?

Inept.

His opinion of Mark Sloan was unaffected by the fact that the homicides the doctor solved jacked up the DA's conviction rate. The glory went to Sloan, even if the doctor avoided the limelight and always gave credit for his accomplishments to the detectives and prosecutors. The damning, though unspoken, subtext was still there: The LAPD and the DA's office aren't as bright as some elderly, amateur sleuth.

Dr. Sloan probably didn't intend to send that message, though Burnside couldn't be entirely sure, especially now, at the onset of what was certain to be a hotly contested mayoral campaign.

Burnside wondered if perhaps the doctor's avuncular personality was actually a disarming ruse to disguise the cunning political gamesman he really was.

He'd underestimated Dr. Sloan many times before. Doing so again now could have disastrous consequences.

All of which made the box on Burnside's desk as dangerous as it was tantalizing.

Burnside stared at it. So did his campaign manager, Rhea Dickens, and his most trusted prosecutor, Owen Penmore, the man he was grooming to take his place.

Burnside spoke first. "A string of major arrests and convictions between now and election day would make me look like a confident, aggressive, and successful prosecutor."

"Who owes it all to the work of a blackmailer. How's *that* going to look?" Penmore folded his arms across his broad chest. He came from a wealthy family and had a St. Bart tan and a double-breasted, tailored suit that were beyond the means of any other civil servant at his pay grade.

"Stryker is dead and may never be found." Dickens paced in front of the desk, casting a glance at the box each time she passed it. "Forget about him."

"He obtained this evidence questionably at best and illegally at worst," Penmore said. "He defrauded his clients and blackmailed the targets of his investigations. His character, or lack of it, taints every document, photograph, wiretap, and video in that box."

Dickens rejected his concerns with a dismissive wave of her impeccably manicured hand. "He's not a factor anymore."

"He will be when they find his corpse," Penmore said.

"Who says they have to?" Dickens cast a conspiratorial glance at Burnside, who pretended, for Penmore's benefit, not to notice.

"Either way, Stryker isn't going to be available to be impeached on the stand," Burnside said. "So who is to say exactly how he obtained this evidence or what he was doing with it?"

"The high-powered lawyers all his victims are going to be hiring after we arrest them," Penmore said. "They will make him the story."

"A tiny, two-paragraph news brief on the back page of Section B, while the coverage of their clients' crimes will be splashed all over the front page of the *Los Angeles Times* and will be the lead item on every local newscast, especially after we leak some of the wiretaps and video evidence to the press," Dickens said. "Nobody is going to care where it came from. They'll be too busy being shocked by the sound bites and the video clips. Whatever noise they have to make about Stryker can't possibly compete with that."

She leaned across the desk to face Burnside. "Think of all the media attention these cases will bring you without costing the campaign a dime."

Burnside had thought about it. He also liked the idea of ending his tenure as district attorney with a string of headline-grabbing convictions that would overshadow his past missteps.

He motioned to the box. "We may only have to introduce a fraction of this stuff in court, Owen. What are these files, really? It's no different than someone phoning in a tip or reporting a crime. We can use what Stryker has gathered as a starting point and obtain the evidence we need for conviction on our own."

"That's true," Penmore said. "We can cherry-pick the best stuff from his files and corroborate the rest ourselves."

Dickens looked at Penmore. "If you've got a video of a politician taking bribes, in the court of public opinion nobody is going to care where it came from or how it was obtained."

"That's not where I try cases," Penmore said.

"It's where I do, sweetie," Dickens said, wagging her finger at him. "These files are a godsend for our campaign."

"Stryker may actually have accomplished something worthwhile with his miserable life," Penmore said. "Shame he had to die to do it."

There was another benefit to making cases on Stryker's files. Nobody had brought it up yet, but Burnside knew his campaign manager was certainly aware of it. The arrest of Lieutenant Sloan's top suspects in Stryker's murder would be personally disastrous for two of Burnside's rivals in the mayoral race.

A big police-corruption scandal involving the Major Crime Unit could torpedo Chief John Masters's campaign long before election day.

And the revelation that Delmar Campos, a good friend and appointee of the mayor's, took bribes from a Mob-connected contractor could derail the entire reelection campaign.

But Penmore was right—there was a risk of blowback for Burnside. Aligning himself with a blackmailing scumbag like Stryker could have unforeseen consequences, especially if the investigation into the murder unearthed even more unsavory secrets in Stryker's past.

Burnside cleared his throat and sat up straight in his seat. "We have to put my campaign considerations aside."

"We do?" Dickens said.

"Rhea, my first obligation is to the pursuit of justice. We've received irrefutable evidence that serious crimes have taken place, and it's our obligation to prosecute the offenders, no matter what," Burnside said. "Owen, I want you to start getting whatever warrants are necessary. If you need help, pull people off of other cases. This takes priority."

"What about the Stryker murder investigation?" Penmore asked.

"I'm sure the facts concerning whatever happened to Mr. Stryker will eventually come to light in the course of our prosecutions of these offenders," Burnside said.

"Lieutenant Sloan may not agree," Penmore said.

"He'll be too busy working on the task force I'm creating to deal exclusively with closing these cases," Burnside said. "Get him in here right away."

"What makes you think the chief will go along with forming this task force?" Penmore said.

"Because it will look a hell of a lot worse for him if he doesn't," Burnside said.

"I'd see to that," Dickens said. "And Masters knows it."

"I'm counting on you, Owen," Burnside said. "My future and yours depend on you now."

"I won't let either of us down," Penmore said and hurriedly left the room.

Rhea Dickens looked at Burnside and smiled in admiration. "You're good. I have a feeling that becoming mayor of Los Angeles may just be a stepping-stone to much bigger things for you."

He smiled back confidently, but he knew there was still a wild card that could disrupt everything.

Dr. Mark Sloan.

What was the doctor's motivation in all this? Was it to remove Chief Masters from the political playing field? Or was there a booby trap hidden amidst the files that Mark Sloan knew would blow up in Burnside's face?

It was a risk he'd have to take.

That uncertainty was another good reason to put Steve

Sloan on the task force. In fact, maybe Detective Sloan should *lead* it.

The more Burnside thought about it, the more he liked the idea, if for no other reason than the clear message it would send to Mark Sloan.

If I go down, Doc, your son goes with me.

After meeting with Stryker's lawyer, Steve dropped Mark off at Community General, promising to call if there were any new developments. They both knew that Steve couldn't act on the information in the files until he got the go-ahead from his captain or the DA's office. And there was nothing left for Mark to do on his own.

So Steve decided to go back to his office and concentrate on backtracking Stryker's movements, using his phone records and credit-card statements as a guide.

Stryker's various home, office, and mobile phone records were waiting for Steve on his desk, but the PI's credit-card and bank statements hadn't come in yet.

The first thing Steve noticed was that Stryker hadn't made any calls from any of his phones in the last four days. That in itself was an ominous sign.

He started sorting through the list of calls Stryker had made over the past several weeks. Most of them meant nothing to him at first glance.

Except one.

It was the number for arranging visits with death row inmates at San Quentin.

Steve was reaching out to call San Quentin himself when the phone rang.

The call was from Chief Masters, ordering him to drop everything and report to the district attorney immediately.

CHAPTER SEVEN

Mark waited for Steve that night at Barbeque Bob's, the small restaurant his son and Dr. Jesse Travis bought a few years earlier from the original owner. The purchase price included the recipes to Bob's three sauces and his secret smoking techniques, all of which his cattle-driving ancestors supposedly honed on the trail in the 1880s and brought west with them when they finally settled in California. From the looks of the restaurant, most of tables and benches and even the sawdust on the floor dated from the same period.

Steve and Jesse like to call Barbeque Bob's a throwback to simpler times, which was their catchall excuse for not spending any money to fix the place up. While the decor may not have earned them a spread in *Architectural Digest*, the barbecue they served was widely regarded as among the best in Southern California.

Their pecan pie wasn't bad either, especially when paired with a scoop of vanilla ice cream the size of a softball.

Mark was enjoying a slice of that pie when Steve showed up forty minutes late and slid into the booth across from him.

"Sorry I'm late," Steve said, setting a file down on the table between them. "I had a long meeting with the district attorney about Stryker's files."

"So did he give you the green light to start acting on Stryker's evidence?"

"I've been temporarily reassigned by the chief to an inter-agency task force created to oversee all the investigations springing from Stryker's files," Steve said without enthusiasm. "It's being run out of the DA's office by me and Owen Penmore, Burnside's pet prosecutor."

"That's a good thing," Mark said. "Isn't it?"

"I'm not working the Stryker homicide anymore," Steve said.

"Who is?"

"Nobody," Steve said.

"But you can't just ignore a murder," Mark said.

"You can when there isn't a body."

Mark pushed his half-eaten pie away. He'd lost his appetite. Steve pulled the plate in front of him and picked up where his father left off. His appetite, apparently, was unaffected.

"The DA says whatever happened to Stryker will emerge in the course of our other investigations," Steve said.

"You buy that?"

"No," Steve said. "But I'll question everyone we arrest about Stryker's disappearance and the torching of his office."

"Question them with what?" Mark asked. "The DA isn't allowing you to gather any facts in the case."

"You don't work for the DA," Steve said. "No one is stopping you from gathering facts."

"The only leads I have came from those files," Mark said. "Without them, I have nothing to go on."

Steve slid the file on the table to his father. "Now you do. These are Stryker's phone records. Two weeks ago, he called San Quentin and arranged a visit with a prisoner on death row."

"Who?"

"Bert Yankton," Steve said. "I arrested him a few years back for hacking his business partner up and burying the body parts in the desert."

"The partner must have done something pretty awful to make Yankton so angry," Mark said.

"He slept with Yankton's wife and embezzled ten million dollars from the company's clients," Steve said.

"That would do it," Mark said. "How does Stryker fit in?"

"He was the PI Yankton hired to follow his wife," Steve said.

"Stryker definitely had a talent for catching people with their pants down," Mark said. "What did Stryker want to talk to Yankton about?"

"I don't know, but I'm sure you'll tell me after your visit with him." Steve gathered the crumbs of the pie and the last drops of melted ice cream into his spoon and ate them with a satisfied smile. "You have an appointment on death row tomorrow afternoon."

Not too long ago, Mark had read about an experiment conducted by the *Los Angeles Times*. The paper sent two reporters to San Francisco to have afternoon tea at the St. Francis Hotel. Both reporters left LA at the same time. One flew, the other made the four-hundred-mile drive.

The two reporters arrived at the St. Francis at the same time.

The experiment only confirmed what Mark and most of his fellow Los Angelenos already suspected.

Between the traffic to the airport, the long lines, and the one-hour advance check-in, the forty-five-minute flight to San Francisco had ballooned to three hours. Add to that the time to rent a car or take a cab and make the traffic-clogged drive into the city, and it became a five- to six-hour journey.

All of which explained why Mark Sloan got himself up at five a.m. the next morning. He wanted to get an early start on the drive to San Francisco and avoid getting mired in the morning rush-hour traffic that otherwise would add hours to his trip.

The shortest route to the Bay Area was to take Interstate 5 north up the western edge of California's San Joaquin Valley. The downside was that it was also the dullest stretch of highway in the state, offering neither scenic charm nor interesting places to visit. The interstate was flat and straight, the journey measured in the miles between the next turnoff to a few gas stations and fast-food franchises cut into the farmland.

Whenever Mark stopped over the years at one of those nameless patches of blight, he wondered where the people came from who worked there. Where did they live? He knew there must be small farming towns somewhere nearby, but beyond the occasional road sign on the highway announcing their existence, there was no sign of them in the distance or on either side of the road.

The four hundred miles of mind-numbing, wide-open road were good for a few things—excessive speeding, quiet contemplation, and listening to music. Mark indulged in all three of those pursuits during the five-and-a-half-hour trip. Mostly he thought about what Steve had told him the night before about Bert Yankton's case.

Yankton and his partner, Jimmy Cale, were successful financial managers for actors, directors, agents, and scores of Hollywood executives. Vivian Yankton was an aspiring actress herself. Her husband began to suspect she was cheating on him and hired Stryker to follow her.

When Yankton saw the pictures of Vivian and Cale together, he flew into a violent rage. He smashed up his house with a sledgehammer, ordered his terrified wife to move out, then supposedly drove down to their weekend home in La Quinta to cool off.

Vivian called her lover, Cale, who arranged to meet her in Marina del Rey at an apartment he kept for his illicit assignations. When Cale didn't show, Vivian got worried and went to his home, which she found trashed inside and covered with blood. Police later confirmed that the blood was Cale's.

Steve's theory was that Yankton stopped at Cale's on his way to La Quinta, killed his partner, and threw the body in the trunk of his car.

Once down in La Quinta, Yankton dismembered his partner and scattered the body parts somewhere in the vast desert near his home. When Yankton returned to Los Angeles on Monday morning, Steve arrested him. The crime lab found bloodstains and one of Cale's toes in the trunk of Yankton's car.

Riverside County sheriff's deputies found Cale's blood on an ax in the garage of Yankton's La Quinta retreat but never discovered where Yankton had disposed of the rest of Cale's body parts.

The affair wasn't Yankton's only motive for murder. Cale had misappropriated millions of dollars in funds belonging to their management clients, funneling the money to secret offshore accounts, most of which were never found.

The jury deliberated for one day before returning a guilty verdict against Yankton and even less than that to decide that he should die for his crime.

Of all the wealthy enclaves of Marin County, this was by far the most exclusive neighborhood of all. It was nestled on a pristine shore, windswept by the sea breeze and offering magnificent views of beautiful San Francisco Bay.

But despite the enviable location, the six thousand residents of this guard-gated community were desperate to leave. All they had to do was get past the iron bars, the high walls, the electric fences, the razor wire, and the armed guards.

The builders of San Quentin couldn't have picked a more picturesque spot for California's first prison, erected in 1852 by the boatload of convicts who would be its inhabitants. Now real estate developers were salivating over the prospect that the budget-strapped state government might demolish the decaying, overcrowded prison rather than invest the $300 million necessary to renovate it.

For now, however, the prison remained home to the largest death row population in the nation. Among those 644 men condemned to execution was Bert Yankton, who sat across from Mark Sloan at a table in a private, windowless visitor's room.

Looking at Yankton now, his arms and legs chained, his sunken face sickly pale, Mark was reminded that someone had once said that the leading cause of death on California's death row was old age. Yankton looked deflated, as if all the air, blood, and spirit had slowly leaked from his body.

"I usually get my physicals at the infirmary, not the visitor's room," Yankton said, sounding as fatigued as he looked. "Or do you have something else in mind for me, Doc?"

"Nobody told you why I wanted to see you?" Mark said.

"My secretary isn't very good about passing along my messages," Yankton replied. "I'm thinking about firing her."

"I don't work for the Department of Corrections or for any law enforcement agency, though you've met my son," Mark said. "He's the one who arrested you."

"I didn't know that Lieutenant Sloan was so concerned about my health."

"Actually, it's Nick Stryker's health we're concerned about."

Yankton straightened up in his chair, his eyes showing the first spark of life since Mark arrived.

"What do you mean?" Yankton said. "What's happened to him?"

"He's dead," Mark said.

Yankton sagged. This surprised Mark because he didn't think it was possible for Yankton to sag any more than he already had after five years on death row.

"He was murdered," Yankton said. "And I know who killed him."

"Who?"

"The same person who killed Jimmy Cale," Yankton said.

"How could you do that from in here?" Mark said.

"I'm innocent," Yankton said. "I hired Nick Stryker to prove it."

"Shouldn't you have done that five years ago?"

"I hired a detective agency that's got offices all over the world. They didn't do anything for me during the trial or afterwards besides suck up cash. I finally realized they were going to string me along until my money ran out," Yankton said, "so I fired them and went back to Stryker. He's not the best, but at least he's a man I can trust."

Mark thought about telling Yankton exactly how trustworthy Stryker really was, but decided the kind thing to do was keep it to himself. He chose his next words carefully.

"What made you think you could trust him more than anybody else?"

"When I wanted someone to follow my wife, I chose Stryker over a big agency because I didn't want everybody in Hollywood to know my business," Yankton said. "Those agencies work with all the big law firms, all the studios, and many of my clients. Stryker was a small-time guy. I figured he'd be more discreet."

Big mistake, Mark thought.

"How did you get in touch with Stryker?"

"Through my new lawyer," Yankton said. "Pamela Swann."

Mark wondered what other things the lawyer had lied about during their meeting. He made a mental note to ask Steve to see if any of the blackmail money that flowed into Stryker's bank account had found its way into the college fund for Swann's daughter. But with the DA restricting Steve's activities on the Stryker case, Mark knew it might be some time before he got an answer.

"Have you heard from Stryker since you hired him?" Mark asked.

"If I walk out of here, it's going to make your son look bad. He might even lose his badge. For all I know, it was the LAPD that killed Stryker to cover their asses. Why should I tell you anything?"

Mark mulled over several replies, finally settling on one that wouldn't tell Yankton more than he needed to hear.

"Stryker prepared a letter that was to be sent to me in the event of his death. He wrote, 'If you're reading this, I'm dead.' He asked me to bring his killer to justice. And I will, regardless of the consequences, because it's the right thing to do."

"I suppose if Stryker trusted you with his last wish," Yankton said, "I can trust you with mine."

"You're a long way from dying." Mark knew that death penalty appeals moved at a glacial pace through the California legal system. Things didn't move any faster at the federal level. It could be another fifteen years before Yankton would take the long walk down the short corridor to the gas chamber.

"I'm dying a little every day," Yankton said.

"We all are, Mr. Yankton."

"Not as fast as I am," Yankton said. "I only spoke to Stryker that one time, but he told me what he was going to do. He was going to treat Jimmy's life like an onion."

"An onion?"

"Peel it open one layer at a time, until he found the killer, no matter how much the truth stung while he did it," Yankton said. "I liked the image. I think about that onion a lot. I see onions in my dreams."

Yankton's eyes were moist. Mark didn't know whether it was from peeling all those metaphorical onions or his own helplessness.

"How was Stryker killed?" Yankton asked.

"I don't know," Mark said, and then explained to Yankton about the monthly phone call Stryker made to his lawyer and what happened after that call didn't come. He left out the part about Stryker's files, figuring Swann could tell Yankton about that if she wanted to. "I'm hoping if I follow his tracks, I'll discover what happened to him."

"What about me?"

Mark gave him a look. "What about you, Mr. Yankton?"

"The only thing that keeps me from smashing my skull against one of these walls is the faint hope that somebody will find whoever killed Jimmy Cale," Yankton said. "Stryker was going to do that. Now you will."

Mark shook his head. "I'm only looking for Nick Stryker's killer."

"Fine. You do that," Yankton said, "and you'll find the man who should be sitting here instead of me."

CHAPTER EIGHT

Limousines were lined up in front of the Beverly Wilshire Hotel, waiting for the attendees of the National Lupus Foundation's Woman of the Year dinner, a black-tie benefit honoring a sufferer of the autoimmune disorder for her courage and fund-raising efforts. It was a must-attend event on the Beverly Hills charity circuit. Tom Jones was flown in from Las Vegas to sing and catch the panties the women in the audience threw onstage. At this event, however, he was more likely to be catching girdles and diapers.

A cluster of men in tuxedos and women in evening gowns stood under the hotel's front awning, lustily dragging on their cigarettes during the narrow window of opportunity between the appetizer and the main course.

One of the men was drawing so hard, in fact, that passing motorists were in danger of being sucked into his pockmarked face. Steve Sloan managed to avoid the deadly vortex by approaching Weldon Fike from behind.

Steve was frustrated, waiting for the authorization to make arrests and for all the search warrants he'd requested to come through. So he'd decided to confront the one suspect in Stryker's murder who wasn't facing arrest on another crime. Weldon Fike. The vicious serial rapist who walked out of prison a free man in exchange for his testimony in the federal case. The man Stryker had blackmailed to keep his new identity secret from his victims.

When Steve spoke up, Fike was busy admiring the surgically upgraded cleavage of a Botox-browed society matron through the fog of his smoky exhalations.

"She's a little old for you, Weldon. I heard you like your prey at least twenty years younger," Steve said. "Unless, of course, they happen to be worth a hundred million."

Fike flicked his cigarette into the street and turned to face Steve.

"Naughty, naughty. Littering is a crime, Weldon," Steve said. "You violated your parole."

"You've clearly mistaken me for someone else." Fike adjusted a pair of cuff links to draw Steve's attention to his ten-thousand-dollar Patek Philippe timepiece. "I'm Kingsfield Turlington."

Steve whistled. "Sounds rich. Did you come up with that moniker yourself, Weldon, or did somebody in the witness-protection program choose it for you?"

Fike grabbed Steve by the forearm and led him out of earshot of the others. Ordinarily, Steve would have instantly pinned Fike's arm behind his back and slammed him face-first into the nearest hard object, but he didn't want to make a scene.

"Who the hell are you?" Fike hissed.

"The guy who is going to break your left hand if you don't let go of me, *Weldon*." Steve smiled pleasantly.

Fike let go of him, his eyes drifting to the badge clipped to Steve's belt. "It's Mr. Turlington to you and all your friends. You got a problem with that, talk to the attorney general."

"What kind of first name is Kingsfield anyway? I bet you picked it just so women would have to call you King, especially in bed, where I'm sure you need all the help you can get. Does hearing her call you King make you feel like a man, Weldon, or do you still dream of raping and torturing teenage girls?"

"That never happened. That man doesn't exist, understand?" Fike stepped close, way too close, and looked into Steve's eyes. Most people would probably have been intimidated. Steve might have been, too, if he hadn't been carrying a loaded gun. "You aren't supposed to even look at me."

"I wish I didn't have to," Steve said. "It's hard for me to keep my dinner down."

"We had a deal." Fike didn't break his gaze. He didn't even blink.

"Which deal are we talking about?" Steve asked casually. "The one with the feds? Or the one with Nick Stryker?"

That made Fike blink. He stepped back.

"Stryker." Fike seemed to gag on the name. "I thought that was finished."

"Might have been, if you'd dug a deeper grave," Steve said. "I once convicted a guy on just a nose hair. Imagine that. A nose hair. Never pick your nose, Weldon, especially when you're committing a felony."

"What are you talking about?"

"Murder, Weldon," Steve said. "I think killing a guy voids whatever deal you had with the government."

Fike smiled. "Stryker is dead?"

"You killed him so you could keep more of your allowance."

"Think whatever you want." Fike was suddenly a lot more relaxed than he'd been only moments ago. "I didn't do it, but I'm glad somebody did. He had it coming."

"King?" A sequined woman in her early fifties seemed to glide towards them on some invisible cushion of air. Steve assumed she was the future Queen Turlington.

"Who's your friend?" she asked, crinkling her nose above her artificial smile.

"A gentleman hitting me up for a smoke," Fike said,

doing his best Thurston Howell impersonation. He reached into his pocket and handed Steve the pack. "Keep it, friend."

"It's a filthy habit," Queen said.

"He has worse," Steve said.

She eyed Steve warily, then looked back at Fike. "Is something wrong, King sweetie?"

"Not anymore, my love." Fike looped his arm through hers, turned his back to Steve, and led his fiancée away.

Steve watched them go. Whatever invisible force had propelled her now carried them both back to the ballroom. Science didn't have a name for it, but Steve did.

Money.

Mark firmly believed that the Internet was one of the greatest threats to individual privacy ever invented. It was also a godsend to detectives.

As soon as he got into his room at the St. Francis Hotel, he unpacked his laptop and went straight for the high-speed Internet connection, turning his back to the sweeping view of the San Francisco skyline that he was paying a substantial premium to enjoy.

He ordered room service and started his work by visiting an online national reverse directory, where he input the numbers on Nick Stryker's phone bills and matched them with names and addresses.

Armed with that information, Mark began the laborious task of running each name and address through databases he subscribed to that, for a small monthly fee, accessed the department of motor vehicles, court records, business entity filings, property tax records, even information input by customers when they registered their electronic products and software with the manufacturers.

Mark never registered anything because he knew it was the equivalent of volunteering to have his privacy invaded, his identity stolen, and his mailbox inundated with sales pitches.

Thankfully, though, most of the people Nick Stryker had contacted didn't feel the same way. By midnight Mark had a list of everyone Stryker had talked to over the last month, and where they lived or worked. In many cases he also learned their ages, their occupations, their marital statuses, their legal histories, their military records, the makes and models of the cars they owned, the Web sites they liked to visit, and the electronics they'd purchased.

He complemented those research results with a basic Google search on each person, to see what Web sites, blog postings, newspaper articles, and Usenet discussions came up.

By two a.m., Mark was able to construct a time line of all the people Stryker had called each day. His last call was made three days before his disappearance, to a number in Kingman, Arizona.

Only four names on the list meant anything to Mark. One was Pamela Swann, Stryker's attorney. The others were Cale's ex-wife, Betsy, their daughter, Serena, and Yankton's ex-wife, Vivian.

Betsy and Serena lived in Capitola, a beach community in the Monterey Bay area, about a hundred miles south of San Francisco. If Mark took the long way back to Los Angeles, down the Pacific Coast Highway, he could stop in Capitola on his way and talk with them.

By the time he was done, he could barely keep his eyes open. He was totally exhausted from his long day, the long drive, and the long hours in front of the tiny laptop. It was only as he fell into bed that he remembered that he'd forgotten to call his son and tell him about his meeting with Yankton.

There was nothing exciting to report anyway. He'd learned that Yankton, through his lawyer, had hired Stryker to prove he was innocent. The fact that Yankton was Stryker's last client didn't change anything, at least not yet. And it certainly wouldn't be a shock to Steve that Swann had lied to them. Steve assumed all lawyers were liars. If Mark had proved she was honest, *that* would have been worth a call.

Mark drifted off to sleep wondering how he could have raised such a cynical son.

The international headquarters of the super-secret, unnamed interagency task force of law enforcement agents was a windowless conference room in the district attorney's office that had previously been used to store old computers and busted copiers.

Steve thought it would have been much cooler if the headquarters had been a sleek underground base that was accessible only through a false wall in a dry cleaner's storefront, but the government's budget for law enforcement just wasn't what it used to be.

He was in his seat in the conference room at nine a.m. He was the first and only member of the crack force in attendance at that early hour. At 9:01, Assistant District Attorney Owen Penmore stuck his head in and pointed at Steve, singling him out from everyone else who wasn't in the room.

"You. Burnside's office. Now," Penmore declared and withdrew his head.

Steve glanced at the empty chairs of his absent colleagues. "Don't get started without me."

He followed Penmore down a long row of cubicles to Burnside's corner office. Burnside was behind his desk, glaring in advance at the open doorway so Steve would get the full force of his fury the instant he walked in.

"What the hell were you thinking?" Burnside said.

"I was thinking that I should have picked up a Cinnabon

on my way to the office," Steve said. "I know they're bad for you, but I like them anyway."

"Last night," Burnside said.

"Oh," Steve said. "When exactly? Because I was thoughtful all night."

A vein pulsed in Burnside's forehead. Either Burnside is putting a lot of effort into his glare, Steve thought, or he's about to have a stroke.

"Don't forget who you're talking to, Detective. Or I will take your badge and give it to my wife for her charm bracelet."

From what Steve had heard in the locker room, Burnside's wife had a lot of badges on it already and they weren't gifts from her husband. He could have said that, but decided he was better off saying nothing.

"The Justice Department called my house before the sun was up," Burnside said. "They were irate. They told me that you stalked, harassed, and threatened to expose a high-level resource in the witness-protection program."

"Weldon Fike is a convicted serial rapist who victimizes teenage girls."

"I don't care if he assassinated John F. Kennedy," Burnside said. "He's been exonerated and is under the protection of the federal government."

"So was the second shooter in Dealey Plaza," Steve said. "Or so legend has it."

"You could have blown Fike's cover and jeopardized his future testimony," Burnside said. "And for what, exactly, Detective?"

"The King was being blackmailed by Nick Stryker, who threatened to tell his victims where he was hiding," Steve said. "He also stood to lose his hundred-million-dollar fiancée. He's also got a proven propensity for violence. I think those are all good reasons for Weldon to have murdered Stryker."

"Weldon Fike is the pivotal figure in the prosecution of a prison gang that's responsible for arranging the killings of two dozen people," Penmore said, his voice quivering with rage. "All of the victims were witnesses scheduled to appear in trials in which their eyewitness testimony would have led to convictions. You would jeopardize that case for the sake of a blackmailer?"

"My job is to investigate homicides, not judge the victims," Steve said.

"Your job is to investigate the evidence in Stryker's files and arrest anyone engaged in criminal activity," Burnside said. "There is no murder investigation. Am I clear, Detective?"

"Transparent," Steve said.

"Good, because if you pull anything like this again, your new profession will require a drive-thru window and a paper hat." Burnside picked up several folded blue documents from his desk and held them out to Steve. "Judge Lancaster issued these warrants this morning. They're good for Detective Harley Brule's home, office, car, and the warehouse full of stolen goods he's got in Chatsworth. Shut him down and arrest every member of the Major Crime Unit."

Steve took the warrants. "Will do. Should I alert the media so we have some footage for your next campaign ad?"

"Don't push your luck, Detective," Burnside said. "You don't have many friends left."

"I wasn't aware I had any," Steve said.

"You're getting my point," Burnside said. "You need the power and the publicity that comes from a string of successful, high-profile convictions much more than I do."

"I don't play politics," Steve said.

"Of course you do," Penmore snickered. "You just do it badly."

Steve turned to go, but before he was out the door, Burnside called to him.

"Are you still thinking about that hot cinnamon roll?" Burnside said.

"Yeah," Steve said.

"Get one for me, too, will you?"

CHAPTER NINE

Mark was awakened by two sharp knocks at his door, but the fog in his head didn't clear right away. His mind was still running through an onion field, searching for something he couldn't name. A crow swooped down and cawed, "Maid service."

It was the jarring sound of the door catching against the chain that finally cleared his head. He'd forgotten to hang the DO NOT DISTURB sign on his doorknob last night.

"I'm here," he called groggily from his bed in the dark room. "Come back later."

Mark heard a muffled apology and rested his head again on the sleep-warmed pillow. The heavy shades blocked out the sun completely. The room was black, illuminated only by the light from the corridor that seeped under the door and the red glow of the numbers on the clock radio on the nightstand.

It was ten thirty in the morning.

So much for an early start, he thought.

It was noon by the time he'd showered and shaved, gone down to the business center, and printed out all the notes he'd made on his laptop the night before. He also e-mailed the notes to himself for good measure.

By twelve thirty, he was on the Pacific Coast Highway heading south to Capitola. It was the perfect day to be skimming along the jagged edge of California, all blue skies, tall pines, cotton-ball clouds, and frothy surf.

Mark stopped for a quick lunch in Half Moon Bay at a ramshackle hamburger stand in a pumpkin patch across the highway from the craggy shore. The cheeseburger was soggy and oversalted, but the pumpkin pie was so good it took all of his willpower not to order a second slice. He was becoming a pie addict.

It was nearly two p.m. by the time he drove down the hill and under a towering wooden railroad trestle into Capitola, a seaside village nestled between two cliffs where the Soquel River met the sea.

Capitola had a unique mix of architecture, setting, and lifestyle that managed to simultaneously evoke a Mediterranean resort, gold rush San Francisco, and sixties California at the height of the hippie movement. Somehow, those sharp contrasts melded together seamlessly to create a place of unusual charm and beauty.

Betsy Cale lived in Venetian Court, a tightly packed hamlet of twenties-era villas embraced by the beach in front, the cliffs behind, a fishing pier on one side, and the mouth of the river on the other.

The beachfront villas looked like brightly colored birthday cakes, frosted with swirls of stucco painted pink, orange, blue, yellow, and turquoise under red terra-cotta tile roofs.

Betsy and her daughter lived in the first row of villas on a concrete promenade that doubled as a breakwater in the winter months, when the beach was often consumed by the churning sea.

On this particular day, the sand was as smooth as sugar, dotted by a few sunbathers, two old men flying kites on either side of the gentle river that cut through the center of the beach, and several giggling children running back and forth through the ankle-deep water.

Mark found Betsy sitting at an easel outside the open door

of her villa, facing the bay and delicately dabbing paint on a canvas. She wore a large straw hat, a paint-spattered denim work shirt and loose-fitting shorts. Her skin was evenly sun-bronzed, right down to the toes of her bare feet. She was in her forties, but could easily have passed for a much younger woman. It was only as Mark got closer that he could see the crow's-feet at the corners of her sea green eyes.

He'd assumed she was painting the beach scene playing out in front of her, but as he looked over her shoulder, he could see that her gaze was directed farther south, to a distant pier leading to a shipwreck in the bay.

"I don't see how anyone with a paintbrush could resist capturing a dramatic seascape like that," Mark said.

"They haven't," Betsy said with a friendly smile. "Around here, painting the Cement Ship is a cliché."

Mark squinted into the distance, trying to bring the wreckage into focus through the sea mist. "That ship is made of cement?"

"The *Palo Alto* is our version of the *Spruce Goose*," she said. "She was one of two concrete tankers constructed in San Francisco during World War One. The war was over by the time they were finished. The *Palo Alto* made only one short voyage before she was towed down here seventy-five years ago and beached to become a dance hall. A fierce storm broke the hull apart a few years later, and that's where she's been resting ever since, becoming home to seagulls, pelicans, crabs, mussels, and fish."

"And the inspiration to generations of talented artists like yourself," Mark said.

"I wouldn't call myself talented yet. Fumbling is more like it. There's something about that wreck that captivates me. I could look at it for hours." She sighed wearily and frowned at her painting. "But whatever it is about her that enthralls me, I haven't been able to capture it yet."

"It looks just like it," Mark said.

She shook her head. "It doesn't look like the ship I see."

He studied her painting more closely. There were no birds, no people, no living things in her portrait of the Cement Ship. Only the ocean seemed alive, but even it seemed to ebb into stillness around the wreck. The Cement Ship on her canvas was a broken hulk, fading into the mist like a lost memory.

"It's sad," Mark said.

"What is?"

"Your Cement Ship," he said. "All the history you told me is right there in your brushstrokes. I see the wasting away of a dream, the ruins of hopes that went unfulfilled."

She studied her own painting, as if seeing it for the first time.

"What happened to the sister ship?" Mark asked.

"The *Peralta*. Amazingly, it's still afloat, up in British Columbia," she said. "It's one of ten rotting old warships anchored together to form a breakwater for a paper mill on the Powell River. I'd like to go up there someday and paint it, too."

"What's stopping you?"

Betsy motioned towards a slim teenage girl in a bikini, lying on her stomach on a beach blanket. The girl was leaning on her elbows, running a yellow highlighter over passages in a textbook, her face a grimace of boredom.

"I know the feeling." Mark nodded. "It's not easy being a single parent."

Betsy set down her paintbrush and turned to give Mark her full attention. "How did you know I'm a single parent?"

Mark offered his hand. "I'm Dr. Mark Sloan, chief of internal medicine at Community General Hospital in Los Angeles."

She shook his hand but looked at him guardedly. "It's a long way to go for a house call, Doctor."

"You met my son a few years ago," he said. "Lieutenant Steve Sloan."

"The homicide detective who investigated my ex-husband's murder," she said. "Jimmy seems to be a popular topic lately."

"I suppose Nick Stryker came down to see you, too," Mark said.

"So that's what this is about," she said. "You're worried that Stryker might prove that your son put an innocent man on death row."

"Do you think Bert Yankton is innocent?"

"The Bert Yankton I knew was a sweet man who was manipulated and betrayed by those closest to him," she said. "I have a hard time imagining him killing anyone, even with the horrible things that Jimmy did to him. That's probably not what you wanted to hear."

"The evidence against him was pretty compelling," Mark said. "Especially when you look at his motive and his state of mind the night of the murder. His wife was lucky he didn't take a swing at her with that sledgehammer."

"If you're convinced he's guilty, then why are you so worried that Stryker will come up with something that will set him free?"

"I'm not," Mark said.

"Then what are you doing here?" Betsy said. "It wasn't to learn about the Cement Ship."

"Nick Stryker disappeared a few days ago," Mark said. "I'm trying to find out what happened to him."

"Why?"

"Because he asked me to," Mark said. He told her about the letter he received from Stryker and his visit with Yankton at San Quentin, but he didn't mention the box of blackmail files.

"You think whatever happened to Stryker has something to do with my ex-husband's murder?" Betsy asked.

"I don't know," Mark said. "I'm following Stryker's tracks, hoping I'll figure out what happened along the way."

"If you do that," she said, "whatever happened to him could happen to you."

Mark smiled. "I try not to think about that."

She regarded Mark anew and, apparently, liked what she saw. "How would you like an ice-cold glass of fresh-squeezed lemonade?"

"That would be very nice. Thank you."

Betsy stood up and led Mark into her villa. While she got out the pitcher of lemonade, two glasses, and some cookies, Mark took a moment to look around, his hands clasped behind his back.

There were only two bedrooms and one small bathroom in the villa, the narrow kitchen separated from the living room by a high counter. All the furniture was wicker, with hand-sewn seat cushions and throw pillows. The walls were paneled in lacquered pine and decorated with photos of Serena and Betsy's paintings of Capitola's many scenic charms.

It was a small space for two people to live in, but Mark thought the location more than made up for the cramped quarters. When Mark's wife had died, he also had moved to the beach to live with his child.

Betsy invited Mark to join her at the table, which was placed in front of the big picture window that dominated the living room. Wooden storm shutters were latched open outside on either side of the window.

As she poured the lemonade, Mark complimented her on her cozy abode.

"This is why I will always do whatever I can to help Bert," she said, settling into her seat across from Mark. "I owe him for giving us this wonderful life."

"What did he have to do with it?"

"The only decent, unselfish thing Jimmy ever did was put

Bert in charge of our finances. Bert made sure that our assets were protected, that Serena and I would always be secure."

Betsy looked protectively at her daughter on the beach. Serena felt her mother's custodial gaze. The teenager put her highlighter down and cocked her head quizzically, as if to say, Is everything okay? Her mother smiled reassuringly and turned back to Mark.

"After Jimmy was killed, investigators discovered that he'd been looting from his clients for years and stashing the cash in secret accounts. Bert had no idea either."

"It's hard to believe that he didn't know," Mark said. "It was his business, too. The police believe it was the one-two punch of finding out that Jimmy was stealing from the company and sleeping with his wife that provoked Bert's murderous rage."

"If Bert had known about the looting, he would have reimbursed the clients himself. That's the kind of man he is," she said. "But he ended up paying for it anyway. The pack of wolves cleaned him out and then they came after me."

"Why you?"

"Because Jimmy willed everything to me," Betsy said. "The army of lawyers and accountants hired by Jimmy's clients found only a small fraction of what he stole. So they pillaged our accounts and made us sell off everything. The house. The furniture. The art. The cars. And the thing he loved most of all—his money."

"His money?" Mark said. "You mean you had to liquidate his investments?"

"No," she said. "I mean I sold his collection of cash. Jimmy loved money the way that James Bond bad guy Goldfinger loved gold. He liked the look of it, the feel of it, the smell of it, and, of course, what he could get from it. He enjoyed looking at the cash in his money clip almost as much as his collection of paper currency."

"He was a numismatist?"

"Not many people know that word," she said. "Even fewer can pronounce it, including me. So I called him a money collector. It fit his hobby and his profession. He had one of the finest U.S. currency collections in the world. He was particularly fond of large-denomination National Bank Notes, gold certificates, and silver certificates."

Mark knew a little about numismatics. As a kid he collected coins, but after a couple years of intense devotion to the hobby, his interest waned. Along the way, though, he learned some things about currency.

For instance, he knew that National Bank Notes were paper money issued by individual banks across the country under a charter from the Treasury Department, a practice that began after the Civil War and continued until the early thirties. What made the currency collectible was its scarcity and its regional character. The bills were emblazoned with the names of their issuing banks. Some of the institutions were obscure and produced only a small number of notes.

While the physical condition of the bills played a large part in determining value, Mark knew there were other important factors that collectors considered, including the denomination, the color and type of the U.S. Treasury seal, the signatures on the note, and the actual size of the bill itself.

Mark shared his limited numismatic background with Betsy, who admitted that her knowledge of the field wasn't much better than his. She was, however, able to describe to him some of the highlights of Jimmy Cale's multimillion-dollar collection.

"The least valuable notes in Jimmy's collection were worth from thirty-five thousand to one hundred thousand dollars," she said. "But his most prized possessions were crisp, uncirculated currency worth nearly three hundred thousand dollars each."

Those bills included a hundred-dollar gold certificate from 1882 with a portrait of Senator Thomas Hart Benton on the face, a five-hundred-dollar legal tender note from 1880 with a red seal and a portrait of Major General Joseph King Mansfield on the face, and an 1882 fifty-dollar gold certificate with a brown seal and a portrait of New York governor Silas Wright on the face.

"Not that I really know what any of that means," she said. "I couldn't tell you why a red seal was any more valuable than a brown once, or vice versa. It seems strange to me that a bill worth fifty dollars at the time it was printed could be worth six thousand times as much now."

She told Mark that it took her ex-husband years to accumulate his remarkable collection through brokers, dealers, auctions, and private transactions between other well-heeled numismatists. But it took her only a single day to auction it all off to keep the slavering lawyers, accountants, and creditors at bay.

"All that was left were the crumbs that Bert wisely set aside for me and Serena years ago," Betsy said. "It turned out to be enough for us to buy this place and support ourselves. It gave me the freedom to be a stay-at-home mom and look after Serena instead of having to apply for a job at Wal-Mart. I shop there, though. It's about all we can afford."

That was when Serena walked through the door, her towel and textbook under her arm, her feet covered with sand. The breeze from the beach carried the scent of her coconut suntan lotion across the room.

"Serena, how many times do I have to tell you to wash your feet before coming in the house?" Betsy said.

"We live at the beach, Mom," Serena said. "There's sand everywhere. That's life."

"Wash your feet," Betsy said firmly.

Serena groaned at the unendurable oppression, tossed her stuff on the wicker couch, and held her foot under the water faucet next to the front stoop. She looked up at Mark as she washed her feet.

"Who's our guest?" she asked. "Another private eye?"

"Have there been more than one?" Mark asked Betsy.

"No, just your friend," Betsy replied, then turned to her daughter. "This is Dr. Sloan. He's helping Mr. Stryker out."

"Nick showed me his ride," Serena said. "A tricked-out Escalade with a DVD entertainment system and chrome spinners on the rims."

"I've seen it," Mark said.

"Do you have a cool car, too?" Serena asked.

"I drive a new Mini Cooper," Mark said.

Serena frowned. "Cool, but not *private eye* cool. More like community college, aspiring actress cool."

"You mean it's more suited to someone like you," Mark said.

"Clever deduction," Serena said mischievously. "Are you sure you're not a detective?"

"I'm not, but my son is a police officer."

"What does he drive?" She dried off her feet by wiping them on the doormat, which made her mother scowl. Mark was sure that was why Serena did it.

"A Ford pickup," Mark said.

"If you don't want him living at home until he's thirty, get him a sports car for his birthday."

It was a little late for that. "What makes you think he still lives at home?" Mark asked.

"He drives a Ford pickup. Unless he's a cop in Mayberry, it doesn't make him much of a babe magnet." She gathered up her things and headed towards the bedroom. "I've got to change for class. Nice meeting you."

"You too," Mark said.

CHAPTER TEN

At the exact moment Lieutenant Steve Sloan walked into the squad room of the West Valley Police Station to address the members of the Major Crime Unit, carefully coordinated simultaneous raids were occurring all across the Southland.

SWAT team members and police officers working under the auspices of the DA's special task force served search warrants at Detective Harley Brule's Chatsworth warehouse, where they arrested Brule's wife, Natalie, and several off-duty MCU detectives and ValTec security officers. Task force officers were also searching their homes, offices, and private vehicles for evidence related to the fencing of stolen goods.

But Harley Brule didn't know that. Nor did the five other members of his unit who were sitting in chairs facing the watch commander's podium, where Steve now stood.

Brule certainly wasn't Jack Webb's vision of an LAPD detective. He'd shaved his head down to the shiny skin on his knobby skull and wore a skintight black T-shirt to show off his prison yard pecs—not that he'd ever been anywhere near a prison yard.

That was going to change, Steve thought. He was surprised nobody had noticed Brule was a crook before. The cop was practically advertising it with his attitude. He slouched in his seat, looking bored, so his crew of MCU cops affected the same disaffected pose.

It was going to be a pleasure taking these arrogant jerks down, Steve thought.

"I'm Lieutenant Steve Sloan. I've moved over from robbery-homicide to lead a joint agency task force working out of the district attorney's office. I'm here because we've uncovered a major crime ring in the West Valley trafficking in stolen goods."

Brule muttered an expletive.

"Did you have something to say, Detective?" Steve asked.

"It's crap, Lieutenant. Nothing happens in the Valley that we don't know about," Brule said. "Usually before it happens."

"I'm sure that's true," Steve said.

"Then why are you here?"

"To clear up the confusion."

"I'm not confused." Brule turned to another member of his team. "Are you confused, Rollo?"

"No, sir," Rollo said.

"See?" Brule looked back at Steve. "No confusion here."

"Then maybe you can tell me why you're clearing thirty thousand dollars a month selling stolen goods online through auction sites," Steve said.

Brule sat up slowly in his seat. He looked over his shoulder at his men, and that was when he noticed the uniformed police officers filing into the room.

"We thought you understood that the Major Crime Unit was supposed to *prevent* major crimes, not commit them," Steve said. "That's the confusion."

"You're making a big mistake," Brule said.

"There's something else I don't want you or your crew to be confused about," Steve said. "You have the right to remain silent. Anything you say can and will be used against you in a court of law . . ."

As he read the men their rights from the podium, the uniformed officers moved in, handcuffed the detectives, and took their weapons.

Brule glared at Steve the whole time. Suddenly the room was alive with the sound of beepers chirping and cell phones trilling.

"You can ignore those pages and calls. I can tell you who's calling," Steve said. "It's your frantic wives and children warning you that cops are tearing your homes and cars and boats apart, that your Chatsworth warehouse has been taken down, and you should ditch anything incriminating that's on you. I'm afraid it's too late for that."

Steve stepped out from behind the podium, walked up close to Brule, and got right in his face.

"We have Stryker's files, Harley," Steve whispered.

Brule flinched as if slapped.

"Your wife is in a cell. Your son is being picked up at school by child protective services. Think about that," Steve said. "Think about your wife in prison and your son in the foster care system. Think about what you can tell me to make life easier for them."

Before Brule could reply, Steve walked away to let the dirty cop marinate in his guilt, torture himself with the horrible fates that would await his loved ones if he did nothing.

After Serena went off to attend her afternoon classes at Cabrillo College, Betsy invited Mark to take a stroll with her on the beach. Mark rolled up his pantlegs and went barefoot, letting the surf wash around his ankles as they walked.

"What sorts of things did Stryker want to know about?" Mark asked.

"You never call him Nick," she said. "The way you talk about him, he doesn't sound like much of a friend."

"He wasn't," Mark said. "To be honest, I don't even like him much."

He doubted she would either if she knew that Stryker made his living as a blackmailer.

"You're going to a lot of effort for someone you don't like."

"If I don't look for him," Mark said, "I'm not sure anybody else will."

"There's probably a good reason nobody wants to bother," she said. "But I guess you already know what that is. And you're looking anyway."

"You think I'm a fool?"

She smiled at him warmly. "It's better to be a man who cares too much than one who doesn't care at all."

"You ever know anybody like that?"

"I married one," she said. "Jimmy was all about Jimmy. For a while, he was the center of my universe, too, so it worked out. But then Serena was born, and that changed my priorities. It didn't change his."

"What were his?"

"That's basically what Nick Stryker wanted to know, what was Jimmy into? He liked to party, smoke fine cigars, and gamble. He'd go to Las Vegas every chance he got. That's where we got married, that's where we had our honeymoon, and that's where he wanted us to go on vacation," Betsy said. "I begged him to go to Europe, but he wouldn't go anywhere he couldn't speak the language. Not understanding what people were saying made him feel horribly paranoid and insecure. The one time we went down to Cabo, we had to come back after only two days because he couldn't sleep. He worked himself up into a panic, convinced that everyone speaking Spanish was ridiculing him, laughing about how they'd ripped him off."

"Kind of ironic, considering he was busy ripping off his unknowing clients."

"I'd say it was his own guilt bubbling up to the surface, but Jimmy didn't have any guilt," Betsy said. "He never even tried to hide his sleeping around."

"When did the womanizing start?"

"After Serena was born," she said. "I think he wanted to make me leave him. I wouldn't do it. Part of it was out of spite. I didn't want to give him what he wanted. Mostly I stayed with him for Serena. I felt she needed her father in her life. But he never was. I finally realized that divorcing him wouldn't change her life that much after all."

They continued walking for a while in silence, crossing the river to the other side of the beach, where his car was parked along the promenade. When they got to his car, he opened the hatchback and retrieved his research notes from his suitcase.

"Very cute," she said from behind him.

"What is?" he asked.

She grinned. "If I said your fanny, would it make your day?"

"My decade," Mark said.

"I was talking about your car," she said.

"Maybe I'll put spinners on the rims to give it some gangsta edge," Mark said.

"That's fine," Betsy said, "but what are you going to do about the driver?"

Mark reached into the front seat, grabbed a pair of sleek Ray-Ban sunglasses, and slipped them on.

"It's a start," she said.

He handed her the list of names and addresses he'd gleaned from researching Stryker's phone bill. "Do any of these names or addresses mean anything to you?"

"Sure," she said. "A lot of these are currency collectors and dealers who sold him bank notes. And I know Jimmy shopped at some of these cigar stores."

"Was Jimmy a big cigar smoker?"

"He had a private humidor at Hampshire's, a Beverly Hills tobacconist, as well as a four-thousand-dollar rosewood humidor at his office. At home, he had a humidified room kept at a constant temperature of sixty-five degrees just for his cigars. Jimmy treated his cigars like bottles of wine. He said they only got better with age. He smoked one every night. God knows how many he went through at the office or the blackjack table. Some of my clothes still smell like his damn cigars."

She handed the notes back to Mark.

"Thank you so much, Betsy," Mark said. "You've been an enormous help."

"Let me know how things turn out, okay?"

"Absolutely." Mark shook her hand.

She turned and started walking back towards the beach. Mark got into his car, sat on the edge of the seat, and wiped the sand off his feet.

"Hey, Doc," Betsy called out.

Mark looked up.

"Your fanny is pretty cute, too."

He felt himself blush. He couldn't remember the last time that had happened.

She smiled, amused with herself, and continued on her way.

Mark did the same.

CHAPTER ELEVEN

Harley Brule didn't look too comfortable sitting in the lop-sided chair reserved for suspects in the interrogation room. The hard-assed arrogance was still there, but now the effort that went into sustaining it was showing.

Steve sat across from Brule and didn't have to put any effort into looking relaxed. He was. He didn't feel any tension at all.

"You know how the game is played," Steve said. "So I'm not going to waste any time. Here's where things stand. We've got you. We've got your wife. We've got your entire crew. We've got all the evidence we need. This will be the easiest case the DA has ever prosecuted."

"Then why the hell are you here?" Brule said.

"I'm thinking about your wife and kid," Steve said. "We're going to come down hard on you no matter what you tell us. We have to make an example out of you. But maybe we can get your wife probation so she can take care of your kid. All depends on whether you talk."

"If your case is so good, what do you need me to talk about?"

"You could plead guilty, save the taxpayers some money," Steve said. "You can also tell us who capped Nick Stryker."

"Nick who?"

Steve leaned forward, resting his arms on the table. "The

guy who was blackmailing you. The guy who said if anything ever happened to him, his files would go to the police. I've got a news flash for you, Harley. He wasn't bluffing. We've got the photos, the videos, the phone taps, and the stolen goods he won in your eBay auctions."

"You know that, then you know I paid him," Brule said. "We gave him ten percent off the top to keep quiet."

"Harley, you've seen what prison does to a woman. Do you really want your wife to go through that? Think what kind of life your son is going to have in foster care. You can save them."

"I didn't kill Nick Stryker," Brule said.

"I'm sure you didn't," Steve said. "You got someone to do it for you. I want a name, Harley."

"I don't have one to give you because I didn't kill the sonofabitch."

There was a knock from the other side of the interrogation room mirror, behind which was an observation room where people could watch without being seen.

Steve rose from his seat. "A man takes care of his family. I guess you're not much of a man."

"I can give you something else," Brule said. "I can tell you who sold us the merchandise."

"We arrested the ValTec security guards, too." Steve shook his head and walked to the door. "You'll have to do better than that."

Owen Penmore was waiting for Steve in the corridor, a file in his hand. The ADA looked very pleased with himself.

"The raids were a complete success. We've gathered enough stolen goods to fill a moving truck and apprehended every member of Brule's unit except one."

"Who?"

"Detective Arturo Sandoval."

"How did he get away?"

"He didn't," Penmore said. "Sandoval hasn't showed up for work in three days."

"Has anybody else see him?"

"Nobody knows where he is. His girlfriend hasn't heard from him in a week," Penmore said. "She figured he was working undercover or something."

"Is he?"

"The MCU isn't running any undercover operations," he said. "They're too busy robbing people. We've put out an APB on his car."

Steve thought for a moment. "Can you pull his jacket for me? I want to know if he's ever been shot in the shoulder."

"I can tell you that right now." Penmore opened the file in his hand and flipped through a few pages. "Yeah, he took a bullet five years ago. Why?"

Steve smiled to himself. "I think we're going to have to amend the charges against Brule."

"To include what?"

"The murder of Nick Stryker," Steve said.

It was late afternoon by the time Mark left Capitola. He decided to put off the five- to six-hour drive back to Los Angeles until the next morning. There was no point in exhausting himself. He chose instead to spend the night in Monterey, the former Spanish colonial capital of California.

He checked in at the Portola Plaza Hotel, located on the harbor in the center of town, right at the base of Old Fisherman's Wharf. The desk clerk won Mark over immediately by giving him two hot chocolate chip cookies in a little Baggie along with his room key.

Mark took his overnight bag to his room, plugged in his laptop, and sat down to make a few calls to the people on Stryker's phone bill. But first he needed to figure out what lie he was going to tell.

The truth was too complicated to explain and unlikely to win the cooperation of those he was calling.

After a moment he came up with a lie that was close enough to the truth that maintaining the deception wouldn't tax him too much. It was also the kind of lie that could prove alluring to the people he was calling.

He began by calling the currency dealers. He introduced himself by his real name, explained that he was writing a book about the Jimmy Cale murder case, and wanted to learn more about the man as a "three-dimensional person" rather than simply an embezzler and adulterer. Part of understanding Cale meant learning more about his passions, and there was nothing the man loved more than his money.

With the exception of passing himself off as a writer researching a book, Mark's pitch was pretty close to the truth, and everybody he called was eager to help him.

He learned that Cale was well known in numismatic circles and had a collection that was the envy of many in the field. But Cale made a lot of enemies on the way to accumulating that collection, using his wealth to pummel his opponents. Few could afford to outbid him, and he thought nothing of overpaying for an item just so he instead of someone else could possess it.

When Cale's collection went up for auction after his murder, it created a feeding frenzy among the wealthiest numismatists, though their identities remained secret and their bids were made anonymously through brokers or front men.

This was not unusual. Because the paper money fraternity was quite small, Mark learned, it wasn't in any collector's best interest to let his specialities become too well known. So to shield their anonymity, and get the best price, the wealthiest collectors worked through middlemen.

Some of the collectors who were outbid at the auction still hadn't given up on getting what they'd lost.

When an uncirculated hundred-dollar brown seal, 1882

series gold certificate believed to have been part of Cale's collection had recently come back on the market, a broker acting for a secret buyer nabbed it for a whopping three hundred thousand dollars, well over its actual value. The same broker bought an 1880 series hundred-dollar silver certificate signed by Register of the Treasury Glenni W. Scofield and U.S. Treasurer James Gilfillan, like one Cale owned, a few months earlier.

The broker's name was Sanford Pelz.

Mark wasn't surprised to find that Pelz appeared several times on Stryker's phone bill. Pelz was also the last person Stryker had called before disappearing.

When Mark tried to call Pelz, all he got was an answering service. The broker's address was a post office box in Kingman, Arizona.

He glanced at his watch and was surprised to see that it was nearly eight o'clock. His stomach growled, reminding him that all he'd had to eat since lunch was two chocolate chip cookies.

Mark e-mailed his notes to himself, shut down his computer, and left the hotel in search of some dinner. He strolled down Fisherman's Wharf, which was lined with souvenir shops, candy stores, and seafood restaurants. The air was heavy with the smell of salt water, fried fish, and roasted nuts. In the harbor, barking sea lions piled up on buoys and sailboats chugged slowly to their moorings.

At one time, Monterey was one of the largest suppliers of sardines in the world, shipping two hundred thousand tons a year, until the ocean was finally fished dry. Now the once bustling Cannery Row, immortalized by John Steinbeck, was an outlet mall. There was no place for history in America, Mark thought. But there could never be too many outlet malls.

Mark didn't consciously pick a place to eat. He kept walking until he came to the restaurant at the end of the wharf. He didn't feel like turning around to see what restaurants he'd missed, so he went inside without even glancing at the menu displayed out front. The restaurant had a marvelous view of the bay and, as it turned out, served decent seafood, too.

His mind was a blank while he ate. He was letting the events of the day, and all the facts he had accumulated, churn in his subconscious without any prodding from him.

He'd set out to discover what happened to Nick Stryker by following the detective's trail until he disappeared. But now Mark realized he had to do more than that. He had to follow the man's *thinking*.

Bert Yankton hired Stryker to prove he didn't kill his best friend, Jimmy Cale, the man who betrayed him by plundering their business and seducing his wife. Mark knew Stryker wasn't interested in correcting a miscarriage of justice. Stryker took on only work that had a potential for blackmail. So what was the blackmail potential in this case?

Did Stryker actually believe Yankton was innocent? Or was he stringing Yankton along until the money ran out? That was the most likely scenario, but it didn't explain why Stryker actually seemed to go to work on the case.

If Stryker believed Yankton was innocent, did he intend to blackmail the real killer and let Yankton remain imprisoned for a crime he didn't commit?

Why did Stryker bother talking to Betsy? What did Stryker hope to learn from her? What *did* he learn? Mark didn't know. All he knew was that after talking with her, Stryker spent the next several days contacting currency dealers all over the United States.

What was Stryker looking for?

Why was he so interested in Cale's money?

One obvious conclusion occurred to Mark: Jimmy Cale wasn't killed by Yankton. He was murdered for his currency collection.

*   *   *

Steve was reasonably certain who killed Nick Stryker and why. The only thing left to do now was prove it.

While Burnside and Penmore were busy hustling more search warrants against other criminals in Stryker's files, Steve contacted Dr. Amanda Bentley at the morgue. He told her about Arturo Sandoval, the missing member of the West Valley Major Crime Unit who once took a bullet in the shoulder.

Amanda said she would pull Sandoval's dental records and medical files and compare them with the unidentified charred corpse in her freezer.

In the meantime, Steve interrogated the other members of the Major Crime Unit. None of them would cut a deal to testify against Brule or their fellow cops. And none of them would admit to any involvement in Stryker's murder. The ValTec security guards, the ones who did most of the actual stealing, weren't any more helpful, mainly because their involvement in the scheme ended once they sold their stuff to Brule.

Steve would have to crack Brule. He'd left Brule alone and handcuffed in the interrogation room to stare at his own reflection and wonder what would become of himself and his family.

It was nearly six p.m. when Amanda finally called Steve with her results: The charcoal man was definitely Detective Arturo Sandoval. Now all the pieces fell into place. There was a homicide case to close, and Steve was going to close it.

Steve returned to the interrogation room to confront Brule with the new information.

Brule was sitting in his chair, legs stretched out, feigning sleep as Steve came in.

"About time," Brule said. "I've been in here for hours."

"Would you prefer a cell?" Steve took the seat across from him and set a file down on the table.

"I'd prefer a bathroom," Brule said. "You know how long it's been since I've taken a leak?"

"No," Steve said, "but I know what happened to Arturo Sandoval."

Steve pulled a picture of Sandoval's charred corpse from the file and slid it across the table to Brule.

"He torched Stryker's office a couple nights ago and managed to torch himself in the process."

"So?" Brule slid the picture back to Steve.

"Sandoval was one of your crew," Steve said. "You ordered him to kill Stryker and destroy his files."

"You can't prove that," Brule said, nervously shaking his leg. Steve wasn't sure whether Brule was doing it out of anxiety or to control his bladder.

"Stryker was blackmailing you and the crew. You were Sandoval's commanding officer in the MCU and on the street. Stryker was murdered, his office was burned down, and Sandoval's body was found at the scene. Come on, Harley, how do you think that's going to look to a jury? They'll connect the dots and end up with a pretty picture of an electric chair—with you strapped into it."

Both of Brule's knees were bouncing now. He leaned forward, sweat glistening on his bald head.

"Look, Artie hated giving that parasite Stryker a percentage," Brule said. "I said it was the cost of doing business, but Artie didn't see it that way. He wanted us to kill Stryker and torch his office. I said no, it was too big a risk. What if Stryker's threat was real? What if the files weren't in his office? Artie says so we make him tell us where the files are and *then* blow his brains out. I told him to live with it. I guess he couldn't."

"You're saying Sandoval acted alone," Steve said.

"Yeah, that's what I'm saying," Brule said.

"You expect me to believe he'd defy you and risk the consequences?"

"What choice do you have?" Brule said.

Steve shrugged. "I can pin it on you."

"Go ahead and try."

"Tell me where the body is," Steve said. "That's your only bargaining chip."

"I told you, I don't know," Brule said. "But I'll testify to whatever you want against Artie and you can close the Stryker case. It's a win-win for you."

"You think that's all you've got to give us to get your wife probation?"

"It's a good deal. The doubleheader of arresting me and solving Stryker's homicide will play well in the press. The DA will make the deal whether you like it or not," Brule said, then turned and looked directly into the mirror. "Now will somebody take me to the goddamn bathroom before I wet myself?"

CHAPTER TWELVE

"Brule's right," Penmore told Steve later as they stood in District Attorney Neil Burnside's office. "It's a good deal."

"See?" Burnside said to Steve. "I told you the facts surrounding Stryker's murder would shake out in the normal course of events."

"Brule is lying," Steve said. "He ordered the hit and he's letting a dead man take the fall. So are we."

Burnside shrugged. "So what?"

"He's getting away with murder," Steve said.

"He's doing time. Nobody is getting away with anything. Do you have any idea what it's like for a cop in prison?" Burnside said. "It's going to be living hell for ten long years."

"If he survives," Penmore said.

Steve couldn't argue with that. And yet he still was uneasy about the deal. Burnside seemed to read his mind.

"The fact is, Detective, even if Brule ordered the hit, he sure as hell didn't pull the trigger," Burnside said. "Sandoval did that. This is the best outcome we could possibly hope for without Sandoval's testimony against Brule."

"I know," Steve said. "I don't know what my problem is."

"I do," Burnside said. "It's not that Brule isn't being charged with murder. It's that he's getting what he wants. He won the contest in the interrogation room."

Steve sighed. "I hate to admit it, but yeah, you're probably right."

"It would bug me, too. I like to win. But you've got to look at the big picture, Detective," Burnside said. "You closed two big cases today and we're going to reward your efforts with two big convictions. And this is just the beginning."

"There are a lot more files where this one came from," Penmore said. "Tomorrow we're arresting city housing chief Delmar Campos for corruption and his contractor buddy Douglas Lorusso for bribery. And that's just for starters. Campos will crack and Lorusso's little crime family will collapse. We've wanted to take Lorusso down for years. That day is finally here."

Steve shook his head. "Hard to believe we owe it all to a blackmailer."

Burnside smiled. "Hell, when this is over, Stryker may deserve a statue in front of City Hall."

After his dinner on Fisherman's Wharf, Mark cruised by the front desk of the hotel, hoping to be offered two more hot cookies, but apparently that was a perk reserved exclusively for people checking in. He gave up after a few passes, went up to his room, and called his son at home.

Steve answered on the first ring.

"You're not going to believe why Nick Stryker was visiting Bert Yankton," Mark said.

"It doesn't really matter anymore," Steve said. "We've solved Nick Stryker's murder."

"You found his body?"

"Not yet," Steve said. He went on to tell his father about the arrest of Detective Harley Brule and the discovery that the charred corpse in Stryker's Dumpster was one of Brule's men, Detective Arturo Sandoval. "We've got a sworn deposition from Brule saying that Sandoval wanted to kill Stryker and burn his files rather than pay him off. Between the deposition and the circumstantial evidence, the DA and my captain are satisfied. The homicide investigation is officially closed."

"You're going to close the case without a body," Mark said.

"And without the hassle and expense of a trial. Sweet, isn't it?" Steve said. "But we're confident that if Sandoval was alive, we could have convicted him of murder."

"So you're satisfied, too."

"You say that as if you aren't," Steve said. "What more do you want?"

"A corpse," Mark said.

"We've convicted killers before without ever finding the bodies of their victims. Bert Yankton, for instance. What difference would it make if we found Stryker's body now?"

"The way Stryker was killed and forensic clues at the scene could possibly exclude Sandoval and implicate somebody else," Mark said. "I would hate to see someone get away with murder simply because it's more convenient for the DA and the police to hold a dead man responsible."

"Dad, do you really think if that was what was going on that I'd play along with it?"

"No, of course not."

"The truth is, I think Brule may have ordered Sandoval to kill Stryker, but I can't prove it," Steve said. "So I'll settle for this. It's an empty victory for Brule. He's still in for a long stretch in prison. Justice is being served."

"I suppose you're right," Mark said.

"So why do you sound so glum?"

"I'm just tired," Mark said. "I'm heading home first thing in the morning. If you're free at noon tomorrow, I'll buy you lunch at Barbeque Bob's."

"When have you ever paid for a meal at Barbeque Bob's?"

"Never," Mark said. "That's why it's my favorite place to take people to lunch."

Some people believe that dreams are a manifestation of the mental filing and sorting of experience, emotion, and knowledge that's necessary to keep the mind organized and running smoothly.

If that's true, then Mark's mind was trying to organize a lot of mental clutter as he slept that night.

He once again found himself running through an onion field, only the onions were made of tightly rolled vintage currency.

The crows were there again, too, gathered on the shoulders of a Nick Stryker scarecrow and holding smoking cigars in their beaks. One of the crows dropped his cigar down the scarecrow's faded overalls and set the straw man ablaze.

Mark awoke at five in the morning, the dream still vivid in his mind. Instead of going back to sleep, he decided he'd might as well get up. His alarm was set for six anyway. He showered and shaved, made a quick visit to the hotel's breakfast buffet, and was on the road by the time he'd originally intended to wake up.

He managed not to think about Nick Stryker, Bert Yankton, or Jimmy Cale for the next forty minutes, distracting himself by listening to National Public Radio and appreciating the verdant farmland on either side of Highway 101.

And then the fields of lettuce, artichokes, and tomatoes gave way to the guard towers, razor-wire fences, and barracks of the Salinas Valley State Prison, located along the freeway leading into the farming community of Soledad. A sign on the highway warned drivers not to pick up hitchhikers, particularly those, Mark thought, wearing orange prison jumpsuits.

The sight of the prison immediately reminded him of his visit with Bert Yankton at San Quentin. Soon Mark found himself tormented again by all the unanswered questions about Nick Stryker's activities in the days before his murder.

Even though those questions didn't really matter anymore, he couldn't help pondering them anyway. They were a mystery, something Mark couldn't resist. He needed something to occupy him for the next few hours. What difference did it make whether he thought some more about Stryker or listened to public radio? At least if he thought about Stryker, he wouldn't be nagged every twenty minutes to make a generous pledge.

Mark turned off the radio and let his mind work. He thought about Bert Yankton and his actions the night of Cale's murder. He thought about how Jimmy Cale was killed and the evidence that had convicted Yankton. He thought about his conversation with Betsy Cale and the kind of man Jimmy had been. And he thought about all the calls Stryker had made to currency dealers and brokers.

That was when Mark remembered it wasn't only Cale's currency collection that Stryker was interested in.

Stryker also called cigar stores, including Hampshire's, where Cale maintained his own private humidor.

Why did Stryker call cigar stores? What was the point of that?

There was only one way to find out, but it was still too early to call any cigar stores. They wouldn't be open for another couple of hours. So he waited, mulling over everything again. And again.

Around nine o'clock Mark stopped in Solvang for gas. The station had a windmill on its faux-thatched roof. It wasn't that unusual. Everybody had a windmill in Solvang, a town built by Danish settlers in the early 1900s that exactly emulated the architectural style of their homeland. Little did the settlers know they were creating California's first theme park. All that was missing was a roller coaster.

After filling his tank, Mark figured the cigar stores were

probably open. He parked his car, rolled down the window for some air, and called Hampshire's Cigar Shop, where he told Hugh Tiplin, the proprietor, the same lie he'd told everyone on the phone last night.

Like the others, Tiplin was glad to help the writer. Nobody could resist the opportunity to be acknowledged and immortalized in a book, especially a scandalous, true-crime tale rife with sex, money, and gory murder.

Tiplin described Cale's taste in cigars as refined and expensive. Cale once spent three hundred fifty dollars for a single stick from a box of pre-embargo Padron Cubans.

Cale loved the Havanas, but otherwise enjoyed double corona or Churchills made in the Dominican Republic using tobacco grown from seeds smuggled from Cuba before Castro took over.

To ensure that he got a steady supply of Fuente Opus X, a cigar made in limited quantities, Cale donated hundreds of thousands of dollars to the Fuente family's favorite charities.

He liked Partagas Salamones and Padron Anniversarios and Aston VSG, rare cigars that are so pricey they are usually bought one or two at a time. Cale bought them by the box.

Tiplin then began rhapsodizing about the pleasures of a relatively new cigar, the Davidoff Zino Platinum Crown, that Cale would have loved. It was a luxurious smoke of two different Dominican seeds, Piloto Cubano and San Vicente, blended with Peruvian tobacco, all wrapped in a semi-dark Connecticut seed grown in Ecuador.

All of that meant nothing to Mark. But he got the general idea. Cale had exacting standards when it came to choosing his cigars.

Mark thanked Tiplin for his help and hung up, looking at the barely legible notes he'd made during the conversation and wondering why he'd bothered to take them at all.

What did he hope to learn from a bunch of cigar brand names?

About as much as he'd learn from his list of vintage paper money.

So he'd learned some trivial facts about the late Jimmy Cale. Big deal.

Knowing some of Cale's hobbies and personal pursuits wasn't going to get him any closer to figuring out what Nick Stryker was doing before one of the corrupt cops he was blackmailing decided to kill him.

It didn't matter anymore anyway.

The Stryker case was closed.

It also wasn't going to get him any closer to figuring out if Yankton was an innocent man, a cause that Mark wasn't convinced was worth pursuing.

Mark tossed his notes onto the passenger seat and started up the car again. He was about to back out of his parking space when he felt the tickle, the tingle on the back of his neck that occurred when whatever was percolating in his subconscious finally emerged into his awareness.

All the disparate facts he had collected over the last two days suddenly coalesced into a truth that revealed itself to him with startling clarity.

Stryker wasn't looking for Jimmy Cale's killer.

He was looking for Jimmy Cale.

CHAPTER THIRTEEN

Mark was already sitting at his usual booth at Barbeque Bob's, nursing his second root beer, when Steve came in at noon.

"You look tired," Mark said as Steve slid into the booth across from him.

"While you've been taking a driving tour of the Golden State, I've been busy arresting people," Steve said. "I've discovered that working Stryker's files is a full-time job."

"It's amazing the information he gathered," Mark said. "Stryker had an incredible instinct for ferreting out criminal behavior."

"Because he was a crook *and* a ferret."

Steve waved over a waitress and ordered a root beer for himself and two slabs of ribs, hot corn bread, and baked beans for him and his father to share.

"Over the last few days I've developed newfound respect for Stryker's investigative skills," Mark said.

"You're joking."

"Not at all. He was a remarkable detective. Truly gifted."

"And corrupt, unethical, and immoral."

"That, too," Mark said. "Bert Yankton hired Stryker to find Jimmy Cale's killer."

Steve raised his eyebrows. "What did Stryker say, 'Look in the mirror'?"

"Stryker took the job."

"Of course he did. How could he resist? Yankton was asking to be ripped off. It was found money for doing absolutely nothing."

"That's just it, Steve. Stryker was working the case."

"What case? Yankton killed Cale."

"But let's say he didn't," Mark said.

"He did," Steve said.

Mark explained how Stryker began learning about all of Jimmy Cale's hobbies and passions, from smoking cigars to collecting paper money.

"I don't see the point," Steve said.

"I didn't either at first," Mark said. "But then I found out someone has been quietly re-creating Cale's currency collection—if not the actual bills, then ones just like them."

"So?"

The waitress arrived at the table with their food and plenty of napkins. She'd seen them eat before. Mark tucked a napkin into his shirt collar like a bib and picked up a rib.

"What if Cale is still alive?" Mark said, starting to eat.

"He was hacked to pieces and buried in the desert," Steve said. "You're the doctor, you tell me. Could he have survived?"

"Let's say there never was a murder," Mark said.

"Cale took Yankton's wife and his money," Steve said between bites of pork ribs slathered in barbecue sauce. "Cale's blood was all over his house, all over Yankton's house, all over Yankton's hatchet, and all over the trunk of Yankton's car, where, incidentally, we also found Cale's toe."

"What if Cale faked his death and framed Yankton for it?"

"Why would he do that?"

"I don't know," Mark said. "But what if he did? What if he ran off, had massive plastic surgery, and created a whole new life for himself somewhere else, leaving Yankton to rot in jail?"

Steve wiped some barbecue sauce off his face and tossed a rib bone into the basket he and his father were filling.

"You think that's what Stryker was onto?" Steve said.

Mark nodded. "He may have been a repugnant human being, but he understood people. He realized a man can change his face and his identity but he can't change who he is. Whoever Cale is now would indulge in all the same passions he did before he created his new life. He would still love money. Making it, collecting it, and gambling with it."

"So you think Stryker intended to find Cale and then blackmail him," Steve said. "That's a mighty big leap based on no evidence at all."

"It's based on Stryker's phone bills and my intuition."

"Like I said, no evidence at all." Steve said. "But let's take a step back. What made Stryker arrive at the conclusion so quickly that Cale is alive?"

"I don't know," Mark said. "Whatever happened to Vivian Yankton?"

"If you think she ran off with Cale, think again," Steve said. "Vivian became an actress, though I use that term loosely. She ended up doing direct-to-DVD, soft-core porn, starting with *Triangle of Lust*, based on the Yankton case. She played a thinly disguised, and thinly dressed, version of herself, only with much bigger boobs than before."

"You saw it, didn't you?"

"Professional curiosity," Steve said. "I wanted to see the guy they got to play me."

"How come you never told me about this?"

"The character's name was Lieutenant Stockton Stone, and he interrogated Vivian by having sex with her. They ended up running off together at the end," Steve said. "It wasn't the most flattering portrayal."

"I still may want to talk with her," Mark said. "Did you ever get Stryker's credit-card statement?"

"Yeah."

"When and where was his last purchase?"

"Four days ago at a gas station in Victorville," Steve said.

"Interesting," Mark said.

"Why?"

"Because his last call was to Sanford Pelz, a currency broker in Kingman, Arizona, which isn't far from Victorville," Mark said. "I've tried calling Pelz repeatedly and can't reach him. Maybe Stryker had the same experience."

"So what's your next step?"

Mark sighed. "I'll drive to Kingman to see Sanford Pelz. He may have been the last person to see Stryker alive."

"When are you going?"

"Right after dessert," Mark said.

"Why bother? We know what happened to Stryker. And you don't really believe that Cale is alive, do you?"

"Arturo Sandoval may have killed Stryker, but I need to know if an innocent man is on death row."

"Yankton is guilty, Dad. I should know, I put him there," Steve said. "If word gets out about what you're doing, the press will be all over it."

"I'll poke around discreetly," Mark said. "I'm curious about what Stryker was doing, but I promise I won't let my curiosity jeopardize your career."

"I want you to make me a promise, but that wasn't it," Steve said. "Here it is. If you think Yankton is innocent, I want you to forget that the dumb cop who put him away was your son. Do whatever is necessary to set him free."

Mark smiled at his son. He'd never been more proud of him. "I promise."

"Then you deserve a slice of pecan pie," Steve said. He signaled the waitress, who came over and took their order. After she left, Steve let out a deep breath. "Looks like Burnside was right."

"About what?"

"I may need all the glory that comes from these Stryker

file arrests more than he does," Steve said. "If you're right about Cale, they may be the only thing that can save my career."

The five-hour journey to Kingman, Arizona, was memorable only for how unmemorable it was, marked by seemingly interminable periods of crushing boredom, particularly along the Pearblossom Highway, a two-lane California road that cut across the empty desert scrub between Lancaster and Victorville.

It was so dull that people often dozed off at the wheel and drifted into oncoming traffic. But even if a driver managed to stay awake on this deceptively peaceful, straight stretch of desert highway, there were other dangers. Bored drivers in a hurry to put the dull road behind them, or perhaps just to quicken their deadening pulse, would attempt to pass the cars in front of them by speeding up in the westbound lane. They frequently miscalculated the speed they were traveling, the amount of open roadway they needed to pass the cars, and the time left until the oncoming tour bus smashed into them head-on.

The result was miles of highway shoulder lined with faded crosses and piles of dried flowers, makeshift memorials to the dead. It was why the highway was better known as Bloody Alley.

Mark Sloan managed to stay awake and alert, despite his many hours on the road, and reached Victorville without incident. He headed north on the interstate, which had the benefit of being wider and safer than Bloody Alley but wasn't any more interesting when it came to scenery.

At least there weren't crosses along the road here.

Before long, he came to the eastbound transition to Interstate 40, which replaced the famed Route 66, now fondly remembered by some as the Mother Road and by others as America's Main Street.

Most of Route 66 was either paved over in the sixties and seventies for new highways or bypassed entirely, leaving towns that once thrived on the cross-country traffic to decay into ruins not even worthy of mowing down for outlet malls. A few of those once prosperous towns managed to survive as out-of-the-way tourist traps, celebrated by road junkies in search of kitsch and motor-home retirees eager to relive the good old days.

The interstate ran right through Kingman. It's main attraction as a place to live was that no one else could imagine living there. It was far away from everything and offered neither natural beauty, historical interest, nor kitsch appeal. The town seemed to exist simply to service the basic needs of travelers who found themselves stuck midway between where they'd been and where they wanted to go. Presumably, some never left.

It was always a place meant to be passed by. Long before the advent of highways, Kingman had served as a way station for railroad travelers and, before that, probably for Indians on the move across the dry, brown Hualapai Valley.

The post–Route 66 architecture in Kingman was roadside basic with a blandness that transcended time, style, or place, buildings made to be forgotten even as you were looking at them.

They achieved their purpose.

Mark stopped at the post office where Sanford Pelz kept a box for his mail. The building was a sun-bleached gray that blended perfectly with the sidewalk, the parking lot, and the street to create one seamless block of dullness. The post office might have been built in 1950 or a week ago—it was impossible for Mark to tell, at least from a design standpoint.

No one except the postman was inside. He sat behind a chipped and yellowed Formica counter on a rickety stool that was strategically placed so it was in the crosscurrent of the office's three whirring fans.

The postman embodied the same blandness as the building he occupied. It was as if he'd been assembled at the same time out of the leftover building supplies. Maybe thirty or forty years old, he wore his pale pudginess like a soggy coat. The name tag pinned to the breast pocket of his fading postal uniform read: DWAYNE.

"Can I help you?" Dwayne asked with an unbridled lack of enthusiasm.

"I'm Dr. Mark Sloan, chief of internal medicine at Community General Hospital in Los Angeles." Mark showed Dwayne his hospital identification.

"Uh-huh," Dwayne said. "Would you like to purchase some stamps today?"

"I'm here about one of my patients, Sanford Pelz," Mark said. "I understand he keeps a post office box here."

"Yep."

"Has he been in lately to pick up his mail?"

"Not for a few days," Dwayne said. "Hasn't even come in for this month's issue of *Bank Note Reporter*. It arrived yesterday."

Mark didn't like the sound of that. Pelz had stopped coming in for his mail around the same time Stryker was killed. The coincidence troubled him.

"I'm worried about him." That much was true, but what Mark said next certainly wasn't. "He missed an important appointment with me at the hospital and I haven't been able to reach him on the phone."

Dwayne gave him a blank look. "So you drove all the way up here from LA?"

Obviously. There was a reason this man was working in a post office in Kingman.

"Mr. Pelz is very sick. He needs immediate medical attention," Mark said. "Do you know where he lives?"

"We aren't supposed to give out that information," Dwayne said. "It's private."

"I understand," Mark said. "But do you think I would have come all this way if it wasn't an emergency?"

"Rules are rules," Dwayne said.

"Which would you rather have on your conscience? The violation of his privacy or his death?"

Dwayne pondered that for a while. A long while.

"He lives in a trailer up in the Black Mountains," Dwayne said. "We don't have mail service up there."

"I'm not from around here," Mark said. "Do you think you could draw me a map?"

Dwayne sighed, as if drawing that map would be an extraordinarily strenuous undertaking involving hours of complex drafting and years of cartography experience. But after the sigh, he quickly drew a crude map on the back of a vacation-hold card and handed it to Mark.

"Thanks. I appreciate your help," Mark said, though he didn't think the map would be much help at all, not for someone who was unfamiliar with the area to start with. He would need something with more detail.

Mark got in his car and drove to a Chevron station he'd passed earlier on his way in from the interstate. He filled up his tank, then went inside the tiny convenience store to ask for a map to Oatman and some directions.

The gas station attendant was a stout woman with a pony-tail face-lift, her hair pulled back so tight that her eyebrows became her bangs. Her name tag read: SHARONA.

Whoever made name tags in Kingman must be doing brisk business, Mark thought.

"Excuse me, do you know how to get to Sanford Pelz's place?"

"Sure," Sharona said. "Who are you?"

"Dr. Mark Sloan," he said. "Mr. Pelz is my patient. Do you know him?"

"Everybody does," Sharona said. "He's one of those people who expects the Trilateral Commission and the Secret World Government to take over the United States any day now."

Mark had thought the conspiracy theories about the Trilateral Commission, a secret body of business leaders who supposedly controlled world affairs, died with mood rings and Afros. Apparently he was wrong.

"You his shrink?" she asked.

"No, I'm his physician."

"Wishful thinking on my part. He lives up in the mountains between Sitgreaves Pass and Goldroad."

"So I've heard," Mark said. "What's Goldroad?"

"An old gold mining settlement. It's nothing but rocky ruins now," she said. "Are you planning to go out there?"

"If I can find my way," Mark said. "I'd appreciate some directions. The map I was given isn't too clear."

Sharona took out a map from a display behind her, spread it open on the counter, and showed him the way, a wiggly scribble up into the mountains to Oatman, a decaying old mining town that survived as a scrappy tourist trap. She marked the approximate point where he'd find the dirt road that led to Pelz's trailer. The only way to spot the road, she said, was to be on the lookout for the weed-covered footings of the long-since-demolished trading post.

"You be careful on Bloody 66, Doc," she said.

"Why's that?" Mark figured it was never a good sign when "bloody" was used to describe a road, but he didn't think it could be any more dangerous than the Pearblossom Highway and he'd survived that.

"It's fearsome," she said. "The ghosts of many a dead traveler wander in the shadows of those cliffs."

Sharona explained that the old road was part of Route 66 until 1953, when it was replaced by a new stretch of highway that avoided the mountains and that eventually became Interstate 40. But even in its heyday, the road into Oatman was a terror.

The way she described it, the steady, arduous climb would be hard enough on driver and car alike, but as you neared the dark, brooding peaks, the road tried to trick you with one turn after another, each more deadly than the one before.

If you were fortunate, your car would simply die struggling up the grade and have to be towed the rest of the way by an experienced local. Many drivers counted their blessings when that happened. It meant they didn't have to drive the Bloody 66 themselves. Others simply hired someone in Kingman to take the wheel of their car from the get-go and guide them safely to Oatman or on to Toprock. The local would then turn around and guide travelers heading east over the pass.

"My uncle's uncle Cletus will drive you for thirty bucks," she said. "He's made that drive so many times he could do it with one eye shut, which is fortunate, 'cause he's only got one left."

"He only has one eye?"

"And only one testicle, but that's another story. Uncle Cletus lost the eye in a bar fight in '88. It got plucked out with a pool cue. Rolled across the floor like a marble, they say. He's got it in this pickle jar full of formaldehyde on his mantel. It's his security system. One time a robber broke in, saw that eye staring at him in the moonlight, and got spooked. He ran outside in such a hurry, he tripped over the porch step and broke his neck."

Mark was afraid to ask where Uncle Cletus kept his testicle.

"Well, thank you so much for the directions. I think I'll take my chances on the road myself."

"Say, Doc," she said, "could I ask you a little favor?"

He figured he owed her something for her help and for sharing an anecdote with him that he'd be telling everyone as soon as he got home.

"Of course," Mark said.

She motioned another attendant to take her place at the register, slipped out from behind the counter, and led Mark towards the restrooms.

"It's about my hemorrhoids," she whispered. "It's got so I can read an entire Harlequin every time I visit the john, if you get my meaning."

Unfortunately, he did.

"Think you could take a look at it?" she asked.

Before Mark had a chance to answer, she grabbed a box of rubber gloves from a nearby shelf, shoved them in his hands, and opened the bathroom door, inviting him inside.

CHAPTER FOURTEEN

Mark wasn't too thrilled with the sights in Kingman, having viewed a natural wonder he wouldn't recommend to anyone as a tourist attraction.

After a careful and reluctant examination, he'd urged Sharona to visit a qualified proctologist right away for a hemorrhoidectomy.

She sighed wearily. "Guess I won't have much opportunity anymore for appreciating literature."

"There are other places you can read."

"Not with a husband and six kids," she said.

Mark left the gas station as fast as he could without looking as if he was running. He didn't want to be asked for any more favors.

He set out immediately for the Pelz place so that he'd get there before dark. After his talk with Pelz, he'd find a place to stay in Victorville and return home in the morning.

The narrow, crumbling road that crept up into the Black Mountains turned out to be every bit as treacherous as Sharona had made it seem. It twisted along the jagged hillside, with unexpected hairpin turns around blind corners over sheer cliffs. There were no guard rails, and the blinding glare of the sun in his face didn't help.

Mark was sweating, his back stiff and tense with concentration and anxiety. He found himself wishing he'd taken Uncle Cletus on as a driver after all.

Every so often, as he slowly negotiated a harrowing switchback, he would see the rusted and charred wreckage of cars and trucks at the bottom of the ravine. The wrecks lay there, hundreds of feet below the road, tangled in the mountainous brush like the bleached bones of long-dead animals or embedded amidst the boulders like exposed fossils.

It made his throat go dry.

Mark was so intent on his driving that he almost missed the trading post ruins that marked the top of the unpaved road down to where Pelz lived. The footings were made of native stone, and he easily could have mistaken them for a natural outcropping if he hadn't known what to look for.

He took the turn and bounced along the rutted, rock-strewn road until he finally emerged into a clearing surrounded by saguaro cactus.

Pelz's compound was a ragged collection of weather-beaten, rusted-out mobile homes joined together by corrugated metal breezeways and shacks, apparently built from materials salvaged from the ruins of other buildings. The hulks of several old Cadillacs were lined up behind a giant satellite dish like silent sentries, their hoods raised in salute, their engines long since gutted for parts. A five-year-old Cadillac, a Frankenstein of Caddy parts covered in dirt and dents and someday destined to join its organ donors, was parked in front of one of the mobile homes.

Mark parked beside the Caddystein and got out, relieved to finally be off the treacherous road. It was hard for him to believe it could ever have been part of Route 66, much less the principal highway into California. He dreaded the rest of the drive back to the interstate beyond Oatman.

He took a deep breath of fresh Arizona desert air and immediately wished he hadn't. His stomach recoiled, and he coughed the breath right back out of his lungs, nearly bringing his lunch up with it.

The air was heavy with the sickening scent of decaying flesh. It was the scent of death.

Mark turned apprehensively towards the mobile home, knowing what he would find inside. Holding a handkerchief to his nose, he walked up to the screen door without bothering to knock or announce his presence.

The door opened with a mournful, agonized creak, as if he was causing the old mobile home pain, stretching muscles and tendons instead of rusted hinges. He stepped inside, startling a thousand flies and sending them buzzing all around him.

Mark swatted them away and examined his cramped surroundings. There were currency reference books and pricing guides going back years lined up on the kitchen counter. There were stacks of yellowed currency auction catalogs and back issues of the *Bank Note Reporter* along the walls and on the dinette table. He guessed that this mobile home served as Pelz's office and that one of the others must be his living quarters.

As he neared what had once served as the master bedroom he saw a man, facedown on the floor, his body grotesquely bloated from decomposition, a bullet hole in the back of his head.

Mark crouched beside the body and turned the man's head so he could see his face. It wasn't Stryker. The man was in his late fifties, his nose was bulbous, red, and looked like a cauliflower. The dead man had suffered from rhinophyma, a disfiguring skin ailment exacerbated by alcohol consumption.

Using his handkerchief, he reached gingerly into the dead man's back pocket, pulled out his wallet, and glanced at the Arizona driver's license.

The dead man was Pelz. And judging by the degree of

decomposition, Mark figured he was killed around the same time that Stryker disappeared. He sorted through the rest of the wallet's contents: a hundred dollars in crumpled bills, several phone cards, and a single credit card.

Mark jotted down the account numbers of all the cards on a piece of paper and slipped the wallet back in Pelz's pocket. And then he stood there, trying to decide what to do next.

The murder of Sanford Pelz, perhaps on the same day that Stryker was killed, raised all kinds of troubling questions, none of which Mark was prepared to deal with at the moment.

He thought about searching the office, but what would he be looking for?

A phone would be a start.

After a few minutes of looking around, though, he concluded that Pelz didn't have a phone, at least not in his office. So he took out his cell phone and tried to call 911, but he couldn't get a signal.

Now Mark understood why Pelz had so many phone cards in his wallet; he used them when he went to town to make his calls.

Mark would have to drive to Oatman and notify the authorities there. That was fine with him. He couldn't wait to leave.

He took one more quick glance around the place to make sure he wasn't missing any vital clues, then hurried out—not that time was of the essence. Pelz wouldn't be getting any less dead.

The urgency Mark felt was the need to escape, to get as far away from the violence and the rot as he could. He'd seen a lot of corpses in his life, so that wasn't what disturbed him. It was this place, the desolation of it, and the omnipresent sense of doom around each hairpin turn.

Mark got into his car and drove away, careful not to give

in to the urge to speed. Hurrying along this road could be fatal.

He returned to the main road and headed west, into the setting sun, which made the dangerous drive even more harrowing. His sunglasses weren't much help against the glare, and he was afraid to lower his visor for fear of critically limiting his view.

The road became even narrower and curvier than it had been before. As he was making yet another unexpectedly sharp turn, a flash of light stabbed him in the eyes. He slammed his foot on the brake pedal in surprise and nearly lost control of the car, which came to a screeching, rubber-peeling stop at the edge of the cliff.

Breathing hard, his heart pounding, Mark looked back to see what had caused the reflection that nearly killed him.

At the edge of the curve, at the perfect angle to catch the light of the setting sun, was what appeared to be a bright silver propeller about the size of a large pizza. It took Mark a minute to figure out that it was a spinner ripped from the rim of someone's tires. The driver had probably shaved the exposed, craggy face of the rocky mountainside while negotiating the tight turn.

That had to hurt. Steve had looked into getting a set of rims with spinners for his truck, and Mark knew they could cost thousands of dollars. Whoever lost the spinner must have been pretty upset when he reached the interstate—but not enough to brave a return trip up Bloody 66 to retrieve it.

Mark got out of the car, surprised that his legs were shaking, and went over to get the spinner. He didn't want anyone else to be blinded by it. As he leaned over to pick it up, he saw dozens of skid marks on the asphalt. One of them was surely his own.

At the same moment, he remembered something Serena Cale had said to him in Capitola.

"Nick showed me his ride. A tricked-out Escalade with chrome spinners on the rims."

Stryker's last call was to Pelz. His last purchase was in Victorville. And he'd been missing about as long as Pelz appeared to have been dead.

With growing trepidation, Mark followed a set of skid marks to the edge of the cliff and peered over the side into the ravine below.

There was a trail of freshly scraped dirt, flattened scrub, amputated cacti, and dislodged rocks that stretched for fifty yards. And at the bottom of that trail was an Escalade SUV, crumpled like a discarded soda can amidst the boulders.

Mark ran back to his car, tossed the spinner inside, and grabbed his medical bag. As an afterthought, he also brought his portable earthquake kit, a large backpack that contained first-aid supplies, nonperishable food, bottled water, running shoes, flashlights, batteries, a folded tarp, duct tape, rope, and an assortment of other survival essentials. Like many Los Angelenos, he had earthquake kits at home, in his car, and at his office.

It took him a few minutes to find a place where he could reasonably attempt to get down the ravine without killing himself, and then he spent nearly an hour carefully working his way down, losing the daylight. He flicked on a flashlight and continued on, slipping several times in the darkness and sliding into the thorny brush, but he made it safely to the bottom with only a few scratches.

He swept the beam of his flashlight over the wreckage. The Escalade had been nearly flattened by its end over end tumble down the cliff. As he got closer, he could see the SUV was resting at an angle against several boulders, creating a cave underneath it.

Mark aimed his light into the space under the SUV and

saw the body of a man, his clothes torn and blood-splattered. He took off his backpack and crawled inside.

The man was Nick Stryker. His eyes were closed, his breathing shallow, his lips cracked and bloody from dehydration, but he was alive.

Mark opened Stryker's shirt and in the glow of the flashlight saw blue-purple discoloration on each flank and around his belly button, indicating a broken pelvis and internal bleeding. Stryker's left leg was badly lacerated and, judging by the purple skin and swollen calf, he'd broken his fibula.

Those injuries were the least of Stryker's problems. Over the last five days, Stryker must have endured severe thirst, crippling fatigue, excruciating muscle cramps, and lapses into delirium from the blood loss and dehydration. Even the simple act of breathing robbed his body of water.

Mark assumed that he was dangerously close to kidney failure, perhaps only hours away from lapsing into a coma and dying.

He checked Stryker's neck and head for injuries and felt a drop of water hit his cheek. Stryker had dragged himself underneath the cracked windshield wiper reservoir. Soapy water was, Mark supposed, better than no water at all.

"Nick, can you hear me? It's Dr. Mark Sloan."

Stryker groaned, which was about the best response Mark could have hoped for. At least he wasn't in a coma yet.

"You're going to be all right," Mark said. He didn't know if Stryker could hear him, but he figured some reassurance never hurt. "I'm going to help you."

Mark reached for his backpack, unzipped it, and removed the bottled water. He held it to Stryker's lips and poured. As soon as the moisture touched his lips, Stryker reflexively opened his mouth and greedily sucked in the water.

"Easy. There's plenty more where that came from."

He let Stryker have only a little water. Too much, and Stryker would vomit, worsening his dehydration. He moistened a towel and considered his next move as he gently dabbed Stryker's face.

There was no signal, so calling for help on his cell phone was impossible.

He couldn't carry Stryker back up to the car himself, and, even if he could have, it was too dangerous.

There was really only one thing he could do: Stabilize Stryker as best he could and leave him behind, climb back up the hill, and drive to Oatman for help.

Stryker would just have to hang on for a few more hours.

Mark cleaned and disinfected Stryker's wounds, then began looking around the wreckage in the bright moonlight for the materials he needed.

He used some foam padding from the car seats, hard plastic from the door panels, and duct tape from his earthquake kit to fashion a splint for Stryker's leg.

He was giving Stryker another sip of water before leaving when he heard the growl of an engine on the road above.

And then he remembered his car. He'd left it parked on the road, on the blind side of the tight curve.

In the dark.

Mark scrambled out from under the Escalade in time to see a motor home rounding the curve too fast and smashing into the rear of his Mini Cooper, launching the small car off the cliff.

Directly at him.

CHAPTER FIFTEEN

Everything happened within seconds, but for Mark Sloan, everything slowed to a crawl. He dove back under the Escalade, grabbed Stryker by the ankles, and dragged him away as fast as he could.

At the same moment, Mark's car smacked into the hillside and careened towards them in a wave of dirt, rocks, and scrub.

Stryker's screams of agony were drowned out by the earthshaking thunderclap as Mark's car plowed into the Escalade and exploded in a roiling fireball that punched into the night sky like a coiled, flaming fist.

Mark fell backwards, losing his grip on Stryker and hitting the ground hard. He rose shakily to his feet to see the two vehicles consumed by flames. Through the black smoke, he could see people standing illuminated in the glow of the headlights of their motor home, looking down at the flames.

He checked on Stryker, who was moaning pitifully. At least he was still alive.

Mark stepped clear of the smoke and yelled to the people on the road.

"Is anyone up there hurt?" he yelled.

A grizzled old man wearing an eye patch and cowboy boots hobbled to the cliff's edge. Behind him stood a family of four—a man, his wife, and their two teenage daughters.

The four of them, all in pleated khaki shorts and brightly colored polo shirts, were very shaken and stood huddled together, keeping their distance from the one-eyed man.

"We're fine," the one-eyed man yelled back. "What the hell were you doing parking your car on the road?"

"Never mind that. I'm a doctor and I've got a man down here who is critically injured. We need to get him to a hospital. Is that motor home in any condition to drive safely?"

The one-eyed man glanced back at the land yacht. The front grill was smashed, but everything else seemed intact.

"Your car was just another bug on this baby's windshield," the one-eyed man said.

"Then I need you to come down and help me bring this man up," Mark said. "We have to get him out of here."

The Dinino family brought sheets and blankets from their rented motor home when they came down the cliff. With their help, Mark fashioned a litter and dragged Stryker up to the road. The family's driver, Cletus Mabry, waited for them in the motor home, unwilling to risk his remaining eye and testicle by negotiating the steep slope on foot at night. He was watching out for any other traffic on the road.

They laid Stryker on the bed in the master bedroom and Cletus steered them the rest of the way into Oatman. The road was too narrow, and the vehicle was too large, to risk turning around to go back to Kingman, though Cletus offered to drive backwards the whole way.

"I've done it before," he said before heading, almost reluctantly, towards Oatman.

Mark stayed at Stryker's side, mostly to care for him, but also so he didn't have to watch Cletus drive.

When they finally reached the ramshackle town, Mark looked out the window and was surprised to see wild burros wandering the dusty streets and sidewalks in front of the wooden frontier storefronts.

Cletus parked the mobile home on front of the Oatman Hotel, a two-story adobe-block building. Mark got out, eased past an overly friendly burro, and used the phone at the front desk to call 911.

Within minutes, the burros were stampeding up the sidewalks, baying madly, terrified by the Mohave County Search and Rescue helicopter that was landing in the street, the rotors kicking up a huge swirl of dust.

Two medics jumped out of the chopper and Mark rushed to meet them, briefing them quickly on Stryker's medical condition.

Within minutes, Mark, Stryker, and the medics were back in the chopper, on their way to Kingman Regional Medical Center, where a trauma team was waiting for Stryker and sheriff's deputies were waiting for Mark.

Stryker arrived at the hospital unconscious and suffering from severe dehydration, renal failure, internal bleeding, a shattered pelvis, and a badly broken fibula.

The trauma doctors, under Mark's watchful eye, began rehydrating the patient with IV fluids, gave him a blood transfusion to counter his anemia, and started him on dialysis before wheeling him into surgery.

It would be a long time before Stryker was on his feet again.

While Stryker was in the operating room, Mark went down to the cafeteria, refusing to talk to the deputies until he'd had some dinner, figuring if he was going to be interrogated, it might as well be a catered event.

While he ate a hamburger and fries, he was questioned by Sam DeWitt, a thirty-five-year-old sheriff's department homicide investigator who carried himself with an almost military bearing. DeWitt sat ramrod straight in his chair, probably because he had no choice. His uniform was starched as stiff as cardboard.

Mark gave DeWitt a radically abridged version of events, starting with the letter he'd received. He left out the details of Stryker's blackmail activity and focused instead on recounting Stryker's investigation into Jimmy Cale.

"So let me see if I have this straight," Deputy Sam DeWitt said, referring to his notebook. "You're a doctor from LA. You received a letter from a private detective named Nick Stryker that said, basically, 'If you're reading this, I'm dead.'"

"That's exactly what it said."

"You then proceeded to retrace Mr. Stryker's activities prior to his disappearance. You discovered he'd traveled to Kingman to talk with Sanford Pelz, a broker of collectible bank notes, in regards to an ongoing investigation he was conducting. Is this accurate so far?"

"Yes."

"You visited Mr. Pelz's residence and found him shot to death. On your way to report the murder to authorities, you happened upon an auto accident and rescued Mr. Stryker, who'd been laying injured under his vehicle for several days. Is this also correct?"

"Those are the broad strokes," Mark said.

"I see." DeWitt closed his notebook. "That's the damnedest story I've ever heard."

Mark wasn't sure what to make of that and said so. "Is that a good thing or a bad thing?"

"I haven't decided yet," DeWitt said. "You mentioned your son is a homicide detective on the LAPD."

"Yes, he is."

"I'm going to be giving him a call," DeWitt said.

"I'd appreciate it if you'd do more than that," Mark said. "Could you send him the ballistics report on Sanford Pelz, his autopsy, and an inventory of the items recovered in his trailer?"

"Why should I do that?"

"Professional courtesy?" Mark said.

DeWitt snorted. "For all I know, Doctor, you murdered Mr. Pelz."

"Why would I?"

"For his money."

"He didn't look very rich to me," Mark said.

"Pelz has nearly a million dollars in his account at the Bank of Kingman," DeWitt said. "He got a finder's fee and a percentage of the final sales price of all the currency deals he brokered."

"If he was so rich, what was he doing living out there in such squalor? What was he saving all his money for?"

"A rainy day," DeWitt said. "Or the overthrow of the United States by the storm troopers of the shadow government."

"Sounds like you knew him," Mark said.

"Kingman isn't Los Angeles," DeWitt said. "I know everybody. Pelz was a colorful character."

"I'm surprised he trusted the bank."

"He owns it," DeWitt said. "It's been in his family for generations. Doesn't mean he trusted it entirely, though."

"You might want to see if his account has received any major wire transfers in the last few months. I have a feeling more than a few came from offshore banks. I'd be curious to know exactly where they came from."

DeWitt stared at him. "With all due respect, Doctor, I work for the Mohave County sheriff. At this moment, you are a person-of-interest in a homicide."

"Sanford Pelz has been dead for days," Mark said. "I have no motive and can account for my whereabouts at the time of his murder."

"Maybe you hired Stryker to kill Pelz and take his money," DeWitt said. "Stryker had a car accident leaving the scene. When you didn't hear from Stryker, you were afraid he might have run off with the money himself. So you came out here looking for him."

It hadn't occurred to Mark before that Stryker might have killed Pelz, but he rejected the notion right away. Somehow it didn't feel right. Stryker was a blackmailer, not a killer, and he wouldn't gain anything from murdering Pelz, at least not as far as Mark could tell.

"Interesting theory," Mark said, "but there are some big problems with it."

"Such as?"

"Forgetting for a moment that I never heard of Pelz until the day before yesterday, if his money is in the bank, what good would it do for me to send Stryker to rob and kill him?"

"Lots of folks think Pelz has money buried at his place in case his bank and its assets are appropriated by the shadow government during the overthrow."

"Even if that was true, why would I rescue Stryker and go call for help?"

"You didn't have a choice after Cletus hit your car and everything blew up," DeWitt said. "If that hadn't happened, you might have left Stryker there to die."

"You refer to Cletus as if you know him."

"He was a sheriff's deputy here for thirty years," DeWitt said. "Got injured twice in the line of duty."

Mark didn't want to hear the story behind the old man's other injury.

"Well, if you're going to arrest me for this fiendish plot, you better read me my rights," Mark said. "Otherwise, I'd appreciate it if you could recommend a decent hotel for the night."

"I'm waiting to hear back from the forensic boys at Pelz's place and the accident scene," DeWitt said. "I don't want you going anywhere until I get some answers. I'll have deputies posted at the exits."

Mark didn't intend to leave Kingman until he had a

chance to talk to Stryker anyway. "As you may have noticed, I don't have a car, a change of clothes, or a toothbrush. How far could I go?"

That seemed to satisfy DeWitt for the moment. He rose from his seat. "We'll talk again, Dr. Sloan."

The doctors at Kingman Regional Medical Center were a lot friendlier to Mark than local law enforcement had been. They extended to him full staff privileges, allowing him to shower in the locker room and change into a borrowed set of surgical scrubs to replace his dirty clothes.

Fed and refreshed, Mark went to the doctors' lounge and called Steve, reaching him on his cell. Steve was still at work, writing up his reports on the day's arrests.

"You can't charge Arturo Sandoval posthumously with murder," Mark said.

"I know you have reservations, and so do I, but it's legally sound."

"Not anymore," Mark said. "Nick Stryker is alive."

"Don't tell me you think he faked his death, too."

"Stryker had a car accident in the mountains and has been trapped in the wreckage for days," Mark said. "He's in surgery right now at Kingman Regional Medical Center."

"Oh hell," Steve said, then added quickly, "It's not that I wish he was dead, it's just that this really complicates things."

"I understand," Mark said. He knew Steve was worried about how this development would affect the cases they were pursuing on the basis of Stryker's blackmail files. "But while you think about that, there's more you should know."

Mark told Steve about the murder of Sanford Pelz and Deputy DeWitt's theory about what happened.

"I'll take care of DeWitt," Steve said. "Is there anything else?"

Mark reached into his pocket for the note he'd jotted

down in Pelz's trailer. "I copied down the account numbers from some phone cards. I'd sure like to know who he was calling."

"You want me to intrude on a homicide investigation in another state," Steve said. "What do you think will happen when DeWitt finds out I've been checking into Pelz's phone records? Since Pelz doesn't have a phone, don't you think DeWitt might wonder where I got the account information?"

"He didn't ask me if I looked in Pelz's wallet," Mark said. "Besides, I thought you said you were taking care of De-Witt."

"I meant I would get him off your back," Steve said.

"Well, then, this should work. He'll be on your back, not mine."

"Gee, thanks," Steve said.

"There's one more thing," Mark said.

"I'm afraid to ask."

"I need our insurance agent's phone number," Mark said. "I had a little accident with my new car."

"How bad is it?"

"It went over a cliff and blew up," Mark said.

Steve caught his breath. "Oh my God, Dad. Why didn't you say that to begin with? Are you all right?"

"I'm fine. I wasn't in the car at the time," Mark said, deciding not to share the details of how the accident happened. It would be hard enough telling it to the insurance agent. "I'm at the hospital now, waiting to talk to Stryker when he comes out of recovery."

Steve gave him their insurance agent's number. "Let me talk to the DA and see how he wants to handle this. Sit tight. Try not find any more corpses or blow anything else up, okay? I'll call you right back."

"I'll be here," Mark said wearily.

CHAPTER SIXTEEN

Mark called his insurance agent and told him about the demise of his Mini Cooper. The agent fussed and fretted as if Mark had lost an arm instead of a car. It didn't strike Mark as strange. In Los Angeles, people saw their cars as an extension of themselves. The arm, however, wasn't the extension most of them had in mind.

The circumstances of the accident were unique, and the agent couldn't determine how much Mark was covered for, or if he was even covered at all. He asked Mark to fax him a copy of the police report on the accident as soon as possible so he could get the paperwork on the claim started.

But he wasn't hopeful that things would go in Mark's favor. This was the second car Mark had totaled in a year. Even if he could get Mark reimbursed for the loss of his car, it was going to be very difficult to find him a new carrier at anything less than exorbitant rates.

"That accident last year happened because I was exhausted and forced at gunpoint to drive my car against my will," Mark said. "How can they hold that crash against me?"

"Because they are an insurance company," his agent said. "It's what they do."

After Mark hung up, it occurred to him that he'd lost more than his car. He'd also lost his laptop computer and his notes.

It was a good thing he'd e-mailed himself a copy of his work before leaving Monterey.

But he'd still have to buy himself a new laptop, which was another twelve hundred dollars out of Steve's inheritance. This investigation was getting very expensive.

Mark went to the surgical ward to get a progress report from the head nurse on Stryker's condition. She said the surgery was going smoothly and that she'd notify him when Stryker was in recovery and alert.

Mark glanced at the clock on the wall. It was nearly eleven p.m., but it felt like three in the morning to him. He retreated to the doctors' lounge again, stretched out on the couch, and thought about the events of the day. It was hard to believe that only that morning he'd been in Monterey.

He was startled out of his thoughts by hearing his name over the loudspeaker. He was being paged to pick up the phone and dial a particular extension. He did. Steve was on the line.

"I'm driving up to Kingman tonight with Owen Penmore, one of Burnside's prosecutors, to sort things out with Stryker and the local authorities," Steve said. "I'll bring you some fresh clothes and toiletries."

"Thanks," Mark said.

"Burnside talked with the sheriff up there," Steve said. "You aren't going to be treated as a suspect anymore."

"That's good to know," Mark said. "Because if the insurance company doesn't cover the loss of my car, I don't think I can afford a good lawyer."

"There's always Pamela Swann," Steve said.

"Have you notified her that her client is alive?"

"That's not my responsibility," Steve said. "If Stryker wants to tell her, that's his choice. Is there anything else you need me to bring?"

"The information on who Pelz called would be nice," Mark said.

"I'm working on it," Steve said. "See you in the morning."

Mark hung up and decided to give the case some more thought. He was asleep within five minutes.

It felt like he'd closed his eyes for only an instant when the nurse shook him out of a light sleep at four a.m. She told him that Stryker was in recovery, awake and stable and asking to see him.

Mark splashed some water on his face in a futile attempt to wash away his grogginess and followed the nurse to the recovery room.

Stryker was lying in bed, his leg in a cast, his wounds dressed, wires and tubes running from his body to the machines and IV stands around him.

"You're lucky to be alive," Mark said.

"I may end up wishing I wasn't," Stryker said, his voice scratchy and weak. "What did you do with that box I sent you?"

"I turned it over to Steve," Mark said. "He's on his way up here with an assistant district attorney."

"Oh goodie," Stryker said. "I wish you weren't so damn conscientious."

"If I wasn't, you might not be here," Mark said.

"True," Stryker said, squeezing the trigger of his morphine drip. "I have my faults, but you've got to admit I'm a good judge of character."

"It's a shame you don't have any of your own."

"How many arrests has Steve made thanks to the files I sent you?"

"Quite a few," Mark said.

"That should go a ways towards rehabilitating my character," Stryker said. "It will certainly help my attorney cut a deal with the DA on any charges he wants to bring against me. After all, the worse Burnside makes me look, the less valuable I'll be to him on the stand."

"I see you've given this a lot of thought."

"I didn't have much else to do for the last couple of days," Stryker said.

Mark found a chair, pulled it up close to the bed, and sat down so Stryker wouldn't have to strain what little voice he had. "You didn't repent and promise God you'd become an honest man if you were rescued?"

"God knows me too well," Stryker said.

"You've brought misery into a lot of people's lives with the rest of those files you sent out."

"A husband cheats on his wife, he's the one who causes the misery, not me. I'm simply an observer."

"And a profit participant," Mark said.

Stryker grinned. "I like you, Mark."

"I don't like you."

"Still, you found me."

"Yes, I did," Mark said. "I'm going to find Jimmy Cale, too."

"You figured out he's alive," Stryker said. "How did you do that?"

"I figured out that *you* thought he was," Mark said. "What I don't get is why you jumped to that conclusion instead of assuming that either Yankton killed him or someone else did."

Stryker nodded towards the bedside table and a Styrofoam cup of water with a straw in it. Mark picked up the cup and held it to Stryker's lips. Stryker sucked some water through the straw, then settled back into his pillows.

"I thought Yankton did it, just like everybody else," Stryker said. "I took the case to see if I could find out where Jimmy stashed his ill-gotten gains."

"And take Yankton for his last dollar he had left in the process."

"I like to be compensated for my work."

"But then you stumbled onto the fact that someone was

quietly buying up the same pieces that were in Cale's currency collection," Mark said. "It's interesting, but not enough for you to have assumed Jimmy Cale is alive. You must have known something else."

"I put him in a tight spot," Stryker said. "I caught him sleeping with his best friend's wife and showed him the pictures. I offered him a way out. He could pay me not to share what I knew with my client."

"You blackmailed him."

"Call it what you will, but he declined my offer," Stryker said. "So I told Yankton what was going on."

"Cale declined because you inadvertently gave him a *better* way out," Mark said. Everything made sense to him now. "You didn't know that Cale was embezzling millions from his clients. It was only a matter of time before he got caught, and he knew it. But then you walked in the door and told him you were going to tell Yankton about his affair. It was great news. Cale *wanted* you to tell Yankton."

"I handed Jimmy the makings of a perfect frame," Stryker said. "I gave Yankton a motive to kill him."

"You gave Cale the opportunity to get away with all the money he stole and never have to worry about getting caught," Mark said. "But to do it he had to make a snap decision to sacrifice his family, his possessions, and his identity."

"Not to mention a pint of blood and a toe," Stryker said.

"It was all worth it to him," Mark said. "Because nobody is going to look for a dead man."

"You looked for me," Stryker said.

"You *asked* me to, remember?"

The rest of the story wasn't difficult to guess. Jimmy Cale went somewhere, had extensive plastic surgery, and created a new identity for himself. For the last five years, he'd been living nicely off the interest from the millions he stole, content in the knowledge that he was completely safe.

But Cale still loved money and couldn't resist using his wealth to restore his beloved collection. There were probably other pursuits he couldn't resist either, like cigars and gambling, and that would be helpful in tracking him down.

"What's the story with Sanford Pelz?" Mark asked.

"He was the middleman for Jimmy, his front at auctions and in private transactions with dealers and collectors," Stryker said, his exhaustion showing. His words were coming slower now and his eyelids were growing heavy. "I would have asked him about all that, but when I got to his place, he was dead. I got the hell out of there and, my damn luck, blew a tire. You know the rest."

"You think Cale killed him?"

"No. He's a swindler, not a killer. He doesn't get his hands dirty, unless it's counting money. I know the type."

"You *are* the type."

"So trust me, it wasn't him, but he's behind it," Stryker was fighting to keep his eyes open. Mark wouldn't keep him much longer. "He must have heard rumblings that I was asking around about his purchases and hired someone to clean up his trail. I'm sure whoever worked on his face and made his new passport is no longer among the living, either."

"Do you have any idea where Cale is?"

Stryker shook his head. Mark had some ideas, though. Something Cale's ex-wife said was coming back to him. He didn't share his thoughts with Stryker.

"What would you have done if you found him?" Mark asked.

Stryker smiled thinly and closed his eyes. "What do you think?"

"You would have taken Cale's money, kept quiet, and let an innocent man remain on death row?"

"I didn't put Yankton there," Stryker said, his voice trailing off into a whisper as he gave in to sleep. "Your son did that."

CHAPTER SEVENTEEN

The deputy posted outside the recovery room door notified Sam DeWitt that Stryker was out of surgery and conscious, but by the time DeWitt arrived, Stryker was asleep and the doctors wouldn't let their patient be disturbed. So DeWitt hunted down Mark Sloan instead.

DeWitt found him in the doctors' lounge, where he was trying to grab another hour or two of sleep before Steve arrived. The deputy had no qualms about disturbing Mark's rest.

"I hear you talked with Stryker," DeWitt said, pulling up a chair beside the couch that Mark was lying on.

"Yeah," Mark mumbled, not bothering to open his eyes.

"What did he tell you?"

"Pelz was dead when he got there," Mark said. "Stryker was heading back when he blew a tire, lost control of his car, and went over the cliff. End of story. Good night."

"He didn't blow a tire."

Mark opened an eye. "He didn't?"

DeWitt shook his head. "You tell me what you've got and I'll tell you what I've got."

"Some quid pro quo," Mark said.

DeWitt shrugged. He obviously had no idea what Mark was talking about.

Mark sat up with a groan and recounted what Stryker had

told him, deftly omitting the blackmail aspects of the story. He would leave it to Steve and the DA to decide if they wanted to share those details with the Mohave County Sheriff's Department.

"Your turn," Mark said.

"We found the bullet that killed Pelz," DeWitt said. "It went through him, through the wall, through the wall of the *next* trailer, through the refrigerator, and into a bowl of leftover spaghetti. The inside of that refrigerator is a mess."

"How could the bullet travel so far?"

"Pelz was shot at close range with a .308 Remington sniper rifle," DeWitt said.

Which meant that Stryker's accident was most likely attempted murder. "Have you found a matching bullet in Stryker's tire?" Mark asked.

"It won't be in the tire, but now that we know what to look for, we'll find it in the ravine somewhere," DeWitt said. "It will just take some time, that's all."

"What about those wire transfers into Pelz's bank account? Any luck there?"

"The bank doesn't open until ten," DeWitt said, "so I haven't had a chance to ask. I didn't see any point in rousting people out of bed for something that can wait."

"You're right, of course," Mark said.

He couldn't blame DeWitt for not feeling any urgency. There wasn't any, really. But Mark felt it anyway. He felt it for Bert Yankton, who he was now certain was innocent. Every day Yankton spent in prison, living in hell, deprived of his freedom, was another day of his life that was being robbed from him.

"There's more to this case than you're telling me," DeWitt said.

"What makes you say that?"

"Because the district attorney of Los Angeles called the sheriff and claimed Stryker is a key witness in a major LAPD and Justice Department investigation," DeWitt said. "Funny, you didn't mention anything about that."

"I'm a doctor," Mark said, "not a police officer."

"The way I hear it, that's a point you're often confused about, except when it suits you." DeWitt rose from his seat. "I'll leave you to get some sleep."

"Thanks," Mark said.

The deputy strode out, closing the door softly behind him. Mark lay down, closed his eyes, and slowly let out a deep breath.

He knew where he'd have to go to find Jimmy Cale; the rest he still had to work on. How would he find Cale out of millions of people? And then what? Ask the suspects to show him their bare feet?

Those were a few of the problems he was still going over in his mind when Steve walked into the lounge an hour later.

Steve was carrying a gym bag, which he set on a table. "Hey, sorry to wake you."

"I wish I could say I was asleep," Mark said, sitting up and glancing at the wall clock. It was six a.m. "You made good time."

"We used the siren," Steve said.

"You're joking, right?" Mark said.

"I wish I was," Steve said. "Penmore insisted. I've got a hell of a headache."

"Where is your friend?"

"Talking to Stryker," Steve said. "Or at least trying to. He's also got some diplomacy work to do with the Mohave County Sheriff's Department."

"What's your job?"

"I'm the driver, the muscle, and the deliveryman." Steve motioned to the gym bag. "There's a change of clothes for you in there. You can come back to LA with us today."

"Thanks, but I'm not going back to Los Angeles yet," Mark said.

"Where are you going?"

"Las Vegas."

"I don't suppose it's because you're in the area and feel like losing some money on the slots," Steve said. "I got Pelz's phone records. He was calling Vegas a lot lately, but you've already guessed that."

"Was he calling anyone in particular?"

"He was calling pay phones up and down the Strip," Steve said. "Whoever Pelz was talking to must have worked out a prearranged calling time with him and supplied the number. You think it's Jimmy Cale."

"I can't prove it," Mark said. "Not yet anyway."

"How did you guess he'd be in Vegas?" Steve said. "You'd think Cale would have left the country."

"You can change your face, but you can't change who you are," Mark said.

"So you keep saying."

"Betsy Cale told me her ex-husband felt uncomfortable, to the point of crippling paranoia, in places he couldn't speak the language," Mark said. "So that ruled out Europe or Mexico. But he enjoyed gambling and loved Las Vegas."

"So if he's alive, and if he's living in Las Vegas, how are you going to flush him out?"

"By calling in some favors," Mark said.

The Las Vegas Strip was like a high-priced Hollywood hooker—seductive and seedy, frequently renovated, and bedeviled by high traffic.

Only a few years ago, legendary hotel magnate Roger Standiford's T-Rex casino was the biggest attraction on the Strip, with its giant animatronic dinosaurs, erupting volcanoes, and massive hotel towers seemingly carved out of solid rock.

But then the London resort casino opened a block away, offering tourists the chance to visit re-creations of Big Ben,

Buckingham Palace, Piccadilly Circus, and even the Underground, a subway that shuttled guests from one end of the massive hotel to the other. The Tube stops were authentic right down to the smell, fabricated at a cost of eleven million dollars by fragrance experts poached from Chanel.

Now London had been trumped by Standiford's newest mega-resort, the Côte d'Azur, a lavish hotel and gambling palace that evoked a bygone era of elegance, class, and exclusivity. The shimmering golden towers beckoned everyone but accepted only a privileged few. Côte d'Azur wasn't for the all-you-can-eat-buffet tourists or for the retirees who liked to play nickel slots. They were politely turned away before they even reached the lobby doors.

Standiford was interested only in wealthy vacationers looking for a decadent retreat and high rollers seeking the ultimate gambling experience. But most of all, Côte d'Azur courted the whales, gamblers who thought nothing of wagering a million dollars or more a night.

To create the right atmosphere, and actively discourage the less well heeled, black tie attire was required at all times in the Côte d'Azur's casino, restaurants, nightclubs, and bars. Men wore tuxedos and women wore evening gowns. Guests interested in casual dining could eat in the privacy of their sumptuously appointed staterooms or find it elsewhere in the city.

For those who didn't bring the right clothes, a stop at one of the hotel's many fine merchants was recommended. The designer shops included Louis Vuitton, Cartier, Christian Dior, Hermès, Oscar de la Renta, Gucci, and Manolo Blahnik. Any man who showed up at the casino in a rented tux would be politely escorted to the nearest exit by hotel security. The only places the dress code was relaxed were in the lobby, the pool, and the spa.

All the other necessities of life could be found at the Côte d'Azur. It even included a private medical facility that rivaled many of the nation's finest hospitals. Why recuperate from surgery in a drab hospital room when you could rest instead in a luxurious suite with a breathtaking view of the Las Vegas Strip? Why eat hospital food when you could dine on gourmet creations from the world's finest chefs? The hospital specialized in orthopedic, cardiovascular, and plastic surgery, though it dealt as well with the assorted ailments, accidents, and health emergencies of the resort's wealthy, privacy-minded guests.

As posh and elegant as Côte d'Azur was, there was one area where Standiford pandered to superficial, mass-market appeal. Throughout the hallways, garages, and elevators of the hotel, John Barry's brassy music from the first seven James Bond films played on a constant loop. It was tacky, but it worked. Standiford knew that every man, no matter how rich and powerful, wanted to think he was as smooth, capable, and dangerous as James Bond and every woman wanted to be the femme fatale who was his undoing.

If anybody who stayed at the Côte d'Azur thought the 007 music was silly or monotonous, they never said so. It became an almost subliminal part of the Côte d'Azur experience.

The exclusivity even extended to the parking lot, a showcase of the finest automobiles from around the world. Taxis and airport vans were not allowed on the property. Limousines were welcome, as long as they were luxury cars, unadorned with advertising, and gleaming.

When Dr. Mark Sloan drove up in his rented Ford Five Hundred sedan, the valet and the security guard both looked as if he'd arrived in a manure delivery truck.

"We don't accept vehicles of this nature on our property, sir," the valet said. He was only in his twenties, but already he was a master of smug superiority.

"I'm sure you can find a place to hide it," Mark said cheerfully, handing his keys to the valet. "Perhaps in employee parking? Or do you drive a Lamborghini to work?"

Mark turned his attention to the security guard, who was dressed in a suit and tie, a wire running from inside his jacket to his earpiece. "I'd like to see Roger Standiford, please."

"I'd like to see Jessica Simpson naked," the man said, "but that's not going to happen either. You can get back in your car, make a U-turn. Circus Circus is right up the street. Have a pleasant stay in Las Vegas."

"Tell Mr. Standiford that Dr. Mark Sloan is here."

"Don't make me insist, sir," the man said. "You wouldn't like me when I insist."

"I'm not terribly fond of you now," Mark said without losing any of his cheer.

The man started to take a step towards Mark and then abruptly stopped, as if stung by an electric shock. He touched his earpiece, listened for a moment, then looked up at a surveillance camera mounted on one of the marble pillars.

"Please follow me, sir," the security man said, plastering an insincere smile onto his face.

"My pleasure," Mark said.

The security guard led him into the massive lobby, with its marble floors, exquisitely carved columns, and soaring ceiling topped with a stained-glass skylight handcrafted in Italy. The walls behind the expansive mahogany check-in counter were adorned with original masterpieces by Gauguin, Matisse, and Cézanne.

Nate Grumbo, Standiford's head of security, was standing in the center of the lobby, waiting for them.

He was an ex–FBI agent with a buzz cut, square jaw, no neck, and a permanent squint he'd mastered by watching Clint Eastwood movies over and over again. Grumbo looked like a caveman who'd been professionally groomed and forced into a tailored silk suit.

Mark knew from experience that it would be a mistake to underestimate Grumbo based on his Neanderthal appearance. He took it as a given that Grumbo was well aware of the debt Roger Standiford owed him.

"Thank you, Dean." Grumbo dismissed the security guard with a glance, then offered Mark his gigantic paw. "Dr. Sloan, this is a surprise."

They shook hands. Mark was grateful that Grumbo chose not to pulverize his hand and ruin his surgical career.

"Mr. Standiford is in Macao and won't be returning until tomorrow," Grumbo said. "Is there something I can help you with?"

"Perhaps there is," Mark said. "Is there somewhere we can talk where I won't feel so underdressed?"

Grumbo gave Mark a thin smile. "Of course. Let's go to my office."

Mark followed Grumbo to the elevators. Once inside, Grumbo inserted a key into the control panel, typed a code into a keypad, and the elevator descended, which was odd, since according to the display, they were already on the lowest possible floor.

"Don't believe everything you read," Grumbo said, picking up on Mark's thoughts.

The doors opened to far less opulence. In fact, to no opulence at all. The underground corridor glowed with fluorescent light and was painted a flat white. The floors were linoleum. Casually dressed workers rushed to and fro, filled with intent.

Grumbo approached a door secured with palm-print and retinal scanners. He placed his palm on the scanner while a red laserlike beam probed his eyeballs. The James Bond mind-set of the casino clearly filtered down to the security system as well. A moment later the door hissed open, and Grumbo motioned Mark inside a vast, dark room that looked liked a miniature version of NASA Mission Control.

What little light there was in the control room came from strategically placed pinpoint halogens and the glow of the dozens of flat-screen monitors. Individual security agents sat in front of as many as four screens each. Three of the screens showed views of particular gaming tables, dealers, and players. The other monitor took screen grabs of players' faces, lifted from the surveillance camera feeds, and compared them with photos in a database of known cheaters, professional gamblers, and card counters.

Grumbo led Mark to an office a few steps above the control room, where a broad window allowed him to gaze down at the technicians below. On Grumbo's desk was another bank of flat-screen monitors. Some of the screens showed the casino floor. Others focused on individual technicians in the control room.

Even the watchers were watched.

Mark took a seat in a plush green-leather chair across from Grumbo's desk.

"Feeling more comfortable?" Grumbo asked.

"Not really," Mark said, glancing at Grumbo's monitors. "They watch us. You watch them. I suppose someone is even watching you."

Grumbo gestured over Mark's shoulder to a tiny camera mounted in the corner of the room. "We're all being watched, Dr. Sloan."

"I don't know how you can live that way."

Grumbo shrugged. "You do."

"I'm not under surveillance all day."

"Of course you are, Doctor. From the instant you step out of your Malibu beach house."

Mark noticed the casual, and totally intentional, way Grumbo let it slip that he knew exactly where the doctor lived. Grumbo probably also knew what was in his refrigerator, how often he flossed, and what he had watched on TV last Thursday night.

"There are exterior security cameras on the house next door to you. There's also a traffic camera at the intersection of Trancas and Pacific Coast Highway, as well as multiple security cameras in the parking lot of the market across the street," Grumbo said. "Using intersection and freeway traffic cameras and tapping the feeds from cameras at the stores, ATMs, and parking lots that you pass, I could chart your drive all the way to Community General. Of course, once you're in the hospital, I have my choice of dozens of cameras I can watch you with. None of this includes the hundreds of video-enabled cell phones and camcorders, or an array of other cameras that could be trained on you, without your knowledge, at any given time."

"Nobody has any privacy anymore," Mark said. "And they don't even realize it."

"They realize it," Grumbo said. "The same way they realize that crossing the street is insanely dangerous and that a 747 is too damn big and heavy to fly. But they don't care. They ignore the dangers because the benefits are greater than the risks, the gains bigger than what we lose. There are some advantages to being able to gather so much data on a person."

"Funny you should mention that," Mark said. "I need a favor from you."

"What kind of favor are we talking about?"

"I need your help finding a dead man," Mark said.

CHAPTER EIGHTEEN

"I know you keep detailed files on high rollers, not just here but the ones who patronize everybody else's casinos, too," Mark said. "You know their hobbies, the foods they like to eat, the brands of clothes they like to wear. You know their favorite colors, how they like their drinks mixed, even the kind of shampoo they use."

"We know a lot more than that, Doctor," Grumbo said. "A *lot* more."

"Because you want to entice them to play in your casino and make them as happy as possible once they are here."

"We like satisfied customers."

"Especially when they're losing tens of thousands of dollars at your tables," Mark said. "I'm looking for one of those customers."

"We protect the privacy of our guests, Dr. Sloan," Grumbo said. "Surely you can understand that."

"This one won't mind," Mark said. "He's dead."

"What's his name?"

"James Cale," Mark said.

Grumbo swiveled around in his chair and worked his keyboard. After a moment, Jimmy Cale's picture came up on the screen, along with a bunch of information in print too small for Mark to read from where he was sitting. He didn't need to read it anyway. He knew what it said.

"Here he is. Used to play over at the Bellagio," Grumbo said. "Glad I could be of help."

"That's not what I need," Mark said.

"I had a feeling it was too easy," Grumbo said.

"There's another gambler—I don't know who he is yet—who showed up here for the first time about four years ago. He likes a lot of the same things that Jimmy Cale did," Mark said. "He smokes Partagas Salamones and Cohiba Esplendidos, but if you really want to be nice, you offer him a Padron Anniversario imported before the embargo. Either he lives in Las Vegas or spends at least half his time here. He pays for everything in cash and is very secretive about his past. Your efforts to find out more about him have come up blank."

Grumbo stared at Mark. "I thought you said you were looking for a dead man."

"I am," Mark said. "One who has come back to life."

Grumbo thought for a moment, came to a decision, and started typing on his keyboard. A few moments later, a face and a name appeared on one of the flat-screen monitors.

The man looked younger than Cale and had more well-defined features. He had a prominent chin, a neatly kept mustache, and capped teeth that gleamed unnaturally white.

"His name is Robin Mannering," Grumbo said. "He's single and lives at an estate out in Summerlin. He calls himself an entrepreneur and an investor, though I haven't been able to identify any of his businesses or investments. All his cash appears to come to his Las Vegas bank via offshore accounts. Mr. Mannering enjoys ménages à trois and has a suite at his disposal here for those encounters. He never takes a woman home. His gaming preference is poker, though he spends time at the roulette wheel and the blackjack tables. He has a two-million-dollar credit line and has played at Côte d'Azur almost every weekend since we opened."

"Who's ahead," Mark asked, "him or you?"

"He's a skilled gambler, though certainly not a professional.

On average, we only make a couple of hundred thousand dollars off him annually. Over the years, he's lost nearly a million to us. At the moment, he's ahead $122,000, but in the end the house always wins."

"As long as he keeps playing," Mark said.

"That's why we make his visits as enjoyable as possible. He's comped in all of our restaurants and nightclubs, and while he's in the high-roller room, there's a beautiful hostess ready to offer him a fine cigar or whatever else he may desire."

"Can you find out if he has a private humidor at one of the local cigar stores?"

"He has one here," Grumbo said. "We have the finest tobacconist in the West."

Mark leaned over the desk and pointed at the picture of Jimmy Cale on the monitor.

"Can you take that picture of Jimmy Cale, and this one of Robin Mannering, and run them through that software of yours that matches cheaters on your surveillance screens with gamblers in your database?"

"Of course." Grumbo used his mouse to point and click his way through several menus of instructions. The images of Cale on one screen and Mannering on another were layered on top of each other on a third screen. They didn't match up.

"It's not a match," Grumbo said. "But their bone structure is pretty close. According to the computer, there are one hundred ninety-seven points of similarity. They could be related."

"I'm sure they are," Mark said. Now all he had to do was prove it. "This is where the favor comes in."

"I thought I just did you the favor," Grumbo said.

"I want to meet Mr. Mannering," Mark said. "I also need you to help me get his fingerprints and his DNA so I can send them back to LA for analysis."

"Is that all?" Grumbo narrowed his eyes at Mark. "Putting

aside that extraordinary request for a moment, you can't even step into the high-roller room without a five-hundred-thousand-dollar credit line."

"Oh yeah," Mark said. "I'll need that, too."

Grumbo's phone rang instantly and, as he picked it up, he reflexively stole a glance at the camera on the wall behind Mark. He probably wasn't even aware that he'd done it.

But Mark was.

"Hello," Grumbo said and then listened for a long moment. "Of course. Right away."

Grumbo hung up the phone and looked up to see Mark smiling at him.

"Mr. Standiford will see me now," Mark said, then turned and waved at the camera behind him. "How was Macao?"

Most people expected Roger Standiford to be as garish, aggressive, and obnoxious as his mega-resorts, but he was quite the opposite. He was exceptionally polished and polite, greeting guests with a genuinely warm smile, a firm handshake, and the bearing of a statesman.

Standiford carried himself more like a presidential candidate than like one of the richest men in America, the developer admired and loathed for invading the Las Vegas Strip and reshaping it to his own tastes.

But that stately charm and hospitality weren't on display when Mark Sloan was ushered into Standiford's two-story, glass-walled, top-floor office with its breathtaking views of Las Vegas. From here, Standiford could look down upon the city like a Greek god and hurl lightning bolts at those who defied him.

Standiford wouldn't have to strain his arm today. He could smite Mark face-to-face.

"What you're asking goes too far," Standiford said, rising from behind his steel-and-glass desk.

"Not as far as you've gone," Mark said. "I'm not killing anyone."

"I haven't killed anyone either," Standiford said.

"We both know that isn't true," Mark said. "You're morally responsible for what your hit man did. You'd be held criminally responsible, too, if it wasn't for me."

"You didn't have the proof."

"The people who kidnapped and murdered your daughter eluded the FBI and you for years. But I found them. Do you really think it would have been that hard for me to make a case against you?" Mark said. "I chose not to."

Standiford glowered at Mark and sat down behind his desk again. Mark remained standing, mainly because he knew from experience that the steel-and-leather guest chairs that looked so stylish were hell on the lower back.

"You want a five-hundred-thousand-dollar credit line," Standiford said.

"I won't keep a penny of it," Mark said. "Whatever I win belongs to you. I'll try to stick to blackjack or roulette so my losses go back into your pocket and not to another player."

"How generous of you," Standiford said. "I could lose my gaming license if this gets out."

"You mean to tell me you don't have gamblers you're staking to keep the games lively and the pots rich?"

"That's a myth," Standiford said.

"If it is, it won't be after tonight—though I am hardly a professional gambler."

"What's the point of this whole exercise?"

"I believe that Robin Mannering is actually Jimmy Cale with a new face. He faked his murder, framed his business partner for the crime, and ran off with millions of dollars he embezzled from his clients."

"What does this have to do with you?"

"There's a man serving time on death row for a crime he not only didn't commit, but that never happened in the first place. That's an injustice I have to correct. I also believe Cale is responsible for a murder in Kingman last week. He has to pay for that."

"So you want to obtain his fingerprints and his DNA to establish his true identity, to prove Mannering is Cale," Standiford said.

"Yes," Mark said.

"I can do that for you easily enough without giving you half a million dollars to gamble with in my casino."

"I want to meet him in his element," Mark said. "I want to see what kind of man he really is. But I can't get in the door without being a high roller myself."

Standiford grinned. "That's really why you do this, isn't it?"

"Do what?"

"Solve murders. It's not about justice at all. It's not even about the puzzle. It's about pitting yourself against an opponent in a game of wits. You could accomplish what you need to without ever meeting the man, but that would take the thrill out of it, wouldn't it?"

"I like to look my adversaries in the eye," Mark said. "But that's just so I have an accurate sense of who I'm up against."

"You're just another gambler, Dr. Sloan, only you play with much higher stakes than money," Standiford said, his mood lightening considerably. "This is a game I'm going to enjoy watching."

Standiford hit a button on his desk, and Grumbo entered almost instantly.

"Nate, give Dr. Sloan whatever assistance he needs," Standiford said, then turned back to Mark. "If you want to be convincing in the part, you'll need to stay in our hotel and you'll need a new identity."

"Let's not stray too far from the truth," Mark said. "I'm not much of an actor."

"You'll be a wealthy doctor," Standiford said. "No, I have

an even better idea. You'll be a visiting surgeon at our in-house medical center."

"You expect me to work for you?"

"I'm giving you five hundred thousand dollars to play with, aren't I? The least you can do to earn it is hand out a few aspirins. Besides, this way while you're waiting for Mannering's DNA results to come in, it won't seem unusual to anyone if you have the run of the hotel." Standiford gave Mark an appraising glance and clearly wasn't happy with what he saw. "You'll also need to get yourself suitable attire and a nice tuxedo."

"I can handle that," Mark said, though he wasn't sure that his credit card could.

"While you're out shopping for clothes, I'll set everything up," Grumbo said.

"Could you do something else for me?" Mark said. "I'd like you to ask Mannering's lady friends if he's missing a toe. Perhaps they noticed during one of their ménages à trois."

"I find it's hard to keep track of whose foot is whose in those situations," Grumbo said.

"I wouldn't know," Mark said.

"Nate can arrange for you to find out, if you like," Standiford said.

"No thanks," Mark said.

"What happens in Vegas stays in Vegas," Standiford said with a sly grin.

"And in your video vault to be pulled out when it suits your needs," Mark said.

"You're a cynical man, Dr. Sloan," Standiford said.

"Now I know where my son gets it," Mark said.

"I'm going to need a name to establish your new identity and your credit line, book your room, and set you up in the medical center," Grumbo said.

Mark thought for a moment. "Ross. Dr. Douglas Ross. You can call me Doug."

"I'll come down to the casino tonight and make the introductions myself," Standiford said.

"You don't have to do that," Mark said.

"I want to," Standiford said. "I'm a sporting man, Dr. Sloan. I like to meet the players and size them up before I bet on the game."

CHAPTER NINETEEN

Mark couldn't afford to shop at the Côte d'Azur and he couldn't risk being seen driving around Las Vegas in a rented Ford Five Hundred, so he accepted Nate Grumbo's offer of a ride in one of the hotel's fleet of Mercedes limos.

The chauffeur took Mark to the shopping malls at Caesars Palace, the Aladdin, the Venetian, and then, with obvious reluctance, to the outlet mall at the far end of town.

Mark bought himself a week's worth of clothes, careful to select brand names of much higher quality and price than he was accustomed to wearing, and spent more on a tuxedo and dress shoes than he had on Steve's first car.

When they returned to the Côte d'Azur that evening, his room was ready, as was a full set of identification documents to use at the hotel. He was now officially "Dr. Douglas Ross," at least within the confines of the resort complex.

His room was a lavish second-floor suite with a view of the hotel's massive wave pool, the four swimming pools, and the freshwater lake. The interior was opulent, with an elegantly appointed living room full of French antiques, a projection room with theater seating and a collection of classic films on DVD, a study lined with leather-bound first editions, a master bedroom with a four-poster bed and a flat-screen TV, and an elaborate bar fully stocked with vintage wines, fine Scotch, and assorted spirits.

Since Mark had a few hours to spare before Mannering showed up at the casino, he was tempted to stay in the room and read one of the fine first editions or watch a movie in his private theater. Instead, he decided Dr. Ross should probably make an appearance at the Côte d'Azur's medical center.

So he showered and changed into a nice shirt and slacks, clipped his Côte d'Azur ID to his leather belt, and wandered over to the medical center.

When he walked through the door he stopped in amazement. He'd never seen a medical facility like it before. It was to hospitals what the Côte d'Azur was to hotels. The waiting area, elegant, softly lit, with fine art on the paneled walls and plush leather furniture, felt more like a fine private club than the lobby of a hospital. There wasn't anything the least bit sterile-looking or cold about the place. It didn't even *smell* like a hospital.

He approached the front desk and introduced himself to the receptionist, a beautiful and perfectly poised young woman with a bright, warm smile.

She told him the director of the hospital, Alexis Bratton, would be right down to meet him and asked if he'd like a latte or an espresso while he waited.

Mark declined the refreshments but was impressed that he'd been asked. A patient at Community General would be lucky if the receptionist pointed out the drinking fountain—and even luckier if the drinking fountain actually worked.

There was a lot he could learn here. Unfortunately, without Standiford's deep pockets, he wouldn't be able to apply much of that knowledge at Community General.

Mark had heard about places like this, but had never before visited one himself. Specialty surgical hospitals were booming nationwide and were seen by general hospitals to be a serious threat to their continued existence.

He could see why.

If he had a choice between staying at the Côte d'Azur

facility or at Community General, he'd pick this one—and he hadn't even gotten past the lobby yet. But if Standiford's attention to detail and extravagant spending extended to his surgical facilities and patient suites—and Mark was sure that they did—there was no way a full-service hospital could compete.

Alexis Bratton was even more stunning than the receptionist. She wore her lab coat as if it were an evening gown, looking professional, elegant, and sexy at the same time. It was clear to Mark that Standiford used the same standards in hiring his medical personnel that he did in hiring the hostesses on the casino floor. Mark hoped the medical personnel, at least, had qualifications beyond their measurements.

She welcomed him to the facility and expressed her delight that a doctor who had once served as the personal physician to the Saudi royal family had chosen their facility to care for his current patients during their stay in Las Vegas.

Mark just smiled and nodded. He didn't want to be asked any questions about Saudi Arabia, a place he knew nothing about, or the details about his new patients, whom he also knew nothing about, mainly because they didn't exist.

Instead, as Bratton showed him around the facility, he asked lots of questions. What he learned was that the Côte d'Azur facility specialized primarily in elective and preplanned surgeries, as well as any assorted mishaps or ailments that might befall the hotel's guests.

Because the facility focused primarily on orthopedic, cardiovascular, and plastic surgery, it was more efficient and had more state-of-the-art equipment than a traditional hospital. Because it offered a better work environment and higher pay, the Côte d'Azur also attracted superior surgeons and nurses. The ratio of nurses to patients was much lower than in community hospitals.

In specialty surgical hospitals like the Côte d'Azur, Bratton said, patients were twenty times less likely to become infected by other patients, so they weren't hospitalized as long and their medical bills were substantially lower, while at the same time they enjoyed a higher level of care. The length of time patients were hospitalized at specialty surgical centers was twenty-five percent less than at community and teaching hospitals.

As impressed as Mark was by the Côte d'Azur's medical center, he understood the risk that specialized hospitals like it posed to community hospitals, which offered emergency care and basic treatment for a wide variety of medical conditions, as well as outpatient services, anatomical pathology services, clinical laboratory services, and pharmacy services. Those necessary programs were funded, in part, from the revenue generated by the profitable surgeries that the specialized hospitals were luring away. Without that revenue, many general-service hospitals, vital to the well-being of their communities, might be forced to shut down.

But Mark also realized the limitations of the traditional hospital model, which contributed to the soaring costs of health care. Perhaps the increased competition would lead to better medical care for everyone, though for now, facilities like the Côte d'Azur were restricted to only the rich and powerful.

Bratton told Mark that all of the center's services were at his disposal and that the security, privacy, and anonymity of his patients would be assured. Mark knew that his nonexistent patients would rest easier knowing that.

The tour was an eye-opening experience for Mark. He left the Côte d'Azur medical center wishing he had the financial resources to provide the same comfortable, elegant atmosphere and exceptional level of care at Community General.

He returned to his room, had a shrimp salad delivered for dinner, and then changed into his tuxedo. It was time to meet Robin Mannering face-to-face.

As Mark descended the grand staircase into the casino in

his tuxedo, the brassy score of *Goldfinger* playing on the speakers, he couldn't help but feel like James Bond himself.

He'd never felt so cool, so suave, so self-confident, so ready to gamble. The world was his for the taking and he was going to take it.

Mark desperately wanted to play baccarat, 007's game. It didn't matter that he'd never played it before and had no idea what the rules were. He was wearing a tuxedo, he was in a casino, and he looked great. That was all that really mattered.

An impossibly beautiful woman with radiant eyes, lush lips, and bottomless cleavage was standing behind the red velvet rope at the entrance to the high-rollers room. She seemed very glad to see him.

But who wouldn't be, the way he looked, the way he felt? Women would be helpless in his presence tonight.

"The name is Ross, Douglas Ross." Mark cocked an eyebrow and flashed a grin. "Dr. Douglas Ross. Licensed to practice medicine."

"Yes, of course, Dr. Ross," she said. "We've been expecting you. If there's anything I can do to make your evening more pleasant, don't hesitate to ask."

"I can assure you I won't," he said.

She unfastened the rope and motioned him in. As he walked past her, he caught a reflection of himself in a mirror, saw the ridiculous expression on his face, and immediately snapped out of his 007 trance.

What had gotten into him?

He blushed with embarrassment, recalling how foolishly he'd acted with the hostess. How could he face her again after that?

It was amazing the powerful effect that the right clothes, the right music, and the right atmosphere had on a person, Mark thought. All sorts of psychological, emotional, and cultural buttons were pushed all at once. Insecurities washed away and wish-fulfillment fantasies took over.

Maybe when other men saw their reflections as they strode into the high-roller room, it simply reinforced the fantasy. Not for Mark. He was almost disappointed that he'd been jarred back to reality.

But he was grateful to have his wits about him again, because sitting at the poker table behind several large stacks of chips was Robin Mannering.

It would have been a mistake for Mark to confront Mannering with anything less than his full wits about him. Two other men also sat at the table, behind towers of poker chips, waiting for the dealer to begin dealing the cards.

Mark handed his Côte d'Azur ID card to the pit boss. "A hundred thousand dollars in chips, please."

He tried to sound casual when he said it, but all he really managed to do was mumble. The pit boss heard him anyway, ran his card through a scanner, then nodded to the dealer, who counted out the chips and slid the stacks across the table to Mark.

Everything Mark knew about poker he'd learned from watching old *Maverick* reruns. He hoped that would be good enough.

The game was no-limit Texas hold 'em. Every player is dealt two cards facedown. After a round of betting, five shared cards are dealt faceup. The player with the best five-card hand from the seven cards available wins the pot.

In addition to the thousand-dollar ante, there are two forced bets in each hand, called the small blind and the big blind. Before each hand, the dealer slides a button, in turn, around the table. The person to the left of the button pays the small blind bet, the player to his left plays the big blind, which is double the amount of the small blind. The next person to the left is known as the first position, and he must, at the very least, call the bets. That keeps the pot rich and the action hot for every hand. The blinds in this game were three thousand and six thousand dollars.

The ante and blinds alone made Mark's heart palpitate before a single card was dealt.

Just as the dealer was preparing to deal the hand, Roger Standiford walked into the room, and all the action at the various tables stopped to acknowledge his kingly presence. He wore a white tuxedo, which made him stand out from the crowd even more. Anyone else would have looked like a waiter.

The hotel magnate shook a few hands, patted some backs, then made his way to the poker table, where he embraced Mark as if they were old, dear friends.

"Doug, it's so good to see you," Standiford said. "How are the cards treating you tonight?"

"It's too soon to tell," Mark said.

"Try not to bankrupt me, okay?"

"That's why I'm playing poker, Roger," Mark said. "To give the house a break. Just wait until I sit down at the blackjack table."

Standiford forced a smile, then turned to the other men at the table. "Gentlemen, let me introduce you to my old friend Dr. Douglas Ross, a medical genius. He holds the patent to the key technologies behind several medical breakthroughs, including the artificial heart."

"You thinking about getting yourself one, you heartless bastard?" Mannering asked Standiford with a grin.

"Hell no," Standiford said. "A heart, even an artificial one, would be a liability in this business. Maybe when I retire."

Standiford introduced Mark to the other players, but he didn't really pay attention. All he cared about was Mannering, who selected a Cohiba from a silver tray offered to him by the hostess.

"You won't retire until you own every hotel on the Strip," one of the men said.

"Why would I set my sights so low?" Standiford said. "Good luck tonight, my friends."

And with that, Standiford walked out and the cards were dealt. The pot was at $13,000. Everyone folded except Mannering, who raised the ante for Mark to $36,000. Mark glanced at his two cards. A pair of kings. It seemed like a strong hand.

Mark studied Mannering, who was going through the elaborate ceremony of lighting his cigar. He used the first wooden match to simply warm the tip, then struck another, which he held under the cigar until the heat, not the flame, ignited the tobacco.

Mannering was completely relaxed, as if he were betting pennies.

Mark was sweating through every pore in his body and it wasn't even his money at stake. He wondered if he would have been less anxious if he was wagering his own cash, but he doubted it.

A pair of kings was a strong hand, and he'd be a fool not to ride it. He slid $40,000 worth of chips into the pot, enriching it to $76,000.

Mannering puffed on his cigar and studied Mark. "Are you a gambling man, Dr. Ross?"

"I'm here," Mark said.

"That's not what I'm asking," Mannering said.

"You don't go into a profession where you cut into people's hearts, spines, and brains unless you enjoy risk and playing for the ultimate stakes," Mark said. "By comparison, these table games are mere child's play."

"Once you've played for the ultimate stakes, as you put it, it's hard to find something else that even comes close to thrilling you as much," Mannering said.

"You talk as if you're speaking from experience," Mark said.

Mannering smiled enigmatically and tossed in $20,000, raising the pot to $96,000. "I call."

Mark showed his pair of kings. Mannering flipped over

his queen and an eight. Mark was relieved to see he possessed the superior hand, but his opponent didn't seem the least bit rattled.

"Sounds to me like you'd both get a kick out of Russian roulette," said one of the other players.

"But where's the profit in that?" asked another.

"Betting on which one of them lives, of course."

On the flop, the dealer laid out an eight, a four, and another queen, giving Mannering two pairs. Mark felt his stomach roll.

The dealer flipped the turn card, a six. No help there. Mark needed another king. The dealer turned the river card, a seven.

Mannering won the pot.

Mark glanced up at the ceiling, almost apologetically, to the unseen eyes he knew were watching him.

If he kept playing like this, his $60,000 in chips could be gone in the next ten minutes.

Much to Mark's surprise, he was able to hold his own for the next few hours, ending up ahead with $132,000, thanks to very conservative play that didn't pit him directly against Mannering again. He was sure Standiford was relieved. But Mark wasn't concentrating too hard on the game. Most of his attention was devoted to sizing up his opponent.

Mannering seemed to rely less on bluffs than on his unwavering faith in his own good luck. His faith seemed to be well placed. He wiped out another player's pair of aces with a pair of nines that turned into three of a kind on the flop. It earned him $250,000.

"It's unbelievable. You are the luckiest man I know," said the busted player as he rose from the table.

But Mark was certain that Mannering's streak was coming to an abrupt end.

When Mannering discarded the stub of his cigar in his ashtray, the hostess was quick to take it away. Mark knew

Grumbo was waiting to bag the stub for the crime lab. The DNA drawn from that cigar would send Mannering to prison.

In the grand scheme of things, Mannering's luck had run out. He just didn't know it yet.

But Mark did. And he took it as a sign that the cards would fall his way, too.

The blind bets had increased to $4,000 and $8,000. The other player folded, leaving Mark and Mannering to compete over a pot that now stood at $15,000. Mark didn't touch his cards, leaving them as they were dealt, facedown.

Mark called Mannering's bet.

"You didn't look at your cards," Mannering said.

Mark shrugged. "Wouldn't change anything. I have what I have."

"What about strategy? Aren't you interested in playing the odds?"

"Where's the risk in that?" Mark asked. "Poker is as much about instinct as anything else."

"Don't rule out human nature," Mannering said. "That's where the bluff comes in."

"Bluffs play on your opponent's fear," Mark said. "How afraid are you, Mr. Mannering?"

Mannering looked down at his cards, which he hadn't turned yet either. He looked back up at Mark and smiled, leaving his own cards untouched as well.

They were both playing blind.

The dealer dealt three cards faceup. A five, a six, and a seven.

Mark bet $12,000.

"Not a very daring bet. Almost tentative. I didn't think you were a tentative man, Doctor. Perhaps I misjudged you. I'll see your bet and raise everything you've got." Mannering slid $110,000 in chips into the center of the table.

"You're crazy," said the player who'd bowed out.

"And you haven't won a single hand, Ernie," Mannering

said. "Looking at the cards didn't help you much. Besides, it's just child's play, isn't it, Doctor?"

Mark could feel the security camera zooming in on him, Standiford and Grumbo watching anxiously to see what he'd do next. This was, after all, Standiford's money that he was recklessly gambling with. He hesitated, until he saw the hostess use a napkin to take Mannering's empty glass and replace it with a fresh drink.

She was preserving Mannering's prints for the crime lab. They had what they needed to prove who Mannering really was. Jimmy Cale's five-year winning streak was over.

Knowing all of this, Mark *had* to bet.

Mark smiled. "I believe your luck has turned."

He slid all his chips into the pot, bringing it to $265,000, and turned over his cards.

Mark had a queen and an eight. Even with the three community cards, he had nothing.

"Are you sure?" Mannering flipped his cards, revealing a seven and a two, giving him a pair of sevens. It was almost as if he had known all along he had the better hand.

It was unnerving.

It was meant to be.

There were only two more cards to go. Mark needed a queen or an eight or he would lose everything. The odds were not in his favor.

Was Mannering's luck holding?

No, Mark thought, it *couldn't* be.

The dealer dealt the turn card, an ace. Mark's odds of winning plummeted. He was one card away from giving Mannering $100,000 of Standiford's money to squander during his last day or two of freedom.

What kind of luck was that?

The dealer flipped the river card onto the table.

It was an eight.

CHAPTER TWENTY

Mark was so relieved that he'd won the hand with his measly pair of eights that he immediately cashed out. He didn't want to take a chance on losing any of his winnings.

Standiford's winnings, to be exact.

With a return of $165,000 on his investment, he figured Standiford couldn't complain too much about granting his favor.

Robin Mannering was still hundreds of thousands of dollars ahead for the night, so losing to Mark couldn't have caused him much damage. At least not in the wallet, though his ego may have sustained some bruising. But to show he had no hard feelings, Mannering stood up and offered Mark his hand.

"It's been a pleasure, Doctor," Mannering said. "I have the feeling I may have finally met my match."

"I'm certainly going to give it a try," Mark said.

"Then I eagerly await our next encounter at the gaming tables," Mannering said.

Mark left and returned to his room, where Grumbo was waiting, Mannering's glass and cigar stub sealed in Baggies on the coffee table. It was a little unnerving to find someone waiting in his room. Couldn't Grumbo have called first? Or invited Mark to meet him in his office?

"You acquitted yourself well at the poker table, Dr. Sloan."

"I was lucky, that's all," Mark said.

"Using that luck to your advantage is the mark of a true gamesman," Grumbo said. "You're being modest."

"Even if I'd lost the battle at the table, I've already won the war," Mark said, motioning to the Baggies. "We've got him now."

"I'll send these to the Vegas crime lab tonight," Grumbo said. "I have a friend there. We share a mutual interest in bugs."

"Electronic?"

"He prefers the insect variety," Grumbo said. "He'll pass the results through official channels to your son, though it may not be necessary."

"Why do you say that?"

"I spoke to the women Mr. Mannering has invited into his bed," Grumbo said.

"The ones in your employ," Mark said.

"I asked them about his toes," Grumbo said, pointedly ignoring Mark's comment. "He's missing one. He said he lost it in Afghanistan during a particularly aggressive interrogation by his enemies."

"Afghanistan?"

"Men often try to impress women with vague allusions to their secret lives of adventure," Grumbo said. "Implying that one is an ex-spy or a former military operative is a particularly common method of seduction."

"But you've never done that?" Mark said.

"Those of us who actually were in those fields usually don't talk about it," Grumbo said, picking up the Baggies and heading for the door. "Particularly in bed."

"Why?"

"Because as we all know, that's where the best interrogations are done," Grumbo said. "People are much freer with information when they are seeking pleasure than when they are avoiding pain."

Grumbo walked out, leaving Mark to wonder exactly how the Côte d'Azur's security chief had gained his experience, and whether it was as the interrogator or the one being questioned.

Mark went to bed, woke up at nine, and had a leisurely breakfast on his veranda overlooking the Côte d'Azur's pools, lakes, palms, and waterfalls.

He felt relaxed and refreshed in a way he hadn't in a very long time. Perhaps he should consider taking more vacations—though he could hardly count the last week of frenetic travel particularly restful.

And yet, in a strange way, it had been. As tiring as all the driving had been, the rapid change of scenery, from San Francisco to Las Vegas, over so few days was also stimulating, a nice break from the routine of going from his Malibu beach house to Community General and back each day.

Today the fingerprints would come back identifying Robin Mannering as the late James Cale. How could Cale have betrayed his best friend and framed him for murder? What could have made Cale resent Yankton so much? Even more perplexing was Cale's willingness to completely abandon his ex-wife and daughter.

And he did it all for money.

It wasn't as if he didn't have money to begin with. Why did he have to embezzle even more? What was he looking for in life that he didn't already have?

It made no sense to Mark.

The only explanation was that Cale, now calling himself Mannering, was a sociopath.

There were still a few questions that needed to be answered. Did Mannering murder the currency dealer and try to kill Stryker, or did he have someone else do it?

If he hired someone else, who was it and where was this faceless killer now?

Those questions could be answered easily enough once Mannering was in custody, his false life in ruins. Mark was looking forward to that moment, to seeing Mannering's face when his true identity was exposed. After enjoying the satisfaction of seeing the embezzler arrested for his crimes, Mark would drive his rental car back to Los Angeles and begin to sort out his life again.

He'd have to catch up on the backlog of administrative work he'd left behind at Community General, resolve his personal insurance problems, and start looking for a new car.

And, of course, he'd have to make sure the district attorney moved quickly to secure Bert Yankton's complete exoneration and immediate release from prison.

Mark was looking ahead and thinking about how to handle those details when his phone rang. He snatched up the receiver.

"Dr. Ross," he said.

"Good morning, Dad," Steve said. "Did you have a nice sleep?"

"As a matter of fact, I did."

"Sleep—I remember what that used to feel like," Steve said.

"You haven't slept?"

"I haven't had time. We cut a deal with Stryker for his testimony, worked out his extradition with the Mohave County sheriff, then drove back to LA late last night. When we got here early this morning, we walked into a mountain of paperwork on the arrests made on the Stryker file cases in our absence. And there was the matter of Jimmy Cale."

"You got the prints," Mark said.

"Yes and no," Steve said.

"What does that mean?"

"We got the prints you sent us," Steve said. "The only

problem is there are no prints of Jimmy Cale in the system. He was never arrested, and he never served in the military."

Mark sighed. It was frustrating, but not that big a setback. "So we'll just have to rely on the DNA."

"I'm having Cale's file pulled up," Steve said. "It will have all the blood work and DNA information gathered during the murder investigation. As soon as the DNA comes in from the Vegas crime lab, I'll run it through CODIS to confirm the match."

CODIS was the FBI's Combined DNA Index System, a national database of biological evidence gathered from crime scenes and samples taken from convicted sex offenders and killers.

"Great," Mark said. "What kind of deal did you make with Stryker?"

"Three years in a minimum-security prison and restitution to his victims in return for his full cooperation and testimony on the criminal cases arising from his work."

"He's getting off easy," Mark said. "He won't serve more than a year."

"We weighed it against the greater good of all the bigger bad guys we're bringing down thanks to him," Steve said. "Besides, Stryker's going to walk out of prison broke."

"Until the book deal," Mark said. "Or the TV movie."

"I didn't look at it that way," Steve said.

"I can guarantee you Stryker did," Mark said. "He's probably already looking for an agent to start making deals."

"So are you heading back today?"

"No, I think I'll stick around until the DNA match comes through," Mark said. "I want to be here when Cale is arrested."

"What are you going to do until then?" Steve asked.

"I thought I might relax," Mark said. "Find a good book, an empty chaise lounge, and hang out by the pool."

"You mean, like a vacation?"

"Yeah," Mark said. "I think it's time I gave it try. What's the worst that could happen?"

"Somebody will get murdered," Steve said.

CHAPTER TWENTY-ONE

The only victim of murder that afternoon was the English language. That, at least, was Mark's opinion of the mystery novel he tried to read by the pool. Not only did he figure out "whodunit" by page twenty-one, he also knew every word that was going to come out of each character's mouth. There were so many clichés, he wondered if the book had been generated by a computer. It would certainly explain how the author managed to write five books a year.

Mark regretted not grabbing a western from the bookstore instead. He never knew what the horse was going to do next.

He left the book behind on his chaise lounge, swam a few laps, then returned to his room, where he showered and changed into his tuxedo for an early dinner in one of the Côte d'Azur's spectacular restaurants.

He chose Carnivore, a high-end steakhouse that eschewed the traditional dark woods for a modern industrial look of gleaming chrome, glossy whites, and bright lights. He'd just finished ordering a thick rib eye, mashed potatoes, and broccoli when Robin Mannering sauntered up to his table.

"May I join you, Doctor?"

Mannering was, like Mark, dressed in a tuxedo and, unlike Mark, wore it like an extension of his skin. He was holding a martini.

"Of course," Mark said. "I'd be delighted."

Mannering took a seat across from Mark and asked the waiter to deliver the meal he'd already ordered to this table.

"Have you been staying at the Côte d'Azur long?" Mark asked.

"I live in Las Vegas, but I maintain a suite here, courtesy of the hotel, for my personal use," Mannering said. "I use it to change, entertain guests, and for the occasional overnight stay."

"Why not just go home?"

"I like my privacy," Mannering said. "My home is my sanctuary. Besides, this way I don't have to drive here in a tuxedo to enjoy a friendly game of poker. I can shower and change once I arrive. It also allows me to occasionally overindulge in a bottle or two of wine and not worry about being driven home."

"So essentially the Côte d'Azur is like your own private club."

"Considering how much I've given this casino at the roulette and blackjack tables, I believe it's a privilege I've paid for many times over."

"Obviously Roger agrees," Mark said.

"He likes to keep me and my wallet close by," Mannering said with a smile. "What about you, Doctor? What brings you to Las Vegas?"

"My patients. I go where they go. This week they are here. Next week, we could be anywhere on the globe."

"I heard a rumor that you were once the personal physician to the Saudi royal family."

"To confirm or deny such rumors would violate the privacy of my patients," Mark said, appreciating how wise it had been for Grumbo to create and establish a false identity for him at the hotel. Mannering obviously had good sources, and Grumbo knew it. "Maintaining that privacy is one of the reasons they engage my services. Surely you can understand why the CEO of a multinational corporation or the leader of a country would want to guard the details of his personal health from the public."

"Sure," Mannering said. "Learning that a prime minister has syphilis or a CEO has inoperable brain cancer is information that could be used with devastating political or economic consequences."

"Hospitals are notoriously insecure when it comes to sensitive information. Doctors and staff can easily be bribed or coerced to reveal the personal medical condition of their patients," Mark said. "A richly compensated personal physician, however, is more likely to be discreet."

"Is that why you left research?" Mannering asked. "For the rich compensation?"

"Research can be exciting and rewarding, both from a societal and a financial standpoint," Mark said, "but I wanted more adventure."

"And more money," Standiford said.

"The money is nice. I won't deny that," Mark said.

The waiter arrived with their steaks, sizzling and drenched in butter. They were the largest portions of meat Mark had ever seen. Mannering suggested they order a bottle of wine, but Mark declined.

"You don't drink?" Mannering asked.

"I never developed a taste for alcohol," Mark said.

"That's like never developing a taste for women, love, or money," Mannering said.

"I've compensated for my failings by overindulging myself in those other areas."

Mannering grinned, ordered a glass of wine for himself, and sent the waiter went away. Mark took a bite of his steak. It was incredible.

"How do you know Roger?" Mannering asked.

Mark smiled enigmatically. "Our paths have crossed many times over the years. What about yourself, Mr. Mannering? What's your profession?"

"Having fun and taking it easy," Mannering said.

"You were born rich?"

"Oh no. I earned it," Mannering said, cutting into his steak. "But if I told you how, I'd have to kill you."

The rest of their dinner was spent talking about things that had nothing to do with either man personally. They discussed Roger Standiford, his casinos, and the impact he'd had on the amazing growth of Las Vegas over the years.

Mark found Robin Mannering to be an entertaining and friendly dinner companion, and he enjoyed the time they spent together. If Mannering hadn't been a swindler, a deadbeat dad, a liar, a fraud, and possibly a murderer, Mark could have liked the guy.

Mannering insisted on picking up their check.

"Think of it as Roger treating us both," he said. "I'm glad we ran into each other, Doctor. It's been a most enjoyable meal."

"Likewise," Mark said.

"Will I be seeing you in the casino tonight?" Mannering asked.

"Perhaps," Mark said.

"I hope so, because with you at the table, it almost feels like playing two games at once," Mannering said.

"Poker and charades?" Mark asked.

"Poker and cat and mouse."

"So who's the cat and who's the mouse?"

"I don't know," Mannering said. "That's the fun part."

When Mark got back to his room, the message light on his phone was blinking. He called his voice mail and heard two messages from Steve, asking him to call on his cell phone right away.

Mark caught Steve at the task force headquarters.

"What's wrong?" Mark asked.

"It's about Mannering's DNA," Steve said.

"You got the results already?"

"No," Steve said, "but it won't make a difference once we do. There isn't anything to match his DNA against."

"Cale's DNA," Mark said.

"It doesn't exist."

"I don't understand," Mark said. "You used DNA to prove that the toe and the blood you found in Yankton's car came from Cale. You compared it against DNA from a hair in Cale's brush or something."

"That's true. We did," Steve said.

"Shouldn't all that data have been entered into the CODIS database?"

"It should have been," Steve said. "But it wasn't. It appears that there was a clerical error. Someone transposed a digit on the case identification number so that it matched an unrelated case file that was slated for destruction. The Cale file was destroyed before it could be processed into CODIS."

"So go back to the original evidence," Mark said. "Pull a new DNA sample from it."

"We can't," Steve said.

"Why not?"

"Because the evidence was destroyed, too." Steve said. Then he explained how the system worked. "The detective in charge of a case gives a property disposition card, a PDC, to a civilian secretary assigned to the property room. The card orders the property to either be destroyed, returned to the owner, or kept in storage. The civilian property clerk then enters the information, and the case number, into the computer."

Mark sat down in a chair. He couldn't believe this was happening. Mannering's luck was unbelievable. No wonder he lived in Las Vegas.

"So either you or the clerk could have transposed the numbers," Mark said.

"It wasn't me," Steve said. "And it wasn't an accident."

"How can you be sure?" Mark asked.

"The hard copies of the PDCs are kept on file, and the computer entry shows the serial numbers of both the detective who authorized the property disposition and the clerk who entered the information," Steve said. "I matched the card against the entry in the computer. The number I wrote on the card was correct. The number in the computer wasn't."

"What does the clerk say?" Mark asked.

"Nothing," Steve said. "He's dead."

"I have a sinking feeling it wasn't natural causes," Mark said.

"He was killed in a home-invasion robbery about a year after Yankton's trial," Steve said. "I pulled his financial info. Five days before the files and evidence in the Cale case were destroyed, the clerk received a twenty-thousand-dollar wire transfer from the Cayman Islands."

Now there was no way to prove that Robin Mannering was Jimmy Cale. He'd anticipated all the moves, wiping away any tracks, and any person, that could lead to him and his new identity.

"I don't believe this," Mark said.

"I'm sorry, Dad," Steve said.

"Isn't there anything you can do?" Mark said.

"Like what?"

"You could reopen the investigation into Jimmy Cale's homicide."

"There is no basis for reopening the case," Steve said.

"Cale is alive," Mark said. "*That's* the basis."

"There's no evidence at all to support that claim," Steve said.

"Not anymore," Mark said. "Look at what happened to that clerk. You said it yourself—it was no accident."

"But I can't prove it, and neither can you," Steve said. "Any half-decent attorney is going to argue that the clerk's death was a coincidence and that the transposed numbers on the case files was an accident. We're imagining a criminal conspiracy where none exists because we want to believe Cale is alive, even though there is no evidence to support that belief either."

"Robin Mannering is missing a toe," Mark said. "I'll guarantee it's the same toe Cale lost."

"So that means every man in his forties who is missing part of his big toe is Jimmy Cale?"

"Mannering is Cale," Mark said. "I know it. You believe it, too, don't you?"

"What I believe isn't important," Steve said. "It's what I can prove that counts."

"What about Yankton?" Mark said. "Can you live with the possibility that you put an innocent man on death row?"

There was a long silence. Finally Steve spoke up. "You've seen people who've found a way to live while being eaten alive on the inside by cancer. I suppose I'll have to find a way, too."

"This isn't right," Mark said.

Cale was going to get away with the perfect crime, and Bert Yankton was going to be executed for a murder that never even happened.

The game of cat and mouse was over.

Jimmy Cale had won.

CHAPTER TWENTY-TWO

Mark Sloan lay in bed that night staring at the ceiling of his unfamiliar hotel room, unable to sleep. He was too angry, too frustrated, and too disappointed to fall into peaceful slumber.

He'd woefully underestimated the calculating brilliance of his quarry. He should have known that someone capable of devising, within hours of Stryker's blackmail attempt, the complex frame that ensnared Bert Yankton would have an even more elaborate strategy for guaranteeing his own escape.

Even if Mark had recognized the cunning of his adversary, what could he have done differently? He was only following the clues where they led.

It was a weak excuse.

There was no point in rehashing the past. He had to concentrate on the future. Was there any way to prove that Mannering and Cale were the same person?

The only conclusive evidence would be fingerprints, DNA, or dental records. Mark was certain that Mannering had eliminated any points of comparison. Without a doubt, Cale's dental records were gone. And a man willing to chop off his toe would think nothing of having his teeth altered or replaced.

Whoever the doctors were who gave Cale his new face and teeth, transforming him into Mannering, were probably dead, killed by the same person who murdered the LAPD property clerk and Sanford Pelz, the currency dealer.

The killer was the one loose end that Mannering couldn't do without.

Or perhaps Mannering killed those doctors and the clerk himself and brought on the hired gun only recently when he heard that someone had picked up his trail through his currency purchases. Regardless, it was unlikely that the hit man had any idea who Robin Mannering really was.

Nobody would.

Because Mannering hadn't left any of his old self behind. Even his possessions had been sold off by his ex-wife, Betsy, to support herself and Serena.

Mark realized that Yankton, the file clerk, the doctors, and Pelz weren't Mannering's only victims. Mark's son, Steve, was also a victim. He would have to live with the knowledge that he'd doomed an innocent man to years of hell and eventual execution.

What had Steve said to him? He'd said Yankton's fate would eat away at him like a cancer.

Mark would feel the pain, too. He'd feel it as a father, agonizing over his son's needless suffering.

And then it hit Mark.

Steve. Cancer. Flesh and blood.

Suddenly Mark knew what he had to do.

He had to kill Robin Mannering.

Jesse was dreaming of driving on the winding roads above Monte Carlo in a convertible, Susan at his side, a thousand Snickers bars in the backseat, when the phone rang at three thirty a.m., waking him up. He answered it, mumbling a groggy hello, still thinking about those Snickers bars. He didn't even like Snickers bars. Milky Way was his favorite.

"Jesse, this is Mark."

"Mark?" Jesse blinked hard, trying to clear his head. "Where are you?"

"Las Vegas," Mark said. "Is Susan there with you?"

Jesse rolled over, as if he really needed to check, half expecting to find Snickers bars where she was supposed to be. But she was asleep beside him, the covers up to her neck.

"Yeah," Jesse said. "You didn't call to lecture me about premarital sex, did you?"

"Wake her up," Mark said.

"You're going to lecture us both?"

"No," Mark said. "I'm going to plead for your help. But what I'm asking could cost you your careers, and perhaps your lives."

Jesse thought for a moment. "I think we'd prefer the lecture."

It was four thirty a.m. when Steve's phone rang. But he wasn't asleep. Like his father, he was wide awake, tormented by problems he couldn't solve, failures that would irreparably change people's lives.

"Sloan," Steve said.

"It's me," Mark said.

"You can't sleep either."

"I've been using the time to think," Mark said. "There's something we can do about Mannering, but there could be consequences."

"Worse than an innocent man being killed?"

"You could lose everything," Mark said.

"I may already be losing the most important part of who I am. My soul," Steve said. "What else is there?"

Dr. Amanda Bentley was always up at five-thirty, sitting in the kitchen, reading the newspaper online on her laptop. She cherished these early hours of silence and peace. It was her personal quiet time before her son woke up and she had to get him ready for school, which started at eight.

Her first thought when the phone rang was that somebody had died. Not a friend or a loved one, but a complete stranger. That was often how her day began. It was also how her day usually ended.

But it wasn't the police calling her to a crime scene. It was Mark, asking her to risk her career and her liberty as a favor to him.

She said yes without giving it a second thought.

Mark found Nate Grumbo that morning in the security center, watching a blackjack table on his computer monitor.

"See that guy, sitting in the middle?" Grumbo jerked his head towards the screen.

"Yeah," Mark said. He was a large man in a tuxedo, wearing sleek Italian sunglasses and smoking a thin cigarette. There were other men playing cards on either side of him.

Mark would never have imagined before today that there were people who actually got up and dressed in tuxedos to play cards at eight in the morning. But this was Vegas, a world that spun on its own axis.

Then again, maybe Mark had it wrong. Maybe those men simply never went to sleep. There were no windows in the casino. For all they knew, and for all they cared, it might still be the dead of night.

"He's marking every face card he gets," Grumbo said. "The inside of his ring is putting a dot on them that's invisible to the naked eye but that he can see with his glasses."

"It's not a very sophisticated way to cheat," Mark said.

"He'll win a few hands, but not enough to raise much attention, and then move on to the bar or the slots for a couple hours until the dealers change," Grumbo said. "Or he'll go to another casino."

"How did you catch him?"

"He dresses like a tourist, but he doesn't walk like one," Grumbo said. "Or sit like one."

"But tourists aren't just one homogeneous group," Mark said. "They come from all over the world."

"Once they step off the plane or climb out of the limo, they're tourists," Grumbo said. "You have the rich tourists and you have the herd. But they all have the walk. And the sit. He doesn't."

"What are you doing to do?"

"I'm going to deal with the situation," Grumbo said.

"What does that mean?"

"It means I'm going to convince him that cheating isn't very sportsmanlike and that we don't appreciate that behavior at our casino," Grumbo said. "I'm going to convince him strongly."

"It's a good thing you have a hospital on-site."

"He won't need it," Grumbo said.

"Maybe Roger should build a mortuary here as well," Mark said.

Grumbo smiled. "I think you've got me figured all wrong, Doctor."

"I hope not entirely," Mark said. "How do you feel about covert ops?"

"It's what I do," Grumbo said.

"Just here?" Mark said.

"What do you have in mind?" Grumbo asked.

"I want to kill a man," Mark said. "Very slowly."

"I can do that," Grumbo said. "Would you like to see my references?"

Las Vegas was paradise, where any desire, any need, any hunger could be satisfied. Any time. Any day. Any way.

It was made for a man like Robin Mannering.

Anything you could possibly want could be found in this perfect place. The best meals. The best clothes. The best entertainment. The best wine. The best cigars. The best jewelry. The best women.

There were no judgments here. No morality and no ethics. No vice and no perversion. Only desire and fulfillment.

What happens in Vegas stays in Vegas.

That was the city's slogan. But it was much more than that. It was its very reason for being. And it worked because Las Vegas didn't exist in the same dimension as the rest of the world. How could it? All that water, all that comfort, all that glorious excess in the middle of one of the bleakest, driest, most inhospitable deserts on the planet? It wasn't possible.

But there it was. A city apart.

The same could be said of Robin Mannering. He was a man apart, existing in his own realm, one of his own making, answerable to no one.

Mannering loved Las Vegas, a place where you could be anyone you want, do anything you want, live any way you want. Nobody cared. The only thing that had any meaning was money. Big, thick piles of cold, green cash.

Nowhere else was cash so celebrated, so ubiquitous. If not actual currency, then depictions of it, mentions of it, flashes of it, promises of it.

For a man who loved money, who collected it for its beauty, its utility, and its power, there was no place else to be.

Robin Mannering was in his natural habitat. There was no torment or doubt in his life, no regrets. He had no second thoughts about leaving his family or his lover behind or dooming his business partner to imprisonment. Their lives meant nothing to him. His happiness and security were all he cared about. Other people were merely toys to be played with or tools to serve his needs.

The biggest mistake of his life was getting married, a grievous error he'd carelessly compounded by letting his wife have a baby. A child was a pointless acquisition. There was no profit in it, no pleasure. It was a drain on time and money with no tangible upside.

That was when he knew a transformation was in the offing, a move to a new and higher level of being, one free of responsibility for anything but his own pleasure.

He didn't know how it would come about, or when, but he knew that it would.

And then fate drove up to his house in an Escalade and showed him some explicit photos.

It was an epiphany, almost spiritual in its magnitude. He had a vision of his future and knew exactly how to make it happen.

All it took was resolve, some painful sacrifices, and a chunk of his flesh, penance for the mistakes he'd made. The agony when he took the ax to his toe was a release, a rebirth.

Jimmy Cale died in that instant of blinding pain and Robin Mannering, a far better man, was born. The necessary killings that followed—the property clerk, the plastic surgeon, the dentist, the forger—those were all part of maturing, of recognizing that his needs, his well-being, were all that mattered. Once he accepted the worthlessness of any life but his own, killing came easy.

Now he'd reached that higher plane of existence, that perfect life where indulging himself was his full-time occupation.

Mannering did nothing for anyone unless it led to his own immediate enrichment, satisfaction, profit, or amusement. Delaying gratification wasn't an option.

It was an exciting, stimulating, yet oddly restful, life. There was no stress, no demand on him of any kind. He usually partied or gambled until the early hours of the morning and then slept no later than ten, regardless of when he went to bed. Yet he was always full of energy, enthusiasm, and good cheer, ready to take on the day and pleasure himself even more.

His house was his Fortress of Solitude. No one but service personnel were ever allowed inside. Here he could gaze upon his magnificent currency collection, smoke a fine cigar from his walk-in humidor, and enjoy a glass of wine from his world-class wine cellar. Then he could stroll to his seven-car garage and choose a vehicle from his collection—a Bentley, a Ferrari, an Aston-Martin Vanquish, a '59 Caddy convertible, or a massive black Hummer—for the short daily drive to the Côte d'Azur, his personal playground.

At the Côte d'Azur, all his appetites and needs were taken care of. If he wanted a woman, or three women, he could have them whenever and wherever he wanted them. And when he was done with them, they were gone, waiting for him to call again.

Mannering could gamble all night, making fortunes and losing them without a care. He would gorge himself on gourmet food and magnificent wines without paying a cent. This kept him in a very good mood.

To those around him, Mannering was a pleasure to be with, a class act, a wonderful guy.

Why shouldn't he be?

Robin Mannering was the picture of contentment, success, and power, a man at the very top of his game. A man others aspired to be.

Which was why he was troubled now, why the way he'd begun to feel over the last week was so wrong, so *terrifying*.

At first he'd been able to ignore it, to write it off as the consequences of partying too hard.

So he was feeling a little tired after gambling for five hours, drinking three bottles of wine, and wrestling all night with three stunning, very athletic, very demanding, twenty-two-year-old showgirls.

Of course he was tired! It was the best kind of fatigue. Too much of a good thing.

But then he was just as tired the next day, and more so the

day after. He began taking *naps*, something he'd never done in his life.

It wasn't just the crushing fatigue that worried him. It was the weakness. He invited two girls to his room and could barely muster the strength to attend to one of them. And when he was done, he could barely breathe.

Now simply walking across the room left him short of breath, his heart racing. He was growing more and more depressed. It even affected his sense of taste. Soon everything that passed his lips tasted like it was made of chemicals.

Each day it got worse.

Each day it got harder and harder to get out of bed, harder and harder to deny what his mind was screaming.

I'm dying.

CHAPTER TWENTY-THREE

Robin Mannering awoke on the eighth day of his slow death with barely the will, the energy, or the breath to rise from under his sheets.

But it was more than that.

He hated the idea of accepting his weakness, his vulnerability, and seeking help.

It meant stepping out of his carefully controlled, totally secure realm. It meant entrusting his life to someone else, if only for a while.

He'd told himself he would never let that happen.

And now it was happening.

He had to do something. He had to save himself.

Mannering couldn't simply pick a doctor out of the Yellow Pages or stagger into the hospital. There would be questions he couldn't answer, medical history he couldn't provide. They would gather information from him and enter it into databases that he couldn't control. His security would be breached, his carefully constructed world invaded, not to mention his body.

He would be naked and exposed in every sense of the words.

There had to be a way to minimize the risk, to exercise some control over a situation that was frightening *because* it was beyond his ability to control.

And then he remembered his dinner a week ago with Dr. Douglas Ross. He'd seen Dr. Ross a few times since, but not across a poker table. The good doctor didn't have the guts to face him again, preferring to play blackjack, where his only opponent was the dealer.

That was good, because Dr. Ross would have no reason to resent him. He was still flush with the money he'd won from Mannering.

Yes, this was good. Very good.

Fate was playing into Mannering's hands again.

Dr. Ross owed him. And Mannering was going to call in the debt.

That was if, of course, Dr. Ross was still a guest at the Côte d'Azur.

Mannering reached for the phone and made a call.

Dr. Ross was waiting for him in the lobby at the Côte d'Azur medical center. Mannering hated the look he saw on the doctor's face when he shuffled in, short of breath, sweating from every pore on his body. It was a look of pity. His weakness, his vulnerability, was that obvious.

"How long have you been this way?" Dr. Ross asked, taking his arm.

"A week or so," Mannering said, yanking his arm away. He wasn't a damn invalid. Not yet, anyway.

"It couldn't have happened that fast," Dr. Ross said. "It must have been creeping up on you for some time and you just ignored the signs."

"There weren't any."

"I've worked with many rich and powerful people. What I've learned is that people who are used to being in control don't want to accept the slightest hint of their own weakness," Dr. Ross said. "They won't acknowledge it until they have no choice, until it becomes debilitating."

Mannering was flattered to be recognized as someone of

a stature equal to that of the royals and presidents Dr. Ross counted among his patients, so he didn't take offense at the stinging assessment of his failings. He didn't resist when Dr. Ross took his arm again and led him into one of the examination rooms.

To be honest, he felt instantly better around the genial doctor. There was something about Dr. Ross and his natural amiability that made him feel safe in a way he hadn't thought was possible.

The doctor closed the door to the room and asked Mannering to change into a hospital gown.

Then Dr. Ross asked him some general questions about his health and made notes on a clipboard, which made Mannering nervous. The doctor seemed to sense this and set the clipboard aside, though he continued his questioning, probing a bit deeper into his medical history, asking about past illnesses and surgeries, as he examined Mannering.

Dr. Ross gestured to Mannering's feet. "What happened to your toe?"

"Childhood accident," Mannering said. "You should never chop wood barefoot."

"I would think not," Dr. Ross said. "Are you short of breath only when you're doing something, or does it happen when you're at rest, too?"

"I have trouble breathing all the time, at rest or with simple walking. And stairs wear me out. I sleep okay, in fact longer than usual, but I wake up tired and feel as if I haven't slept at all."

"Any swelling of your ankles?"

"Maybe a little," Mannering said. He hadn't really thought about it before.

"Do you have any fever, chills, or cough?"

"I feel cold a lot, but I don't have any real chills," Mannering said. "I thought it was the air conditioning in this place."

"Have you lost any weight?"

"Yeah," Mannering said. "I'm down about five pounds in the last two or three weeks. My appetite isn't very good."

Dr. Ross thought a moment, then asked, "Have you noticed any bleeding, especially from your gums when you're brushing your teeth?"

"Nope."

"Have you been bruising easily?"

"The only serious bruising I've suffered lately was losing that pot to you," Mannering said with a grin, just to keep things light. Dr. Ross grinned, too, but Mannering could tell he was only being sociable. "I ran into the door the other day and bruised my leg. I've done that before, and it didn't bruise any worse than usual."

He asked Mannering a few more question about his symptoms, then sat down on a tiny stool with a heavy sigh.

"Here's what I'd like to do, Mr. Mannering," Dr. Ross said. "I'd like to take some blood and give you an EKG and a chest X-ray."

"What are you looking for?" Mannering asked.

"It's too early to speculate," Dr. Ross said.

"You're keeping your cards close to your chest," Dr. Ross said. "You play doctor the same way you play cards."

"But I'm afraid this isn't a game," Dr. Ross said, a little too grimly for Mannering's comfort.

Mannering had intended, after his visit to the doctor, to play a little poker to lift his spirits. But after the battery of tests, he was exhausted. All he wanted to do was go home, smoke a cigar, and admire his money.

So that was what he did.

He had some Chinese food delivered for dinner, then went to bed early.

The next morning, Dr. Ross called at ten. The tests results were in, and he wanted to see Mannering to discuss them.

"Can't you just tell me over the phone?" Mannering asked.

"I prefer not to," Dr. Ross said. "There's also another test I'd like to perform. Do you have a friend who can give you a ride and take you home afterward?"

"It's that bad?"

"It's a simple test, but I'll need to give you a mild sedative," Dr. Ross said. "That's why I don't recommend that you drive."

"Tell Roger to send a limo for me," Mannering said. "Have him make it quick."

Mannering hung up and noticed that his hands were trembling. He stared at them as if they'd betrayed him.

Dr. Ross didn't even attempt to soften the bad news behind a genial smile. This time, the doctor was dead serious as they sat in the exam room together.

"Your white blood count was abnormally high, and your platelet count was way off," Dr. Ross said. "And your clotting time was too slow."

"What does it mean?"

Dr. Ross took a deep breath. "It could be leukemia."

The one thing Mannering had never considered was that his body might one day fail him. He'd mastered the rest of his universe, he'd always assumed his body would simply fall into line with everything else. His health was something he'd simply taken for granted.

Leukemia?

It wasn't part of his master plan. It couldn't be permitted to happen.

"How can you be sure?" Mannering asked.

"I'm not. That's why I need to do a bone marrow exam, which isn't as scary as it sounds," Dr. Ross said. "It's done by taking a large-bore needle and inserting it, using local anesthesia, into the hip bone along the side of your waist. I can do it here, right now."

"Then what are you waiting for?"

Dr. Ross nodded, reached behind him, and took a clipboard off the counter. "You'll have to sign this."

He handed the clipboard and pen to Mannering. It was some kind of release form.

"I thought you said this was a simple procedure," Mannering said. "Do we really need to be so formal?"

"Yes, we do."

"If it's for insurance purposes, don't worry. I'll be paying cash."

"That's not the issue," Dr. Ross said. "It's a legal release. I can't perform the test, and neither can anyone else at this or any other medical facility, without that signed document."

"I'm a man who guards his privacy," Mannering said.

"I understand," Dr. Ross said. "As you know, I consider protecting my patients' privacy my foremost obligation. I've made it the keystone of my professional life."

Mannering felt his hand begin to shake again and signed the document quickly to hide the tremor from Dr. Ross. There was no need for the doctor to know how scared he was.

Dr. Ross took the clipboard, tossed it on the counter, and put on a pair of rubber gloves. "Let's get to it, shall we? I'm going to bring in a nurse to assist me."

"Can't you do it on your own?"

"Don't worry, Mr. Mannering," Dr. Ross said. "She's on my personal staff. She flew in early this week to assist me with my current patient, the one I accompanied here to Las Vegas."

"You never mentioned who that was," Mannering said.

"No," Dr. Ross said with a tight smile, "I didn't."

The nurse was an African American woman who introduced herself as Cleo Jones and had an easygoing rapport with Dr. Ross that was obviously the result of a long association. It made Mannering feel much better about her being there.

He was feeling much better all around, a state of mind he attributed to the Valium that Dr. Ross had given him before injecting the lidocaine into his hip. Once everything was numb, Mannering watched with calm detachment as Dr. Ross made a half-inch incision in his hip, down to the bone.

The doctor took a short, thick needle and twisted it into the bone, crunching and grinding until he finally broke through to the cavity. He attached a 30 cc syringe to the needle and pulled back the plunger, slowly drawing out the marrow, which was bright red, pulpy, and filled with tiny bone spicules.

Dr. Ross removed the needle and bagged the ampoule, writing Mannering's name on the label. The nurse covered the wound with an antibiotic ointment and a bandage.

"Is that it?" Mannering asked.

"You'll need to hang around for a couple hours to give the sedative a chance to wear off," Dr. Ross said. "You'll have some residual soreness for a few days."

"When will I get the test results?"

Dr. Ross glanced at his watch. "If we rush it, we can have them later today."

Mannering nodded. "You can find me at the blackjack table."

Dr. Ross reached into his pocket and gave Mannering a hundred-dollar chip. "Play a hand for me."

"Why don't you play it yourself?"

"I like your luck," Dr. Ross said.

So did Mannering. It hadn't failed him yet.

CHAPTER TWENTY-FOUR

Mannering went up to his room, changed into a tuxedo, and went down to the casino. Things started out great. He put the doctor's chip on the table and got dealt a blackjack.

He stuck the doctor's winnings in his pocket, put his own chips on the table, and decided to see what his relationship with Lady Luck was like today.

He lost every hand, one after the other. But he refused to give up, increasing his wager with each hand. His losses mounted.

His luck would turn. It had to. It always did.

But not today. Lady Luck must have found another man to love.

Before Dr. Ross sat down at the blackjack table beside him, Mannering knew what the test results would be. The doctor hadn't bothered to put on a tuxedo. Probably the only reason he hadn't been dragged out by security was his close relationship with Roger Standiford.

"How bad is it, Doc?" Mannering asked.

"Maybe we should go somewhere a little more private," Dr. Ross said, though they had the table to themselves.

"Here is fine," Mannering said, motioning the young and amazingly beautiful dealer to hit his fourteen. She had a seven, and an astonishing amount of cleavage, showing. "The cards are hot."

She slapped a face card down. He busted. She turned her card over. Seventeen.

"First, I need to explain what the test was and what we were looking for. All our blood cells come from marrow. If the marrow is healthy, we expect to see the normal distribution of red blood cells, platelets, and the major types of white blood cells, myelocytes and lymphocytes," Dr. Ross said. "We didn't find that in your marrow."

Mannering bet a thousand dollars. "What did you find?"

The dealer dealt the cards. He had a twelve, she had a king showing.

"You had too many lymphocytes and immature myelocytes," the doctor said gravely. "You have myelogenous leukemia."

Mannering motioned for another card. It was an ace, which gave him either twenty-three or thirteen. His throat was dry as sand and he felt light-headed. If he hadn't been sitting, he would have fallen.

"What's the treatment?" Mannering brushed his cards, signaling the dealer that he wanted another card. She gave him a nine. Twenty-two. He'd busted out. She swept his chips away.

"Aggressive chemotherapy," Dr. Ross said. "But before we can begin, you're going to need a compatible bone marrow donor."

"Why?" Mannering bet two thousand dollars. The dealer began dealing the cards.

"The chemo will completely wipe out your bone marrow. You could easily die from bleeding or from infection."

She dealt him fourteen and had an ace showing.

"Insurance?" the dealer asked.

"Where am I supposed to find this donor?" Mannering asked Dr. Ross.

"It has to be a blood relative."

Mannering's hands began to tremble again. He put them in his lap. "And if I don't do the chemo?"

"You'll die."

He never took the insurance bet. This time he did. He put some chips on the table. The dealer turned over her other card. A queen, giving her blackjack. He won the bet. His insurance paid off.

And at that moment, he realized he'd made another insurance bet nearly two decades ago for another terrible hand he'd been dealt today.

He would win that bet, too. Lady Luck was whispering sweet nothings in his ear again. She was unfaithful, but he still loved her.

"If I find a donor," Mannering asked, "can you handle the transplant?"

"I'm going to be here only for a few more days," the doctor said. "But it's not that complex. There are many doctors in Las Vegas who can do it. You could contact the local hospital and—"

"I want you," Mannering said. "And I want to do it here."

"At the Côte d'Azur?"

"Is there a reason why I can't?"

"No," Dr. Ross said, "but it's not really set up for that kind of treatment."

"I'll pay for whatever equipment is necessary," Mannering said.

"It's not me you'll have to convince," Dr. Ross said. "I am merely a guest here."

Mannering got up slowly, his anger and determination overcoming his weakness. "I'll handle Standiford. You just tell him what you need."

"Wouldn't it be easier for you to go to a fully equipped hospital?"

"Wouldn't it be easier for your patients to use a doctor here rather than drag you with them all over the world?"

"That's different," Dr. Ross said.

"Not to me. I hate hospitals, and as you once told me, they aren't very secure with their information," Mannering said. "There are business rivals who would take advantage of me if they knew I had a potentially terminal illness. I can't afford to have anyone know how sick I am."

"I would need to bring in medical personnel to assist me," the doctor said.

"I'm sure that if they're people you've used before with your other patients, I can trust them, too," Mannering said, though he didn't entirely believe it himself. But he had no choice.

"How soon can you bring in a donor for me to test for compatibility?" Dr. Ross asked.

"Give me a day," Mannering said. "Maybe two."

He dug into his pocket for Dr. Ross's winnings and set them on the table in front of the doctor.

"You're a winner," Mannering said. "Try to stay that way."

In the elevator up to Standiford's office, Mannering's mind raced through all the possible scenarios and their potential risks. But none of those risks matched the dire consequences he faced if he didn't act fast and decisively.

There was only one person who could save his life. He hadn't seen or heard about her in five years. But she shouldn't be hard to find. She had no reason to hide.

The first thing he had to do was convince Standiford to let him do his chemotherapy and his bone marrow transplant at the Côte d'Azur. And more important than that, he had to make sure the facility was locked down and that the donor never knew who was getting her marrow.

Standiford greeted Mannering outside the elevator, embracing him like they were old, dear friends, and led him into his office.

"This is the first time you've come up to see me, isn't it?" Standiford said.

"Usually you come to me," Mannering said.

"Isn't that the way you like it?" Standiford asked, motioning Mannering to take a seat.

"I'm in a delicate situation," Mannering sat down in one of the guest chairs. "Discretion is essential."

"I'll certainly do my best to help." Standiford sat beside him, putting them on equal footing. It was a gesture Mannering appreciated.

"I've been in to see your friend Dr. Ross. I haven't been feeling well and I'm afraid the diagnosis isn't good," Mannering said. "I have leukemia."

"I'm so sorry."

Mannering waved the sentiment away. He hadn't come here for pity or understanding. "What I need is Dr. Ross and your medical center."

Standiford cocked an eyebrow. "It's not really a medical center. It's a specialty surgical hospital for coronary and orthopedic surgeries and the occasional nip and tuck. We aren't really set up for chemotherapy and that sort of thing."

"So I'll set it up and pay for everything," Mannering said. "I'll need a private room, no paperwork, and total isolation from the other patients and staff. We're talking cash on the table—or under it, if you prefer."

Standiford frowned. "I feel for you, I truly do, but you're asking an awful lot. We could lose our medical license."

"I built that damn hospital with what I've forked over to this casino," Mannering said. "If I die, you lose a long-term revenue stream. I've been good to you and this hotel and I can continue to be. You're in the business of serving the unique needs of your privileged clientele. This is how you can serve me, and it costs you nothing. I'm paying for everything and a bit more for your consideration."

"It's not just about your comfort and security, is it?"

"I'm going to be bringing in a bone marrow donor who can't know who I am or where I am," Mannering said. "To do so may require extraordinary measures. I'll need Nate Grumbo's assistance once the donor arrives on the property."

Standiford studied Mannering for a long time. "It will cost you a flat fee of one million in cash."

Mannering rose from his seat. "Done."

Henderson is a suburban community outside of Las Vegas, about as far away socially, economically, and geographically as Mannering could get from his house within the hour and not be standing in the middle of the desert.

He found a strip mall under the McCarran flight path and parked in front of a pay phone.

This was the first time he'd been to this pay phone, but not the first time he'd made this call. When Mannering had heard that Nick Stryker was asking paper-money collectors about recent auctions he'd been involved with, he'd known the PI was onto him.

So he called the number he'd been given many years ago by a drunken movie star client who liked to brag about his underworld connections.

"Jimmy, you ever get in trouble, you call the Do-er," the star had said.

"What's he do?" Jimmy asked.

"Whoever you want," the star said.

Mannering called the number and wired the funds where the voice on the other end of the line told him to. Half on commencement, half on completion, the Do-er said, or the next person I do is you.

The deal went beautifully.

They both kept their anonymity and they were both satisfied with the transaction. Mannering had hoped he'd never have to use the number again. Certainly not so soon.

This was much trickier than the other assignment he'd

given the Do-er. He would have to arrange this so the Do-er didn't find out who he was doing the job for and why. It wouldn't be too difficult as long as he had Nate Grumbo's assistance.

For a million bucks, he'd get whatever assistance he needed.

Mannering got out of the car, went to the phone, and dialed. The Do-er answered on the first ring. He had a voice like milk chocolate.

"Yes," the Do-er said.

"I have another job for you," Mannering said.

"Who dies?"

"No one," Mannering said.

"Where's the fun in that?"

"It pays the same," Mannering said.

"What do you want me to do?"

"I want you to find and abduct a teenage girl," Mannering said.

"That's fun," the Do-er said. "Do I get to pick her?"

"I already have," Mannering said. "Her name is Serena Cale."

"Is this a kidnapping for ransom?" the Do-er asked. "Because I don't do that."

"No, it's not. You will have to find her quickly and bring her unharmed to Las Vegas," Mannering said. "I'll get what I need from her and give her back to you."

"What am I supposed to do with a teenage girl?"

"Whatever your heart desires," Mannering said.

There was a long pause. Mannering could almost hear the Do-er's grin.

"I can do that," the Do-er said.

CHAPTER TWENTY-FIVE

Victor Gischler, known as the Do-er to the underworld of gun monkeys and casual readers of the classifieds in *Soldier of Fortune* magazine, drove his growling '68 Mercury Cougar up to the Monterey Bay area from his home base in Fontana, California, where he liked to hang out with his fellow members of the John Birch Society, the Aryan Brotherhood, and the Boy Scouts of America.

It took him longer to make the drive than it did to find Serena Cale. He found out all about her from the Web in about fifteen minutes and even managed to pull her picture off another kid's Web site.

Randi Turner was the other kid, and she had a photo page on her site devoted to her and her friends at beach parties, school games, and hanging out. They were hanging out, all right, mostly in the skimpiest of bikinis.

Serena was one of Randi's chums. They were both hot babes, and as Victor made the eight-hour drive, hyped up on X, he entertained himself by imagining the two girls were very, very good friends. It got him so excited that he was toying with the idea of coming back for Randi later, depending on how things worked out with Serena. He would show them both the glorious American eagle tattooed on his belly, its talons clinging to his hairy navel, and they would be overcome by patriotism and lust. They might even fight with each other over who got to have him first.

He drove all night, stopping a couple of times along the way for hamburgers and beers and visits to the bathroom, where he liked to scrawl the phone numbers of ex-girlfriends on the wall. The ones he was kind enough to leave breathing and unmaimed, that is.

Victor didn't look much like an ex-Marine, mainly because he wasn't one, even though he told everybody that he was. He stood five feet five, with a hairline that had receded clear back to the middle of his bullet head. The Do-er compensated by letting what hair he had grow down to his shoulders, where it tangled with the man fur on his back and chest that spilled out around his collar.

All that body hair gave Victor a unique odor that complicated the more intimate aspects of his profession. On those occasions when he couldn't kill from afar using the rifle in his trunk, his victims usually smelled him before he could get close. If he tried to mask the smell with aftershave or deodorant, it only made things worse. This required Victor to hone his garroting and knifing skills to favor speed over accuracy or stealth.

He got the close-up work done, but often left an unfortunate mess, which was why he preferred the sniper jobs.

This gig, snatching a buxom beach babe, was a new challenge for him. And when he wasn't fantasizing about Serena and Randi together, he gave some thought to how he was going to make the grab.

He settled on the old-fashioned way—soaking a rag with chloroform, following her to a secluded spot, and covering her face with the rag until she passed out. That was how he got most of his dates in the sack anyhow. Roofies were too much trouble and too expensive, especially once he factored in the drinks he had to buy, and all the effort he had to put into witty conversation, in order to drug the object of his affections.

Serena Cale would probably catch a whiff of him before he got close, but he didn't expect that to be much trouble. The client wanted her unconscious most of the time anyway, particularly on arrival at the destination, because he didn't want her knowing where she'd been, in case Victor decided to leave her among the living.

The client didn't have to worry about that. Once the client was done with her, she'd do some partying with the Do-er, then a quick tour of the Grand Canyon, from the top to the bottom.

Victor arrived in Capitola a little after dawn. He parked the car, went out on the beach, and scoped out the place where the kid lived. He found her car, an old Toyota Corolla, parked near the pier and made a note of the Cabrillo College parking tag hanging from the rearview mirror.

No one was up and about, and the only available restroom was at the gas station by the highway, so he urinated on her tire, like a dog marking his territory. This wasn't going to be a good spot to take her. He zipped up his fly, walked back down to the beach, and trudged across the sand to his car.

Since he didn't know her schedule, he'd have to follow her and wait for the right moment. If worst came to worst, he would know where she parked at school. He could hide in the parking structure and take her when she came back from class.

She made it easy for him.

At eight thirty she emerged from the villa in shorts and a T-shirt and went out for a jog that took her through town, along the river, and under the train trestle.

That was where he waited for her, in the dark of the tall wooden pilings that held up the aging structure. He backed his car up nearby, so he could heave her inert body into the trunk.

Victor the Do-er saw Serena Cale coming towards him, running up the dirt path between the ramshackle old houses and the riverbank. He soaked the rag in chloroform, moved behind the post, and waited to make his move.

He could hear the steady, rhythmic *clip-clop* of her feet hitting the ground as she neared him. He felt his pulse quicken, as if to match the rhythm of her run.

The timing had to be perfect.

When she was close enough for him to hear her heavy breathing, he stepped forward. She passed the post, and in the split second that she registered movement out of the corner of her eye, he reached out to cup her face from behind with the rag and drag her away.

But before his rag could make contact, his arm was wrenched back, he was spun around, and a fist smashed into his face, sending him staggering backwards.

He reached behind his back for the knife hidden under his shirt, and the fist smashed into his face again, his nose exploding in blood.

Victor landed on his butt in a sitting position and stared up dizzily at a man pointing a very large gun in his eye.

"If I were you, I'd sit still," the man said.

"Who the hell are you?"

"Lieutenant Steve Sloan, LAPD Homicide."

Two uniformed police officers appeared out of hiding from the front yard of one of the river houses. They kicked his knife aside and yanked him to his feet. The sudden motion made him so dizzy he nearly puked. They pulled his arms behind his back and slapped handcuffs on his wrists, then patted him down. The urge to vomit passed.

"What's this all about?" Victor asked, trying his best to sound righteously aggrieved. "Is it against the law to take a stroll along the river?"

Steve holstered his gun. The officers tossed him Victor's wallet and car keys. The detective examined Victor's driver's license.

"You're under arrest, Victor."

"For what?" he asked with a snort, blood spilling onto his shirt.

"Urinating in public, for starters," Steve said, then motioned towards Victor's car. "Parking in a red zone for another. My gosh, the charges are mounting every second."

Steve started towards the car. Two Capitola police cruisers screeched up alongside Victor's Cougar, and a couple of plainclothes detectives got out. The police station was only half a block away—they could have walked over, but Victor supposed they didn't get much of a chance to screech anywhere.

"Here's your search warrant," one of the detectives said to Steve, handing him a folded piece of blue paper. "You're clear to search the whole car."

Victor glanced at Serena Cale. Her hands were on her hips, and she was glaring at him with pure hatred and not a trace of fear. He wanted to kiss her and smear her face with his blood.

"Did my father send you to do this?" she hissed. "Is he really alive?"

Victor didn't answer, mainly because he didn't know what the hell she was talking about. The officers shoved him towards his car. He stumbled, nearly losing his footing, and blew her a kiss. It would have to do.

Steve used Victor's keys to open the trunk. It was filled with magazines, dirty clothes, six-packs of beer, and, underneath it all, a Remington sniper rifle.

"Well, look at that," Steve said, turning to Victor with a smile. "I've got a feeling we're going to be adding a murder charge or two to your list of grievous offenses against society. What do you think, Victor?"

He'd thought he would go down in a blaze of bullets, blood, and glory, holed up in some house surrounded by cops. This wasn't a climax befitting the Do-er, a man with an American Eagle on his stomach.

Victor wished he could wipe his nose. "Let's talk about a deal."

The Do-er told Steve the whole plan. Steve walked out of the interrogation room of the Capitola police station and into the observation room, where Dr. Jesse Travis and his girl-friend, Susan Hilliard, were watching.

"You get all that?" Steve asked Jesse.

"Seems simple enough," Jesse said.

"You better be sure," Steve said. "Mannering will be watching every move when you get there."

"Good thing Mannering has never seen this guy," Jesse said.

"You mean because the whole plan would go to hell?" Steve asked.

"Because he'd be as disappointed as I am. C'mon, look at that guy. *He's* the Do-er? He doesn't look like a Do-er to me." Jesse glanced at Susan, whose arms were folded across her chest. "Does he look like a Do-er to you?"

"He looks like scum to me," she said with a scowl.

"Exactly," Jesse said. "Hit men are supposed to be smooth, slick, preferably European. I think Robin Mannering is going to be a lot happier when he sees *me* instead of *him*."

"Because you're smooth, slick, and European," Steve said.

"I can be," Jesse said.

Steve handed Jesse the keys to Victor's car. "Don't try to act, okay? Just deliver Serena to Las Vegas and follow Mannering's orders." He turned to Susan. "Are you ready to be Serena Cale?"

"As long as I don't have to ride in the trunk the whole way," Susan said.

Steve looked at Jesse, who was now squinting, Eastwood-like, at his reflection in the glass.

"They call me the Do-er. One bullet from now and they're going to call you the Done. Or the Did." Jesse frowned and turned to face everyone in the room. "Which would it be, the Done or the Did?"

"I don't know, Jesse." Steve motioned to Victor on the other side of the glass. "Why don't you go in and ask him?"

"Okay." Jesse started for the door and Steve grabbed him.

"Tell me you weren't actually going to ask him," Steve said.

Susan sighed. "Maybe the trunk isn't such a bad idea."

CHAPTER TWENTY-SIX

Robin Mannering had thought the Do-er would be a lot taller, a lot more imposing, than the short man who stepped out of the Cougar at the service entrance of the Côte d'Azur hotel.

Perhaps it was because he was watching it all on the security monitor in Nate Grumbo's office.

"Does the security camera make everybody look so small?" Mannering asked.

Grumbo shrugged. "Everyone looks small to me."

Mannering could believe that. He watched two of Grumbo's security men push a wheelchair out to the car. The Do-er popped the trunk and lifted a woman out. She was blond and unconscious, her long hair swept across her face. She was Mannering's daughter, but he felt as much of an emotional connection to her as he did to Grumbo's desk. The Do-er set her down in the wheelchair and the security men pushed her into the building. The Do-er got back into his car and drove off.

"She'll be taken to a room in the clinic," Grumbo said. "When she wakes up, we'll call Dr. Ross to begin his tests. What can we expect from her?"

"Complete compliance," Mannering said. She'd been told that if she asked for help, made any attempt to escape, or refused to cooperate in any way, her mother would be raped, tortured, and killed. "But if there's a problem, can Dr. Ross be counted on for discretion?"

"The doctor's patients have included dictators and despots," Grumbo said. "I'm sure he's been involved in less pleasant situations."

It was welcome reassurance.

As soon as he got word that Serena was conscious, Mannering went to his room at the Côte d'Azur medical center to await the results. He was confident that she would be a perfect match.

He was also pleased that he'd been able to work out a solution to his problem so quickly. It was a tricky situation, but he'd handled it with his usual brilliance and aplomb.

The hardest part would come later, when he had to systematically silence all the people who knew too much. Certainly Dr. Ross and all the medical personnel involved in his treatment would have to go, as well as the two security guards who had brought Serena in. He would eventually have to find someone to do the Do-er as well.

Unfortunately, he'd probably have to live with Standiford and Grumbo, but he wouldn't like it.

There was a knock on the door.

"Come in," Mannering said. He was sitting on the edge of the exam table.

Dr. Ross bounded in, looking very pleased with himself. "Good news. She's compatible."

"That's good to know," Mannering said.

"You must have been certain," Dr. Ross said. "After all, she's your daughter."

Mannering's face flushed with anger. How could Dr. Ross have known?

"Did she tell you that?" Mannering asked, knowing full well that she couldn't have.

"The DNA test did, of course."

"You never said anything about a DNA test," Mannering said, getting to his feet. "What DNA test are you talking about?"

"The one that proves without a doubt that you're Jimmy Cale," Dr. Ross said.

Mannering felt as if he'd taken a fist in his stomach. He couldn't breathe. He couldn't swallow. All his fears about submitting to a medical exam had come true. Roger Standiford had used his vulnerability as an excuse to unlock the secrets of his blood and use it for blackmail.

But how had Standiford found out who he was? Mannering paid an LAPD file clerk to destroy the DNA evidence and make sure it never entered the national database. There should have been no trace of Jimmy Cale left anywhere.

Mannering managed to find his voice and enough air in his lungs to spit out one question.

"Is this some kind of shakedown?" he asked, taking a seat again on the edge of the exam table.

"No," Dr. Ross said and opened the door of the exam room. A man walked in, an LAPD badge clipped to his belt. "It's an arrest."

Mannering gripped the table. The revelations were hitting him like a beating, each word a savage blow with brass knuckles to tender parts of his anatomy.

He knew now he didn't have leukemia. It was all an elaborate con. But he took no solace in the fact that he wasn't going to die. If anything, he felt even more anxiety than he had before.

"Who are you?" Mannering asked Dr. Ross. "Are you even a doctor?"

"I'm Dr. Mark Sloan, chief of internal medicine at Community General Hospital, and this is my son, Lieutenant Steve Sloan, LAPD Homicide."

Mannering knew who Steve Sloan was—the detective

who'd put Bert Yankton away. The name Mark Sloan sounded familiar, too.

"There are some other law enforcement types from the FBI and Las Vegas police that you'll be meeting in a moment," Mark said. "But first, let me introduce you to the cast."

"The cast?" Mannering said.

The Do-er, his daughter, and Nurse Cleo Jones came into the room and, as if they were onstage, took their bows.

"The Do-er is Dr. Jesse Travis. He's also the one who took the blood sample from your daughter a few days ago that we used to compare with your DNA."

So his DNA never did get into the system, Mannering realized. This was all a con to get from him what he'd so carefully erased from existence.

"Technically, we could have arrested you as soon as we had those results, but we wanted to flush out your hired assassin and tie him to you," Steve said. "By the way, he agreed to testify against you after we matched the rifle in his car to the bullet that killed Sanford Pelz."

Mannering closed his eyes. This couldn't be happening. Mark Sloan went on, clearly enjoying every second.

"The lovely lady to Jesse's left is Susan Hilliard, who kindly took the place of Serena so that your daughter would never be in any danger."

"Not that you gave a damn about her," Susan said, practically spitting on him. "The hit man told us that you said he could have her when you were through with her. What kind of monster are you?"

A very rich one, he thought. But he didn't say anything. He shifted his gaze to Mark, who continued with his introductions.

"And finally," Mark said, "the woman you know as my nurse, Cleo Jones."

"That's Cleopatra Jones, sugar," Amanda said with a smile. "I always wanted to be her."

"You called yourself Cleopatra Jones? I remember her. She was like the black female version of Shaft," Steve said. "Shouldn't you be wearing an Afro and a mink coat?"

"Mark wouldn't let me," Amanda said, jauntily adding with plenty of seventies jive-talking sassiness: "He said it might spook the honky sucker."

"This is Dr. Amanda Bentley, a Los Angeles County medical examiner and chief pathologist at Community General Hospital," Mark said. "She conducted the DNA tests that confirmed your identity."

Mannering felt his breath coming back, his heart rate returning to normal. During the course of Mark's blathering, he had begun to see a way out. But there was a little more he needed to know. He applauded, a smirk on his face.

"Very nice, ladies and gentlemen. A grand performance. But what about my symptoms? How did you manage that?"

"We've been drugging your food and beverages here at the resort and at your home with Propanolol, a beta blocker usually prescribed for high blood pressure, angina, and cardiac arrhythmias," Mark said. "The side effects match the symptoms of leukemia."

So *that* was why his food had begun to taste like chemicals, Mannering thought. He was actually tasting the drugs they were giving him.

How could he have been so stupid?

"I suppose Grumbo was the one who broke into my house and spiked my food and drinks?"

Mark nodded. "Roger Standiford and his staff have been an enormous help."

Perfect, Mannering thought. That was his escape.

"I'll be sure to remember them in my lawsuit," Mannering said, puffing out his chest with bravado. "You've gone to an awful lot of effort for nothing. There is no case here. Any competent lawyer can get the DNA evidence thrown out. It was taken against my will using fraudulent means."

"*You* asked us to take it." Mark showed Mannering the clipboard and the release he'd signed. "You even acknowledged that the symptoms you were suffering might be fraudulently induced by drugs you unknowingly ingested. You absolved us of that and a myriad of other liberties we took with your privacy. We even have a security video of you signing the document to prove you did so without coercion."

Mannering sagged, what little bravado he'd managed to muster evaporating in an instant.

"You really should have read the fine print," Steve said. "The district attorney went to a lot of trouble to word it just right so it would be foolproof in court."

Jesse whispered to Susan, "I love this part."

"Is it always this much fun?" she whispered back.

"Why do you think I'm always so eager to volunteer to help Mark?" Jesse replied. "It's so I can enjoy the moment when everything comes together."

"I'm afraid your days as Robin Mannering are over, Mr. Cale," Mark said. "So are your days as a free man."

Robin Mannering was dead. Jimmy Cale could feel his identity peeling off like dead skin. He half expected his face to start melting, his flesh mutating back to the way it was before the plastic surgery, dental work, and hair implants.

"Why did you do this to me?" Jimmy Cale stared at Mark Sloan with tear-filled eyes. "What did I ever do to you?"

"This is about what you did to Bert Yankton, your ex-wife, and your daughter. It's about all the people you killed in your greed," Mark said. "If there's any justice, you'll get Yankton's cell on death row."

Steve grabbed the front of Cale's shirt and lifted him out of his seat, pulled his arms behind his back, and handcuffed him.

"You have the right to remain silent," Steve said, continuing to read Cale his rights as he led him out into the lobby, where Las Vegas police officers and FBI agents were waiting.

Mark turned to the others. "Thank you so much for your help. I couldn't have done it without you."

"We were glad to do it," Amanda said. "A man like that has to be stopped."

"Besides," Jesse said, "it was a lot of fun."

"Sure beats cleaning bedpans," Susan said.

"As a small token of my appreciation, I've reserved suites for all of you here for the weekend," Mark said. "You deserve a vacation."

"Hey, I've got an idea," Jesse took Susan's hand. "You want to get married?"

Susan stared at him in astonishment. "Excuse me?"

"You know, holy matrimony? Wedded bliss?" Jesse said. "They've got a chapel right here in the hotel. We could be husband and wife before dinner."

"Are you serious?" she asked.

"All of our closest friends are already here," Jesse said. "They're more of a family to me than, well, my family is. Your globe-trotting parents are on safari someplace in Africa for God knows how long. So, yeah, I guess I am."

"You *guess*?" she said, socking him in the shoulder.

"I'm serious," Jesse said, rubbing his shoulder. "Will you marry me, Susan?"

Mark and Amanda stood in complete shock, silent and staring at Jesse, waiting in suspense for Susan's answer.

A tear rolled down Susan's cheek as she turned to Mark. "Would you give me away, Dr. Sloan?"

He nodded, a big smile on his face. "Only if you'll finally start calling me Mark."

Susan turned and threw herself into Jesse's arms, nearly knocking him over.

"Yes," she said. "Yes, yes, yes."

Read on for a preview of
Mark Sloan's adventures in the next
Diagnosis Murder novel

The Double Life

Coming from Signet
in November 2006

The first thing Mark became aware of was the pain. He grabbed it like a rope and used it to climb his way into awareness. The closer he got to consciousness, the greater the pain became, until it felt as if an ax were buried in his skull.

He wanted to shrink away from the pain and fall back into the senseless depths from which he'd risen. But he fought the temptation. He held his grip on the rim of consciousness by trying to recognize other sensations sharing the bandwidth with his pain.

He smelled the aroma of disinfectants, soap, and rubbing alcohol, and recognized it as what passed for fresh air within the walls of Community General Hospital. The realization grounded him, strengthening his hold on consciousness. He was in the hospital.

Was he asleep on his office couch?

No, the sounds were wrong. He was hearing electronic hums, clicks, and beeps, the cicadas of the Intensive Care Unit.

Had he fallen asleep in a chair while watching over a patient? Was his head aching from lolling for too long at an uncomfortable angle?

No, he was lying flat. His head was against a pillow.

As the murk in his mind began to clear, he became aware

of other irritations: the catheter, the IV in his left arm, the electrodes on his chest, and the oxygen cannula in his nostrils.

With those sensations came an obvious realization that nonetheless came only gradually to him: He was a patient in the ICU ward.

How could that be? What had happened to him?

He tried to open his eyes, but it was like bench-pressing weights with his eyelids, an effort that took the full measure of his meager concentration and nearly sent him plummeting back into unconsciousness.

What saved him from slipping back was someone dabbing a wet towel against his brow. He focused on that, the moisture and the relief, and then his eyes opened and he found himself trying to focus his blurry vision on a woman's face.

Mark blinked hard and the image sharpened. It was an ICU nurse, someone he knew. But he couldn't remember her name; he was having a hard enough time just keeping her face in focus. Seeing her, however, confirmed his conclusions about where he was and his present circumstances.

The nurse was a slender Asian woman in her early thirties, with a bright smile and perfect teeth.

"Welcome back, Dr. Sloan."

He tried to speak, but couldn't summon his voice. She placed a hand gently on his chest to soothe him.

"Take it easy. I know you've got lots of questions. I'll get Dr. Noble."

She left before he could try to say anything.

Mark glanced at the machines around the room and studied the readout from the cardiac monitor. There was nothing irregular about his EKG or his blood pressure, and there was no breathing tube down his throat.

That was a good start.

Besides his agonizing headache, which probably accounted

for his blurred vision and disorientation, he wasn't aware of any other pain.

He tried flexing his fingers and toes, then lifting his arms and legs. They were stiff, but otherwise normal. No broken limbs or paralysis. He made fists, then rubbed his hands together to test his sense of touch. Everything was okay. In fact, he was even able to reach out, pick up a plastic cup from his bedside table, and take a sip of water.

The headache seemed to be his only ailment. He raised a hand and gently explored his head. There were stitches above his brow and some swelling.

He let his gaze drift around his cubbyhole in the ICU. There were several fresh bouquets, the "get well" arrangement from the gift shop downstairs and two others that were wilting. There were also some gift boxes of candy neatly stacked by the flowers. Two of the boxes had been opened and freely sampled, suggesting someone got bored sitting around his bedside. A paperback copy of John Irving's *A Prayer for Owen Meany*, with a deeply creased spine, was on the chair, suggesting that his visitor wasn't Steve. His son would have left some back issues of *Sports Illustrated* and *Guns & Ammo*.

"So, what's your diagnosis?" a woman asked as she entered his room. The Community General photo ID clipped to her lab coat identified her as Dr. Emily Noble, but the rest of the print was too small for him to make out with his blurred vision.

Studying her slender nose, her sharp cheekbones, and the gentle curve of her chin, Mark could see what Dr. Noble had looked like as a child, a teenager, and as a young woman. Her face was like a painting that stayed the same while the lighting that illuminated it changed. In all phases of her life, she must have been beautiful, as she was now.

There was a certain elegance and authority in her eyes, and yet he saw that smiles came easily to her. The laugh lines gently etched at the edges of her mouth revealed her overall contentment and her age, which Mark estimated to be early fifties. She was wearing a black dress, which seemed a little dressy for making rounds, under her lab coat.

When he tried to speak this time, he was relieved to discover that his voice came easily.

"I've got a whopper of a headache. I'm disoriented, dizzy, and nauseous. I'm suffering from mild photophobia and I've got a nasty contusion on my head," Mark said. "I'd say I've suffered blunt head trauma and a concussion."

He knew that a concussion was simply a catchall description of a blow to the head that causes a brain malfunction, which could be as simple as a headache or as serious as a prolonged coma, and anything in between. The concerns would be internal bleeding and swelling of the brain.

"Judging by the flowers and the candy, I'd say I've been out a few days."

"Three days, off and on. It's nice to know that your deductive skills remain intact."

"What did my CTs and MRIs show?" Mark asked.

"Some mild brain swelling. We've been keeping you on diuretics and Decadron, eight milligrams IV BID twice a day," she said, holding up the index finger of her right hand. "Follow my finger with your eyes."

He did as he was told as she moved her finger this way and that.

"You can save yourself the trouble of doing any more of those basic tests," Mark said. "I just gave myself a neurological examination and I passed."

"Humor me. As I recall, hospital rules clearly state that the doctors are supposed to do the exams, not the patients."

"I am a doctor," he said.

"Glad you remember. That's a good start. Can you tell me your name?"

"Dr. Mark Sloan. I'm chief of internal medicine at Community General Hospital, where I am now residing in the ICU."

She asked him to move his arms and legs for her and to make fists. He reluctantly complied, a scowl on his face.

"I've already done all this," he said.

"Stop complaining, Mark. After three days of lying around, you can use the exercise."

Her overly familiar manner surprised him, but he let it slide. He'd have a serious talk with her about it when he wasn't a patient anymore and was back at work as a hospital administrator.

She tested the strength in his legs by asking him to extend his knees while she pushed against his feet.

"Can we please move on?" Mark said, unable to hide his impatience.

"Not yet. Besides, in your current mood, you'll like this one," she said. "Stick your tongue out at me."

He did.

"I think you liked that so much, you want to grin. Go ahead, indulge yourself."

He did what she asked, giving her an exaggerated grin, knowing she wasn't teasing him but rather testing his cranial nerves. This was a test he'd forgotten in his own quick self-exam. There was another one, too, that he'd overlooked, so before she could ask, he extended his left arm and touched his nose with his finger and then repeated the exercise with his right arm. The actions tested the functioning of his cerebellum.

"Very good," Dr. Noble said. "You must have smacked your head against concrete before."

"Is that what happened to me?"

She stiffened, as if she regretted the words immediately after she'd spoken them. "What do you remember about how you got hurt?"

Mark searched his mind. "Nothing."

He wasn't concerned by his lapse of memory. Not recalling how the injury occurred was an extremely common symptom among those who'd suffered concussions. The recollection of recent events are wiped away by the trauma, at least temporarily. He often compared it to writing something on your computer when the system crashes. Whatever fresh information you were in the midst of inputting is lost.

He'd treated more than a few car accident victims who couldn't remember leaving home. Their last memory was reading the morning paper and enjoying a cup of coffee. In some cases, that was a blessing.

Dr. Noble began to press his legs, abdomen, and face, asking him repeatedly as she did so if he could feel her touch.

"Yes, yes, and yes," he said irritably. "You can stop these tests now. I'm fine. You haven't answered my question yet."

"There's just one more sensory test I need to perform first," Dr. Noble said, her hands still cupping his face. "Tell me if you can feel this."

He thought she was going to pinch his cheeks. But that wasn't what she did. She leaned down and kissed him gently on the lips, lingering for a moment to look intimately into his eyes.

"Is that always part of your neurological exam, Dr. Noble?" Mark asked.

"Only with my sexiest patients, Dr. Sloan." She smiled coyly.

He didn't know how to deal with this and wasn't in any shape to try. It was time to get rid of her.

"I'd like to see Dr. Travis," Mark said.

She leaned back and hesitated. "Jesse isn't here."

Dr. Noble said Jesse's name as if they knew each other well. If that was the case, why had Mark never heard of her before?

"Then get Amanda," Mark said. "Dr. Amanda Bentley, the staff pathologist."

"I know who she is." Dr. Noble cocked her head at an angle, regarding Mark strangely, her expression bordering on fear.

Was she only now realizing how far over the line she'd gone, how inappropriate her behavior had been? What if she wasn't even a doctor at all but some crazy person pretending to be one?

"Amanda is on her way up. I called her right after I called Steve," Dr. Noble said. "They should both be here soon."

Mark was relieved to hear that, though surprised again by the easy familiarity with which she used his son's first name.

"Thank you," he said.

"What's the last thing you remember, Mark?"

He thought for a moment. "The wedding."

"Whose wedding?"

He wondered if he should say, since Jesse and Susan might not appreciate him spreading the word before they got a chance to announce the news themselves. All it would take was Dr. Noble telling one nurse or doctor, and the whole hospital would know about the nuptials within the hour.

"A fellow doctor's, up in Las Vegas. It was sort of a spur-of-the-moment thing."

Jesse and Susan had been in Las Vegas, along with Steve and Amanda, helping Mark in an elaborate plot to trick a murder suspect into confessing. The trick worked, and within moments of solving the case, Jesse asked Susan the big question.

"You're talking about Jesse and Susan's wedding," Dr. Noble said.

"You've heard about it?"

She nodded. The color seemed to drain from her face. Mark wondered if maybe he should squeeze the call button and get a doctor for her.

"An Elvis impersonator performed the service," Dr. Noble said. "Then Jesse serenaded Susan with his own version of 'Love Me Tender.' You started to sing along until Steve nudged you to be quiet."

Word had traveled even faster than he expected. Everyone in the hospital already knew. Jesse and Susan must have started calling people from their honeymoon suite at the Côte d'Azur resort casino. Either that, or Amanda leaked the news after the ceremony. There weren't a lot of other suspects. Mark, Steve, and Amanda were the only guests at the couple's impromptu wedding, though it wasn't as rash a decision as it seemed. Jesse and Susan had been dating for years. The only surprise was the moment Jesse had chosen to ask Susan to marry him and his eagerness to do it right way.

"Did I have an accident on the drive back to Los Angeles?" Mark asked.

He would have been driving an unfamiliar car on the Pearblossom Highway, a notoriously dangerous two-lane stretch of road across the California desert that was lined with makeshift crosses and memorials honoring the scores of people who'd left their blood on the asphalt. If all he'd suffered in a collision was a concussion, he'd been very, very lucky. Though trashing two cars—one on the way to Las Vegas and one on the way back—couldn't have made his insurance agent too happy.

But what if he hadn't been in the car alone? Mark felt his heart start pounding and heard his cardiac monitor beeping to the same beat.

"Was anyone else hurt? Was it my fault?"

She shook her head. "That's not what happened."

"Then why do you have that troubled look on your face?" Mark said. "There's obviously something important you're not telling me."

She sighed. "Their wedding was almost two years ago, Mark."

He stared at her, his vision blurring again. He blinked hard and tried to stay calm. Retrograde amnesia was common with head injuries. It could wipe away anything from hours to years and, in some very rare cases, an entire lifetime of memories. In most of the cases Mark had seen, the memories came back, albeit slowly and in maddeningly incomplete pieces.

But not always.

Sometimes the memories never returned.

He was missing two years.

Though a lot could happen in that amount of time, he figured it was just a small fraction of his sixty-three years. A mere blip in the timeline of his life.

How much could have changed?

Mark hadn't lost his mental capabilities, so it wouldn't take long to adjust to whatever had occurred. He'd simply devour newspapers, magazines and medical journals that were published over the past twenty-four months, educating himself on what he'd missed. His life could go on as before—even if his memories of that brief period never returned.

Mark was alive. His mental capabilities were unimpaired and he wasn't paralyzed.

That was enough.

"Do you know who I am?" she asked softly.

"Dr. Emily Noble."

"If I wasn't wearing this name tag, or if the nurse hadn't mentioned my name before, would you have recognized me?"

Mark studied her. "Have we met?"

She sat down on the edge of the bed and took his hand in hers, giving it a squeeze. This time it wasn't another neurological test.

"Mark," she said, looking into his eyes. "I'm your wife."